DEATH AND THE FAMILY TREE

A TRUDY ROUNDTREE MYSTERY

DEATH AND THE FAMILY TREE

LINDA BERRY

FIVE STAR

An imprint of Thomson Gale, a part of The Thomson Corporation

THOMSON

★ ™

GALE

Detroit • New York • San Francisco • New Haven, Conn. • Waterville, Maine • London

Berry
Linda

LIBRARY OF CONGRESS CATALOGING-IN-PUBLICATION DATA

Berry, Linda, 1940–
    Death and the family tree / Linda Berry. — 1st ed.
       p. cm.
    ISBN-13: 978-1-59414-526-1 (lg. print : alk. paper)
    ISBN-10: 1-59414-526-1 (lg. print : alk. paper)
    1. Police—Georgia—Fiction. 2. Policewomen—Fiction. 3. Georgia—
    Fiction. 4. Large type books. I. Title.
    PS3552.E74745D426 2007
    813'.6—dc22   2007000439

First Edition. First Printing: May 2007.

Published in 2007 in conjunction with Tekno Books and Ed Gorman.

Printed in the United States of America on permanent paper
10 9 8 7 6 5 4 3 2 1

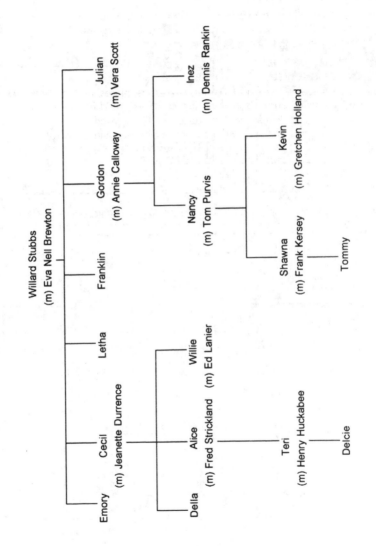

Willard Stubbs
(m) Eva Nell Brewton

Emory   Cecil   Letha   Franklin   Gordon   Julian
        (m) Jeanette Durrence   (m) Annie Calloway   (m) Vera Scott

Delia   Alice   Willie
        (m) Fred Strickland   (m) Ed Lanier

Nancy   Inez
(m) Tom Purvis   (m) Dennis Rankin

Teri
(m) Henry Huckabee

Shawna   Kevin
(m) Frank Kersey   (m) Gretchen Holland

Delcie

Tommy

STUBBS HOUSE

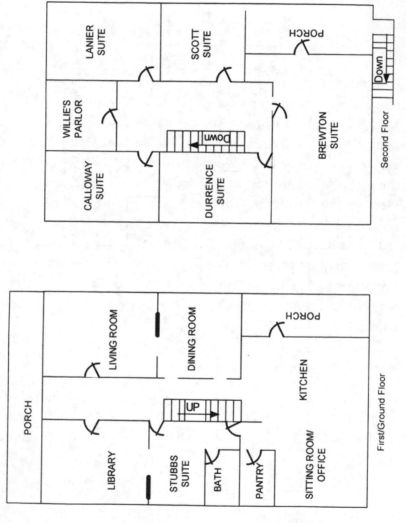

LANIER SUITE

SCOTT SUITE

PORCH

WILLIE'S PARLOR

BREWTON SUITE

CALLOWAY SUITE

DURRENCE SUITE

Down

Second Floor

LIVING ROOM

DINING ROOM

PORCH

LIBRARY

STUBBS SUITE

BATH

PANTRY

KITCHEN

SITTING ROOM/ OFFICE

UP

PORCH

First/Ground Floor

ACKNOWLEDGMENTS

As always, I must acknowledge that I could not put Trudy and Hen on the page without consulting my cousin, Johnny Shuman, Chief of Police in Swainsboro, Georgia, who's been policin' in south Georgia for a good many years. I try to ask him all the right questions, but since I am not a police officer in south Georgia I probably don't get everything just right. Blame me, not him.

I must also thank Bonnie McCune and Suzanne Young, who generously provide commentary and critique at every stage of my writing, and my sister, Dr. Jackie Swensson, who tries to make sure I truly reflect the Georgia we love and that I have commas in all the right places.

Finally, without the unfailing support of Jerry Berry, I wouldn't have the heart even to try to write.

CHAPTER 1

"If I thought I could get away with it, I'd be tempted to commit murder. But I rate Hen too high. And you, too, of course."

The speaker was Lulu Huckabee, my Aunt Lulu. Hen is her son, Henry Huckabee. He's the Chief of Police here in Ogeechee, Georgia, so it shows her confidence in his integrity as well as his law enforcement skills that she wouldn't expect him to let even his mother get away with murder. It's only fair for a mother to think first of her offspring, so I wasn't especially offended that she ranked me as an afterthought. I'm used to it.

I'm Trudy Roundtree, the first and so far only female officer on Ogeechee's police force. Hen's been my boss for several years now, and although he'd probably rather have his tongue cut out and made into sausage than say so, I think he knows I'm an asset to the force. Even if he doesn't feel that way, he wouldn't fire me. In some parts of the world, that's called nepotism. Down here, we call it kinfolkin'.

With the help of Pauline at the Cut-n-Curl, Aunt Lulu marched into her sixties with battle flags flying. The color of the battle flags changes periodically. For the past few months her hair had been a sort of a cranberry color she and Pauline call "Cosmopolitan," and today I imagined the reddish highlights were what put the fire in her eyes as she talked about Della Stubbs.

We were on my back steps. We'd been transferring bag after bag of paper plates, cups, napkins, eating utensils, and paper towels from where they'd been stored in my spacious, mostly unused, pantry to Aunt Lulu's big, heavily used Cadillac, so she could take them to the Anderson Hotel. The hotel, one of Ogeechee's historic buildings, no longer functions as a hotel, but serves as headquarters for the Historical Society and the Visitor Information Center. Two stories, L-shaped, it has porches on both stories all along the inside and the bottom of the L, which faces the courthouse. Like the courthouse, it's a major icon of Ogeechee civic pride and would be the focus of Ogeechee's Bicentennial festivities.

We'd been celebrating the Bicentennial for a year, and tomorrow was what the Bicentennial Committee called the culminating activity, speeches by every living mayor the town had ever had. The speeches would take place on the courthouse lawn, and the Old South Dinner, the final Bicentennial event and the reason for all the paper goods, would be served from the hotel, which was just across the parking lot to the west of the courthouse. Unlike the featureless square boxes that serve many counties, our courthouse is built in a formal style I've heard called Greek Revival, with white stone arches and columns which accent the red brick and form a portico on the ground level as well as the second story.

"Some people," Aunt Lulu continued, "don't know how to work with other people. They have to have their fingers in every little thing. Have to have everything their own way. It's a wonder we ever got anything done. Remind me never to get on a committee with Della Stubbs again."

"Yes, ma'am," I said, even though we both knew it would be ridiculous to suppose my advice would carry any weight. Nothing under the sun would keep Aunt Lulu from having a finger in every civic pie anybody started cooking up. Furthermore, I was sure that if Aunt Lulu had been able to have her own way with things on the Bicentennial Committee, she wouldn't have been so worked up, but I had the good sense not to say so.

"If Della's the one to blame for all the whoop-de-do coming to a peak right here at Christmas, I'll help you kill her," I offered.

"Well, no," Aunt Lulu admitted. "I don't blame Della for that. We all agreed to have it now. December was when the county was officially established, so there wasn't really any discussion about it. When else would you want to do it?"

"When you put it that way . . ."

"You have no sense of history, Trudy."

That wasn't fair and she knew it. One of the projects of the Bicentennial Committee during the past year had been to research old buildings in town and provide those more than a hundred years old with yard signs. I think that project was Aunt Lulu's pet, since she's so proud of the Roundtree house, my house. They gave us all signs that show the name of the house and its date, framed in black-painted scrollwork. The courthouse has a sign and so does the Anderson Hotel. The Stubbs house is old, too, which might be another thing Aunt Lulu and Della Stubbs got crosswise about.

The Stubbs house was built by Willard and Eva Nell Stubbs toward the end of the 1800s. It may be a few years older than my house, but I'm not fighting about it. Their yard sign says the same thing mine does: Circa 1900.

Needless to say, politics got involved when it came to establishing the dates on some of the places, everybody laying claim to the earliest possible date—earlier than the other buildings, at least. I stayed out of that, leaving it to Aunt Lulu to uphold the honor of the Roundtree house. Which is older? I don't really care about that. Circa 1900 is good enough for me.

"Did you know this county was carved out of another one?"

Having decided I had no sense of history, Aunt Lulu was treating me to a history lesson. "That was more than two hundred years ago. Ogeechee came along and got to be the county seat after they made a survey to find the geographic center of the county. This was as close as they could come if they didn't want to put the town in the middle of a river or a swamp."

"Yes ma'am, I knew that, but I wouldn't have before this year and all the marvelous work you and the rest of the Bicentennial Committee has done to educate the masses."

She looked at me with narrowed eyes, rightly suspecting me of insincerity, but reverted to her complaint about Della Stubbs. "Della had to have the last word on everything from picking the topics for essays by the elementary school children right on up to the color of the signs we put up on the highway, and now she's trying to make everybody use her recipe for banana pudding at the Old South Dinner we're putting on after the mayors' speeches."

Ah ha. Bossiness is one thing, but slighting Aunt Lulu's banana pudding is something else. You don't often see Aunt Lulu out of sorts, but this is just the kind of thing that would do it.

"Did you just find out about the banana pudding?" I asked, wondering why she was boiling over right then.

"Yes. I thought it was all settled, but Della decreed that my recipe is too time-intensive—that's exactly what she said, like some kind of efficiency expert, like that would be more important than how it tastes—too time-intensive to make for such a big crowd! Does that make sense to you?"

Actually, it did, but I didn't say that. "Why couldn't everybody just bring their own recipe?" I asked.

She slammed the car door shut with unnecessary force and gave me a scathing look. "Because."

"Oh," I said.

"Della's idea of quality control." Aunt Lulu opened the car

door to frcc a plastic bag that hadn't been completely inside, tucked it inside, and slammed again, not quite so forcefully. "Have you ever tasted Ione Martin's banana pudding?"

"No ma'am, but I see your point. Della must have energy to burn," I said, making an oblique effort to change the subject. "Even with all her work on the Bicentennial, she had time to organize a family reunion."

Aunt Lulu took the bait. Her willingness to support Della Stubbs on this issue demonstrated her essential fair-mindedness. "Stubbses have been part of Ogeechee's history since before there was technically an Ogeechee, so having the reunion at the same time as the Bicentennial made sense. Julian Stubbs is now the oldest living ex-mayor. I always liked Julian. He did a lot for the town."

Just when I thought she was calming down, her pique flared again. "I think that's why Della crammed this speech marathon down all our throats, so Julian could be on the program and all the family would come to hear him and see what she and Willie have done with the house."

What Della and her sister, Willie, had done with the house was fix it up and open it as a bed and breakfast. The grand opening had been just before Thanksgiving, accompanied by generous coverage by *The Ogeechee Beacon* and a spate of small-ish civic and social events on the premises, to introduce locals to what the establishment had to offer, so that they'd feel comfortable promoting it. Any new business takes a while to catch on, I'm told, so it was hard to tell how the Stubbs House Bed and Breakfast was faring.

"Funny you should mention that," I said. "I'm on my way over there. Shawna and Frank Kersey and their little boy are staying there during the reunion. Shawna invited me to come have a tour before the house gets too cluttered up with rela-tives." My lifelong friend, Shawna Kersey, belongs to a branch

13

of the family that fruited into Rankins and Purvises. Della and Willie were Shawna's mother's cousins. I'm not sure what relation that makes them to Shawna.

"Maybe you'll get some fix-up ideas," Aunt Lulu said, patting the crumbling concrete supports beside the steps. "I know Teri would be glad to help." Teri is Hen's wife, and she grew on another branch of the Stubbs tree. Della and Willie were her aunts. I assumed Aunt Lulu didn't speak her mind about Della Stubbs quite so freely within Teri's hearing. Even Aunt Lulu might not want to push the mother-in-law/daughter-in-law thing too far.

"Why isn't Shawna staying with Nancy and Tom?" Aunt Lulu asked, tactfully not dwelling on the renovation theme.

"She said her brother Kevin, the spoiled-rotten, fair-haired son, is staying with them. More likely, she just wanted to check out the bed and breakfast."

"Beats me how Della and Willie think they'll make a go of a bed and breakfast business in Ogeechee. It's not like we're a big tourist destination, after all."

"Don't you think the Bicentennial will attract a lot of tourists?"

"Hasn't so far. Maybe that's why they could fill it up with relatives this week. I wonder if they're charging them. Not that I wish them ill, you understand."

"I understand."

"Thank goodness all this Bicentennial to-do is just about over. After tomorrow we can all relax—might even get through the whole thing without a murder."

"I hope so. Think of the scandal if Hen had to arrest you for murder. Not to mention the gap it would leave in the library board, the garden club, and the leadership of United Methodist Women."

"I'm sure Della Stubbs would step right up," Aunt Lulu said.

Then, brightening, "But she'd be dead, wouldn't she?"

"Even with her alive, after tomorrow you'll get a break from her. You'll be able to get back to your Super Bowl party planning," I said.

For some reason, after Aunt Lulu first mentioned the Super Bowl party a couple of weeks earlier, she'd been uncharacteristically closemouthed about it. I wondered if I'd offended her somehow.

"What are the Geezerettes up to these days?" I had asked.

The Geezerettes is a bunch of Aunt Lulu's friends, not exactly a club but not exactly not a club. They call themselves that, I think, as a way of thumbing their noses at an exclusive men's club, which is exactly a club, which calls itself Ogeechee's Old Gentlemen, but is usually referred to by the irreverent as the OOG or Ogeechee's Old Geezers, or simply The Geezers. As far as I know, the Geezerettes have no regular meeting place or time, and no mission statement, but they know who they are and they get together for fun. They're usually up to something.

When I tell you that sixty-something Aunt Lulu is on the young end of the group, you'll understand my surprise when she told me they were putting together a Super Bowl party.

"Sounds like fun," I had said cautiously, never sure what turn the collective brain of the Geezerettes might take. "But I didn't know the Geezerettes were big football fans."

"There might be a lot you don't know about us, Trudy. We like to keep up with what's going on in the world."

"I'm sure of that, Aunt Lulu. It's just that most Super Bowl parties involve men and a lot of beer. Are y'all branching out?"

She smiled. "We're branching out, but not that far."

"Have you alerted Phil?"

Phil Pittman, the heart and soul, meat and potatoes, and sweat and toil of *The Beacon* is committed to keeping the community informed about everything of possible interest, with hoopla beforehand and pictures afterward. He's one of the best things about Ogeechee in my opinion, right up there with my job. More about Phil later.

"I don't think we need to involve the press yet, Trudy. If we decide to do a fund-raiser, we'll get him in on it."

"A fund-raiser for the Geezerettes?"

"No, for . . . well, a good cause."

"Y'all aren't up to something underhanded, are you? Is your branching out taking the form of something that can't stand the light of day?"

I'd meant it as a joke, but something shifty in her reaction made me wonder if they were up to something that really couldn't stand the light of day.

"Don't get snippy with me, thinking you'll trick me into saying more than I mean to," she said. "I'm Henry Huckabee's mother, you know, and I'm onto tricks like that."

She'd probably taught him some of those tricks.

"The Super Bowl party is well in hand, thank you," she said, bringing me back to the present.

"You don't sound happy about it," I said. "I thought the whole point of the Geezerettes was to have fun."

"It was."

"Was?"

"Ellen Chandler is determined to get Della in on this party. You know Ellen. Everybody's her friend."

"Ah. And Della is not your friend."

"Not a good enough friend to be a Geezerette, but Ellen has some idea for the party that she says she needs Della to help her pull off."

"You could give her a chance."

"Ellen or Della?"

"Both of 'em. Maybe Della's got a good side you haven't discovered."

"If I haven't found it in all the time I've known her, it's pretty well hidden," Aunt Lulu responded, and that was that.

She got in her car and slammed the door one more time.

I watched her drive away, and then I went back inside for my car keys, trying not to notice the peeling paint by the back porch door.

People who think not much goes on in a small town have another thing coming.

CHAPTER 2

When I got to the Stubbs house, Shawna was waiting for me in a cane rocking chair on the narrow porch at the side of the house, where there's room for three or four cars to park on the hard-packed sand, depending on the size of the cars and the steadiness of the nerve of the drivers.

"Aren't you lookin' good!" Shawna said.

"And marriage and motherhood haven't hurt you, either, from what I can tell," I responded as expected. She did look well dressed, well groomed, well cared for, all conditions I sometimes envy. She'd put on a few pounds since I'd seen her, but who hadn't? She was still taller, slimmer, and prettier than I. I did hold against her the aggressive brick-red streaks in her smartly cut blonde hair, which made my short, wavy brown hair feel especially drab. I usually think of my style as "casual," but next to Shawna "boring" was clearly the better word.

"Marriage and motherhood aren't all they're cracked up to be," Shawna said with a pout. "You now, a single career girl, you don't know how well off you are. Policin' and romancin' must be agreein' with you. I'm gonna want to hear all about it."

Shawna and I have been friends for as long as I can remember, but we both left Ogeechee after high school, and it had been a few years since we'd gotten together for a girlish chat. Her marriage and my job with the Ogeechee Police Department as well as a nice romance had come along since then. We had some serious catching up to do. "Well, it turns out

I like the job, and Phil—"

"You closed in your back porch, didn't you?" Shawna inter-rupted, gesturing to the open porch where she sat.

"Grandma did," I answered. "I use it for a TV room. If you can stand the heat and the bugs, an open porch is nice, though."

"You ain't seen nuthin' yet," she said. "Come on in. They've done wonders. I know how interested you are in old houses. Today's a terrific time for us to visit. I talked Frank into taking Tommy to see if they can pull some catfish out of Frank's dad-dy's pond, so they won't be in the way." She giggled. "That'll give me a break from Frank and save me having to spend quite so much time with his folks. All they really care about is Frank and their precious grandson, anyway, and they never have forgiven me for naming Tommy after my daddy instead of Frank's. He gets the Kersey last name, is what I told them."

I appreciated Shawna's tact in not mentioning that a tour of the Stubbs house might give me some ideas for renovation. I know it's time to do what they call up-dating, but it takes more energy and money than I've been able to muster so far, what with fighting crime and all. I should have been warned by the Christmas wreath hanging on the outside of the door, a large wreath of artificial greens with burgundy bows. I hadn't gotten that far into the Christmas season. As soon as we stepped inside, into the kitchen, I knew the tour of the Stubbs house was going to be a mistake. Okay, yeah, they'd had to renovate and dress the place up if they were going to live there and try to run it as a business, but did they have to make it gorgeous? I have hardwood floors, too, but mine, rough and dull, need some seri-ous refinishing. Where my kitchen has disjointed units—sink and cabinet in one place, refrigerator in another, stove sitting all by itself—with a variety of finishes and surfaces that reflect their various dates of acquisition, this room held an integrated array of beautiful pecan-wood cabinets with the sink, stove, dishwasher, and even the refrigerator, built in. I thought my round oak table would have looked better in their kitchen than the butcher-block they had, but that was the only half-point I could award myself.

Through a wide, open doorway on the far side of the kitchen, I saw a sort of family room/sitting room. Della Stubbs was seated in there, at a computer workstation under a window overlooking the backyard. Della's a roly-poly, dumpling-looking woman, with curly hair that makes her look very feminine and a little old-fashioned, not at all the overbearing, hatchet-faced harridan you'd expect if you knew she was a business whiz, or if you listened to Aunt Lulu. Maybe Della and Pauline connive at giving Della an appearance that will make people misjudge her.

"Hey, Trudy," she said, looking up from the sheaf of papers she'd been consulting and smiling to reveal a charming dimple. "How's the crime-fighting business these days?"

"Never a dull moment," I said. "How's the bed and breakfast business?"

"Still too early to tell, but we're going to give it our best shot." The dimple stretched into a grimace. "If we can't make that work, at least we won't be homeless." She tapped the papers she was holding. "I'd better finish up with this before the weekend gets out of control, but Shawna can show you around. I've already given her the tour."

"Thanks," I said.

"And I'd like to see your house sometime, Trudy," Della added. I'm sure she meant to be polite, but my insecurity made it sound like the first move in a game of one-upsmanship. Would my restoration look as good as hers? What restoration?

"Go on then, before anybody else gets here." Della turned back to her computer terminal, dismissing us.

"I don't have to tell you what the kitchen was like before they worked on it," Shawna said, stepping easily into tour guide mode.

"I can imagine," I said. I imagined it a lot like mine.

"You're calling this the Stubbs Suite?" Shawna addressed this question to Della.

"My rooms, yes, the bedroom and bathroom," Della answered. "It says so on the outside of the door to the hall."

"Right," Shawna said, waving a hand in the general direction of the front hall, just as if she'd known about it all along.

"The kitchen is no-man's-land," Della continued. "It helps to have names for the different rooms so when people see the brochure or the Web site they can pick out the one they want to stay in. Willie and I named our own suites after ourselves, so hers is the Lanier Suite. We used family names for the others, too—Brewton, of course, for Grandmother. Durrence for Mama. Calloway for Aunt Annie; Scott for Aunt Vera. Shawna and them are staying in the Brewton Suite." She turned back to her papers.

"Come on through here, Trudy," Shawna invited, gesturing toward a narrow passageway that led toward the front of the house. "See, they've added a bathroom here next to the pantry."

"Wow," I said. Even their pantry was nice, with new shelving. If I ever got around to doing anything, I'd have to think about how much to replace and how much to refurbish.

"One of the main things they had to do was add bathrooms to every bedroom. I don't think there was an inside bathroom at all when the place was built." By now we were in the bedroom, with the hallway, pantry, and bathroom between us and Della, but still Shawna lowered her voice. "I can't imagine what all that cost, but I think Della did pretty well in the stock market, so she had the money. She's got a good head for business, which you'd never guess to look at her. She's taking care of the business end of things here, the way I understand it, and

Willie's in charge of cooking and all the little amenities that will make people enjoy staying here, things like chocolates on the pillows and linens that smell like lavender."

"That would make me want to come," I said. "All I ever find on my pillow is a cat." I was making comments automatically, taking in the beautiful floors, high pressed-tin ceilings, tall windows, and good, solid old furniture.

"Those handkerchiefs were my great-grandmother's." Shawna indicated a framed collection on the bedroom wall. "The library's through here," she continued, trying unsuccessfully to open a pair of pocket doors. "Oh, I guess with a house full of people she thought she'd better lock these for privacy. Let's go around."

She led the way into the wide central hall, empty except for a sideboard against one wall and what looked like old family pictures on the walls.

"Here, take one of these. It's the brochure Della was talking about." Shawna took the colorful brochure from a crystal bowl that sat on a heavily embroidered scarf on top of the sideboard. As I obediently took the brochure, I noted the evergreen swag, decorated with burgundy bows, that lay along the back of the sideboard, and the studied clutter of old pieces serving new purposes. In addition to the crystal bowl/brochure holder, a silver bud vase held ballpoint pens, a china cream pitcher held business cards, a white porcelain hand held a trailing necklace of amber beads set in gold rosettes.

Dazzled, I followed Shawna from the hall into the front room, what she'd called the library. Bookcases—stacked, piled, crammed, jammed with books and papers behind glass doors— lined the walls, and a table with a Tiffany-style—maybe real Tiffany—lamp on it commanded the middle of the room. Two easy chairs in a faded-rose color flanked the Christmas tree near the front window, angled toward each other as if for conversation.

The tree, like the wreath on the kitchen door, like the swag on the sideboard, was decorated with burgundy velvet bows, set off by a variety of crystal ornaments. Beside the pocket doors in the wall separating the room from Della's bedroom was an old-fashioned upright piano with a bright multicolored fringed shawl dripping over the top. A horn and a small drum lay on a pile of pine needles, with burgundy velvet bows, of course, on top of the piano. I could have lived in that room.

"Della told me most of the books came with the house," Shawna said. "And the library table. The piano was Willie's. As much as they could, they used family antiques. I think the tree ornaments are a collection Willie's been working on all her life."

"It's beautiful," I managed to say through my envious daze. "I'm surprised they could track down so much family stuff."

"A lot of it never left here," Shawna said. "Most modern houses have smaller rooms than an old house like this, so even if anybody had wanted it, they might not have had a place for it. I'm not sure of all the ins and outs, but the house and a lot of what was it in was left to my great-aunt Letha, my grandmother's sister, because she never married, and it had always been her home. It was after she died a few years back that Della and Willie bought it. They've been fixing it up, a little at a time, ever since."

"They bought it, didn't inherit it?"

"Right. Bought it from the estate. There was some talk in the family about what would happen to the old place when Letha died. I wasn't in on much of that, but Mama said a lot of people were surprised when it was sold, and really surprised when they found out who'd bought it."

"Surprised? And pleased that it hadn't gone out of the family?"

Shawna's eyebrows took a quick lift toward the heavens. "Mostly. And the heirs liked getting some money from the sale,

I guess. Now across here, we have the living room and the dining room. I have a feeling these rooms are fancier than they were back when my great-grandparents and their six children were living here. Can you imagine trying to keep house with six children? I have one five-year-old, and my house looks like a hurricane zone all the time."

The living room was elegant, with floral curtains picking up the shades of green and gold in a patterned rug, and gorgeous old wood tables and chairs. It matched the library in size, but wasn't nearly as inviting as far as I was concerned. No books handy, no reading lamp, no easy chair. We passed through pocket doors into the dining room.

A china display cabinet, filled with large and small pieces arranged for maximum storage and not for display, dominated the inside wall. The center of the room held a long table, and I counted fourteen dining chairs in at least three different styles. I liked that random touch. It added a smidgen of reality to what was beginning to seem unnaturally perfect.

"Bed and breakfast guests will eat in here," Shawna told me. "Most of the china is Aunt Willie's. I think they're looking forward to using some of this old stuff. If they can make a go of it."

"I hope they can," I said. "They've sure done a good job on the house. I'm impressed with their ambition." I was worse than impressed. I was beginning to be depressed, overwhelmed with the unrealized potential of my own place.

"Ambition," Shawna repeated. "That would be Della. I think she has some business contacts in Savannah that she hopes will send them some business."

We'd come out of the dining room back into the hall, at the foot of the stairs. I followed Shawna up the stairs, which were covered with a carpet runner held against the risers by shiny brass rods.

Squared off like the lower floor, the upstairs had two large rooms on each side of a wide hallway. This hallway was furnished like a sitting room. On the floor at one end of an overstuffed sofa, a shabby leather bag that brought to mind a country doctor was being used as a magazine rack; at the other end, a flat-topped trunk supported a lamp and telephone. Two matching armchairs faced each other across a low chest in front of the sofa.

Featured on the wall at the head of the stairs was a Stubbs family tree, about two feet wide and a foot and a half tall, done in calligraphy and framed in ornate gold.

"Did somebody in the family make this?" I asked, reaching out to touch the beautiful work, then pulling my fingers back guiltily when I saw that it had no glass to protect it.

"Aunt Letha, I think, years ago. That's why it only goes through my mother's generation and I'm not on it," Shawna said. Trust her to assume I was looking for her.

"Where would you fit if you were on it?" Actually, I was interested.

"Here." She pointed. "My great-grandparents, Willard and Eva Nell had six children—Julian, Gordon, Franklin, Letha, Cecil, and Emory. My grandparents are Gordon and Annie, here. They had Uncle Tim, Uncle Daniel, Aunt Inez, and Mama. Tim and Daniel died young. I never knew them. So, if this showed the next generation, Kevin and I would be here, under Nancy and Tom Purvis." She laughed. "Even if Kevin is nearly young enough to be my son."

That gave me a jolt, but I did the math and realized she was right. Since he was still at the University of Georgia, Kevin was probably in his early twenties, at the oldest. I didn't want to consider that with little stretching—and more than a little ir-responsibility—Shawna and I were old enough—nearly old enough—to have children that age. My, my, time was passing me by. Quick, think about something else.

"What relation are Della and Willie to you?" I asked. "Not cousins. Not aunts."

"You're right. Let's see if I can explain it. Della and Willie are my mother's first cousins. That makes them my first cousins once removed. Their children, I mean Willie's children, since Della doesn't have any, are my second cousins. That's where a family tree like this is useful. Somebody explained to me that if it's a straight line across, you're first cousins or second cousins or third cousins. If the line is tilted, then it's once removed."

"Hmm. Let's see if I've got it. Does it mean your son Tommy and Delcie Huckabee are third cousins?"

"Let's see. Tommy would be second cousin once removed to Willie's children, my second cousins. And Teri's in that generation, so her daughter . . . yes, Delcie and Tommy are on the same straight line. Third cousins."

"Do you think anybody can keep all that straight?"

Shawna grinned. "Letha could, I bet. And Willie has all the Daughters of the American Revolution stuff, so maybe she can. We know we're kin and that's the only thing that really matters. It's a good thing we don't have to keep up with all the once removeds."

"A darned good thing," I agreed. "On with the tour?"

"On with the tour," Shawn agreed, turning to face the stairwell and the front of the house. "Willie's room and all the guest rooms are up here."

I opened the brochure. "That would be the Lanier Suite," I said.

Shawna agreed, indicating the brass plaque that confirmed my statement.

"There sure are a lot of suites," I observed.

"I think 'suites' is bed and breakfast code to let people know they have private bathrooms. The little room in the middle of the front of the house is Willie's private parlor. She says she likes to sit there like a cat and watch what's going on outside. It looks to me like it used to be a storage room."

I liked the little room. There was room for an easy chair and floor lamp and not much more. Very cozy. Nearly filling the remaining space, with just room for two folding chairs, was a card table with a partially completed jigsaw puzzle spread out on it, the lid of the puzzle box propped at an angle so that whoever was working on the puzzle could consult it. The picture, like most good jigsaw puzzle pictures, the kind I like, at least, was packed with small details. It showed a Christmas-themed shadow box—nuts and cones, a brightly painted Nutcracker prince, a Christmas tree, Christmas candles, an old-fashioned St. Nick hung with gifts for good little girls and boys, a doll dressed for travel with her traveling bag, a glass candy jar with red and green candies, a pile of gifts, angels, stars, a toy train, a trumpet, a drum. Bits of holly and ribbon flowed and draped from one section to another. The sight of it made my eyes prickle.

Grandma had always kept a jigsaw puzzle going. My fingers itched, and I found myself looking for a piece with gold in it the right shape to add to the beaded swag that wrapped around the candlesticks and hung down into the section where the doll, fatigued from her journey—or maybe waiting to be claimed by a delighted little girl—rested against the edge of the frame.

"But let's don't get out of order," Shawna urged, calling me back from my childhood and Willie Lanier's entrancing parlor. "Come back here."

I returned to Shawna, waiting near the head of the stairs.

"Here to our right is the Scott Suite. Aunt Vera and Uncle Julian, or probably, Great-Aunt Vera and Great-Uncle Julian, are going to be staying here, I think."

A glance inside showed plain dark furniture and several

patchwork quilts in different designs—one covering the bed, another folded on the top of a chest at the foot of the bed, another on a quilt stand, still another covering a wall. A rag rug covered most of the floor.

"The chifforobe against the far wall was Letha's, I'm told, and the rug was one her mother made out of the children's old clothes."

"Wow."

"The quilts came from some department store," my guide said.

"They have the right look," I offered.

"That was the idea," Shawna said, moving on toward the front of the house. "Now Willie's suite."

Dark, formal, mahogany furniture was Willie's choice, with pineapple finials on the bedposts, and a matching chest of drawers and a dresser with mirror. A crocheted white bedspread over a deep-rose-colored undercloth caught my eye.

"Willie brought her own furniture when she sold her house and moved in here. Kind of broke up housekeeping on her own, distributed a lot of stuff to her kids, and settled in here."

"Settled in very comfortably, it looks like."

"There may be a reason she and Della live in different ends of the house, though," Shawna said, lowering her voice. "They aren't very much alike."

"Surely they knew each other well enough to know if going in together like this would work," I said.

Shawna shrugged and crossed to the other side of the house, allowing me only a quick glance into Willie's sitting room as we went past.

"Okay, this one's the Calloway Suite."

Not a suite of furniture, as in Willie's suite. Brass bed. Big, battered old trunk with an arched lid. More old pictures on the walls.

"This is where Aunt Inez and Uncle Dennis will be. Inez's my mother's sister, so she really is just an aunt, not a great. Not even very good, if you want my opinion." She smiled to make sure I got the joke. "And behind it, over Della's bedroom—excuse me, over the Stubbs Suite—is the Durrence Suite. I don't remember if they told me who they're putting in here."

This one had twin beds, what I think are called studio beds, no headboards or footboards, with tailored bedspreads, dark green with white piping, and what looked like dozens of small embroidered pillows. A maple chest separated the beds and a green, white, pink, and black braided rug occupied the floor between them.

"And back here, over the kitchen and office, is the Brewton Suite. This is where Frank and Tommy and I are staying."

"You don't get the Purvis Suite?"

"There isn't a Purvis Suite. Anyway, this is the pick of all the suites. It's bigger, like it might have been a dormitory or something. Come look. Two double beds and a single bed. It's a little more miscellaneous-looking than the others, but look at all the space!"

"Did they go out of their way to decorate the rooms so differently?"

"Good question, Trudy. I asked them that. Willie said they just grouped things together the way they liked them and it sort of came out that way. I think this is the room that got all the leftovers."

It did look like they'd shuffled together remnants of matched sets of furniture. The dresser matched one of the double beds, the chest of drawers matched another. The smaller bed and the rocking chair might have been made from the same wood. What kept the room from looking like a junk/storage room was that all the bedspreads and the curtains were made from the same fabric, cotton with huge pink peonies on a blue background.

"Does Willie consult? Maybe I could get her help if I ever try to fix up my place."

"I don't know about that, but come look at this."

The door opened on to a second-story porch, and we looked down on to the dirt yard where I saw that my car had been joined by another. A staircase with a wooden handrail led from the end of the porch down the back of the house.

"You've found our private entrance," Shawna said. "Tommy loves those stairs. Thinks they're a secret, I guess, put here just for him. Probably supposed to be a fire escape."

At this point in our tour, we were interrupted by a voice that made me think of a chainsaw that had run up against a pine knot.

CHAPTER 3

The strong, grating voice easily carried up the stairs.

"Della? Willie? Anybody here? We came in the front door, since we expect to be treated like guests, not family. Do we get valet service and a bellboy?"

"That'll be Aunt Inez," Shawna said. "Inez Rankin."

"Come on in, Inez. Where's Dennis?" Della's voice, though lower in pitch and in volume, still carried clearly up the stairs and through the open doors.

"He's getting the suitcases. We've been itching to see what you've done with the place."

"She's been itching, she means," Shawna said. "I can't imagine Uncle Dennis giving a hoot."

"Do we get the room Mama and Daddy used to have?" Inez asked.

"No, that's where I live," Della answered.

"Well, where are you putting us?"

"You'll have the Calloway Suite."

"What's that?"

"It's the front bedroom over the library. Aunt Annie said she and Uncle Gordon lived there for a little while right after they got married, before they got a place of their own. Willie thought you'd like that."

"What about that big room in the back?"

"We're calling it the Brewton—"

"I mean, who's got it?"

"Nancy and Tom's daughter, Shawna, and her family."

"Seems like it would have been more respectful to give it to her elders."

"Don't be silly, Inez. Being respectful has nothing to do with it. There are three of them—Shawna, Frank, and their little boy, and they'll need more room."

A deeper voice and a series of thumps suggested that Inez's husband, Dennis Rankin, had joined them.

"Come on up, and I'll show you to your room," Della said.

"I'll carry this one. Think you've brought enough luggage, Inez? It's just for the weekend, isn't it?"

"Wouldn't want to be caught without the right outfit," Inez said.

"And jewels," Dennis added.

"Jewels?" Della asked. "Who do you think you'll impress with jewelry?"

"If you've got it, flaunt it, is what I always say," Inez answered.

"Another whole bag for the right creams, lotions, brushes, soaps, and electrical appliances," Dennis said. "I hope you've had the wiring updated along with everything else, Della."

"Oh! And the plumbing! I do love a nice hot bath," Inez said.

"I think you'll find everything you need," Della said. Something in her tone made me wonder if she was clenching her teeth. "We've tried to think of everything people would need to be comfortable. We've had some special events, you know, and had a few overnighters, but we're still working things out, so you be sure to let us know if there's anything we've forgotten."

"Oh, we will," Inez said.

"You can count on us," Dennis said.

Shawna was easing the door shut. "Here they come."

"It's a family reunion, Shawna. Didn't you expect to spend time with your family?"

"I'll get more than enough of Aunt Inez. Shh!"

Not having had siblings, I can only imagine that Shawna affects me the way a sister would, pulling me helplessly back into old responses and roles. She does not bring out the best in me. Just as I'd always done in high school, often to my regret, I followed her lead. I felt like an adolescent without a hall pass hiding out in the girls' restroom. The door closed with a soft click.

"She doesn't sound happy," I whispered.

"She never sounds happy," Shawna whispered back.

The others thumped up the stairs, right outside our door, and on around to the Calloway Suite.

"Is this Grandmother's trunk, Della?" Inez demanded. "It sure looks like the one she always had at the foot of her bed."

"Yes, I believe it is."

"You believe it is? You don't know?"

"Of course I know. Yes, that was Grandmother's trunk."

"You and Willie think you're pretty smart, don't you?"

"What are you talking about?"

"I'm talking about how you got this house."

"We got this house, if you'll remember, because we bought it when nobody else wanted it. I don't remember you making an offer."

"I wasn't in a position—"

"Don't try to act like you want the place. You wouldn't live in Ogeechee on a bet. You just can't stand the idea that Willie and I have something you don't. You've always been like that. There wasn't anything underhanded about it, and I'll appreciate it if you quit acting like you think there was."

Dennis's voice cut through. "Della, where'd y'all find this shower stall? I've never seen a round one like this."

"Hush, Dennis! Anybody'd think you've never seen indoor plumbing before! Della, I want to know where you got this trunk. And why is it locked?"

33

Shawna and I glanced at each other and stifled a laugh. It seemed obvious that the trunk was locked to keep people out of it, and Inez wouldn't have known it was locked unless she'd tried to open it.

Della's strategy for dealing with her cousin seemed to be selective deafness, but that was having no effect on Inez.

"And while we're at it, I'd like to know where you got that family tree that's out in the hall."

"It came with the house, just like the trunk did."

"Seems like a lot of things just came with the house. Pretty nice for you, I'd say."

"Yes, it was nice." Della's voice, firmly changing the subject, took on a bright, neutral tone, much like Shawna's when she was acting as tour guide. "Y'all going over to Nancy and Tom's for the cookout?"

"You bet," Dennis said. "Tom's barbecuing chicken."

"You haven't heard the last from me about this," Inez said. "Does everybody else know about all the things you just happened to find?"

Della chose to talk to Dennis. "They said we'll eat around six. Go on over whenever you're ready. Well, I think that's all. I won't tell you to make yourselves at home, since I know you will."

"Don't we get a room key?" Inez asked.

"We're working on that," Della answered, "but we don't have them yet. We'll all have to trust each other this weekend. I guess you could pull the trunk up against the door when you go to bed."

"What about during the day, with people in and out?"

"Honestly, Inez!" Even her husband seemed to have had enough of Inez.

Della seemed unruffled. Maybe she was practicing for dealing with the public. "Usually either Willie or I will be here to let you in and keep the riff-raff out."

"The rest of the riff-raff," Shawna whispered. "The non-family riff-raff."

Footsteps and the slam of a door suggested that Della was retiring downstairs and Inez and Dennis wanted privacy.

"That's Inez for you," Shawna said. "Not enough that Della and Willie invited her and Dennis to stay here, she wants to load up her car when she goes home."

"I guess ownership gets a little confused with a big family and everybody feeling like this is the old home place," I said, as much to tease Shawna as to try to be fair.

But she disappointed me. Instead of arguing, she said, "Oh good grief! Look at the time! I told Mama I'd help get things ready for the cookout. I don't know how I let the time get away! As soon as we get a chance, I've got to hear about this boyfriend of yours."

"Phil Pittman," I said.

"Phil Pittman? Really?"

"Really."

"I haven't seen Phil in years and years, but from the way I remember him . . ."

"What? How do you remember him?"

"Oh, sorta cute and a little on the dorky side."

That's not a bad description of him. I started to laugh, but choked on it when Shawna added, with a sly glance, "Maybe I should have gone after him instead of Frank."

"Shawna!"

She laughed. She was always better at teasing me than I was at teasing her. "I'll want all the details! We'll have to find another chance to talk."

"Maybe tomorrow night, after all the to-do. Y'all goin' to hear the mayors?"

35

"Oh, yes. We'll all be there. Uncle Julian is one of the speakers."

"I know," I bragged. "He's the oldest living ex-mayor."

"I'm kind of looking forward to hearing him," Shawna said. "I used to think he was pretty funny, especially if he'd had a snort or two."

When I left, taking the stairs from the porch outside the Brewton Suite rather than going back through the house, I was trying not to be annoyed by Shawna's reaction when I told her Phil Pittman was my romantic interest. Come to think of it, my trying not to be annoyed with Shawna has always been a characteristic of our friendship.

CHAPTER 4

Somebody has to keep the streets of Ogeechee safe, so I had a good excuse for dodging what I couldn't help thinking of as the Mayoral Marathon on Saturday. A speakers' stand and folding chairs had been set up in front of the courthouse and all ten—count 'em, ten—living ex-mayors were given microphone time.

Hen attended, of course. His job shouldn't be political, but is, and even without that nudge in the direction of being seen to be interested in the community, there was the family connection, since Teri's part of the Stubbs clan.

Since this was unquestionably a historic event worthy of *Beacon* coverage, Phil also attended. He would probably even enjoy it.

"You can read all about it in *The Beacon*," Phil assured me with a grin, when I made a crack about enduring speeches by all those present-day or former politicians. He knew I would read all about it. Although I have my faults, lack of loyalty is not among them. And I would probably enjoy reading his account of the event more than I would enjoy actually attending.

Hen's way of gauging if officers on patrol are patrolling or merely hanging out somewhere is to keep track of miles logged on patrol cars, so I was methodically patrolling, keeping an eye on the extra activity around the courthouse and trying to squelch my perverse discontent at being kept away from an event I hadn't wanted to attend in the first place.

One of my sweeps away from the center of town, in recognition of the fact that crime might be going on elsewhere, took me past the Stubbs house.

It sits on the corner of Main Street and (what else?) Stubbs Street, facing Main, a few blocks south of the courthouse. As Inez Rankin's comments had suggested, the door facing Main Street, like most front doors around town, would be considered the formal entry, used mostly by salesmen, strangers, and maybe the preacher, depending on how friendly you were with him. It would be by-passed by friends and family, who would reasonably expect the inhabitants of the house to be somewhere toward the back. They would go to the door at the side of the house, the one leading to the kitchen from the graveled parking area on Stubbs Street, the one I'd used earlier in the day.

I remembered Della telling Inez that either Della herself or her sister Willie would always be at the house for security purposes while they had so many guests. At the time, I'd thought that was quite a commitment, especially in light of the fact that Della had been such a force on the Bicentennial Committee and neither of the sisters would want to miss hearing their uncle speak at the Mayoral Marathon.

So, when I turned the corner on to Stubbs Street and saw a car parked by the kitchen entry and an unfamiliar young man at the door, giving the knob a vigorous shake, it got my attention. He was so focused on what he was doing that he didn't notice me. When he gave up on the doorknob and turned his attention to a window, which he seemed to be trying to open in spite of its resistance, I edged my cruiser close behind the Saturn and burped my siren. Yes, I had created an obstacle to traffic, but police officers can get away with that. The idea was to be an obstacle to the young man's escape, in case he didn't especially want to talk to me. And the siren did draw his attention away from the Stubbs house.

I congratulated myself on my suspicious mind when the white

male, approximately five foot ten and a hundred eighty pounds, probably in his early twenties, with longish curly brown hair, wearing khaki pants and a red golf shirt, turned suddenly, caught sight of me and my uniform, and quickly pasted a smarmy grin over the alarm that had first registered on his face.

"Having trouble?" I asked.

"Uh. No."

"That your house?"

"Uh. No."

"You thinking about breaking in?"

His smile was just as smarmy, but slightly more assured when he said, suggesting an accomplished liar who'd thought of a story, "I was expecting somebody to be here to let me in."

"Who?"

"Huh?"

"Who were you expecting to let you in?"

"Uh. It's funny. I don't remember the woman's name."

"Yeah. That's funny, all right."

"Uh. No. Oh, I see what you're thinking." As if he hadn't known from the beginning. "No, see, I'm from out of town, and my friend arranged for me to stay here."

"Your friend's name?"

He didn't have to stammer over that, at least. "Kevin Purvis."

Shawna's brother. Not a bad answer. "He tell you to come in through the window?"

"No. He said there'd be somebody here."

"And you thought he'd changed his mind about inviting you and talked everybody into being quiet, hoping you'd go away?"

For some reason, I wasn't warming to this man.

"It sounds pretty lame when you put it that way, but I wasn't thinking about it. Obviously, there's nobody here. I guess I'll go see if I can find something to eat somewhere and come back later." He made a move toward the steps, noticed that his car was hemmed in, and, for the first time, seemed to lose confidence. Good.

"Stop right there." I made a gesture toward my Glock. He stopped, holding his hands up and away from his body in the classic pantomime of helpless surrender.

"I guess you think I'm dumb enough to think that just because you can say Kevin Purvis, I'll forget you were trying to break into this house."

"Not break in." Since we were talking again, he dropped his hands.

"Yes. Break in. That's what it's called. Breaking and entering. Doesn't look a bit like sitting in a rocking chair on the porch while you wait for a friend to turn up."

His glance flickered toward the rockers and back to me, still standing on the gravel.

"How do you know Kevin?" I asked.

"We're fraternity brothers."

"Where do you go to school?"

"Athens." University of Georgia. The right answer.

"And what brings you to Ogeechee?"

"I said. Kevin invited me."

"To try to break into a house?"

"No." He bit it off, obviously annoyed but just as obviously unsure how much trouble he was in, given the bad reputation of small-town redneck Southern police forces. He tried to soften it. "He said there was a family reunion this weekend, and mostly they'd be over here if they weren't at his folks' house. I tried there."

"You try breaking in over there?"

"No. And I didn't—"

"I need to see some ID," I told him.

"Why?"

"I think you can figure it out. Now. Fish it out with two

fingers." He did as instructed. "Remove it from your wallet, please. Now, I want you to put it down on that chair and then turn around and put your hands up against the wall there while I make sure you aren't an alligator masquerading as a harmless little turtle. Can't be too careful in my line of work."

In as macho a manner as I could muster, I pushed him against the wall and kicked his legs apart to put him off balance so I could pat him down. "You stay right there, now."

I took my time studying his driver's license, from which I learned that he was Bradley Booth of Columbus, Georgia.

According to the license, both my height estimate and my weight estimate were a little off, but men are notorious for trying to lie about their size when they think they can get away with it.

Noting with satisfaction that Bradley Booth seemed to be uncomfortable leaning against the wall, I carefully made a note of his driver's license number as well as the number on the car's license plate, so I could make a complete record of this encounter later, and so I'd have the information I needed in case he turned out to merit further investigation.

"Okay, you can turn around now."

He did a couple of pseudo-pushups against the wall to ease his arms, and sighed hugely, in case I hadn't noticed how mistreated he was. When he turned, I greeted his frown with a smile as I returned his license to him. "Thank you for your co-operation."

He didn't smile back. In fact, I'd have said he was downright surly as he replaced his driver's license in his wallet and his wallet in his pocket. He was still pouting as he sat in a rocker and began massaging his left calf.

"Why did Kevin think you'd want to come to his family reunion? You related?"

"Not that I know of." He tried a grin. "But you know how

we are here in the South. Probably if you go back far enough, we're all related, one way or another."

"Well, then, cuz, my question stands."

"What question? Oh, why'd I want to come to his family reunion?"

"Uh huh. That question."

"A couple of things, really." He quit massaging his leg and rocked while he considered if he should let me in on it. I waited him out.

"I mean, he's going to make a big announcement to the family, and he wanted me here for backup, like moral support, in case they aren't crazy about it."

That sounded interesting. "You said a couple of things."

"Huh?"

"You're here to help Kevin make an announcement. What else?"

"Oh. Yeah. See, my family's in the antiques business, we really go for that old crap, and Kev said there's a lot of old stuff down here, and maybe I could do some wheeling and dealing. With the school break for Christmas, I figured why not? Maybe I could do a friend a favor and help myself out at the same time."

"Why not? Okay, Bradley, if Kevin will vouch for you, I guess you're off the hook."

"Good."

"Come on. I'll take you to Kevin, and we'll see."

"You aren't taking me to jail, are you?" He was on his feet.

"Not yet. We'll see. Climb in—no, get in the back, please—and I'll take you to him."

"Okay, then!"

It was a pleasant day for outdoor festivities, cool but not cold, and overcast, so that those attending the Mayoral Marathon on the courthouse lawn didn't have to fight the sun.

We got there in the middle of a speech, so we stood behind the rest of the audience to listen. The speaker looked to be in his eighties, a tall balding man with stooped shoulders who had shrunk a bit since he bought the handsome dark suit he was wearing.

"—proudest of what I did to help get a hospital and some good doctors. A lot of you might not be here today if we didn't have that hospital and I hadn't talked Doctor Clifford Holm into giving up the idea of getting rich in some big city to come here. Other people might talk about other things, like the library or the low-income housing, but I'm proudest of the health care. I had the privilege of serving the community for . . . for—"

"Eighteen years," someone from the audience called out.

The speaker smiled ruefully and removed his glasses, folding them and putting them in an inside jacket pocket. "For eighteen years, yes, that's what it says here. I wrote it all down so I wouldn't have to remember it, and then I forgot to keep my place so I can't even find it to read it! Well, now, friends . . . Oh, now Vera's giving me a sign like this—" He drew his forefinger across his throat. "And I guess that means it's time for me to quit talking."

During the applause and laughter that greeted this statement, he turned and made his way down from the speakers' stand. Della Stubbs, beaming, approached the microphone and motioned for the audience to give the old man a standing ovation. "Thank you, Uncle Julian—Julian Stubbs!"

When Julian Stubbs had reached ground level and the applause subsided, Della said, "Thank you all for coming to celebrate our history. You're all invited to come on over to the Anderson Hotel for an Old South Dinner cooked up by some of our civic groups. We've got turnip greens, peas, cornbread, fried chicken, and some of the best banana pudding you'll ever taste."

"Good timing," said my prisoner.

"Don't believe it about the banana pudding," I said.

Hen and Teri had been sitting at the end of a row near the back. He waved and they ambled in our direction.

"Whatcha got there, Officer Roundtree," Hen said in greeting. "Bringing a felon over for a lesson in civic pride?"

"Hey, Hen. Hey, Teri. Enjoying the ceremonies?"

Teri rolled her eyes.

"Best part's coming up," Hen said, pointedly eyeing the growing crowd at the hotel. "We're on our way to reward ourselves for being good citizens."

Far too wise to get between Hen and a meal for very long, I said to my prisoner, "Let me introduce you to my cousin— maybe yours, too, if your theory holds up—Henry Huckabee, our Chief of Police, and Mrs. Huckabee."

"Sheesh," said Bradley.

"Hen, this is Bradley Booth. I just caught him trying to break into the Stubbs house, and he thinks I ought to let him off because he says he's a friend of Kevin Purvis."

"Hey!" Brad said, looking aggrieved.

"Pleased to meet you, son," Hen said, then, to me, "You run him?"

"Hey!" Brad said again, looking from me to Hen and back.

"Not yet. I was thinking I'd deliver him to Kevin. You know where he is?"

"Over there in that clot of people, last I saw," Hen said.

The clot of people Hen indicated was mostly the Stubbs clan, still milling around near the speakers' stand. A laugh with chainsaw overtones drew my attention. Here was a chance to see the woman who matched that voice: a sharp-faced woman with too-dark, spiky hair, was wearing glittering chandelier earrings and a fur stole which the weather didn't call for. Either she'd been away from Ogeechee so long she'd lost her sense of local style or she wanted to demonstrate how far she'd outgrown our backward customs. She tottered on three-inch spikes and had a grip on the elbow of a spindly man far less flashy than she, although the thick, glossy mat of hair—surely a hairpiece!—said he was trying to keep up. This had to be Dennis Rankin.

I spotted Kevin Purvis about the same time he spotted us and loped in our direction with a big grin on his face.

"Brad, my man! I was afraid you were gonna let me down!"

"Who? Me? Have I ever?" Bradley responded.

"Come on and meet my family. Gretchen's over there with her folks."

That would be Gretchen Holland, another UGA student, like Kevin and Bradley, if I remembered correctly. Identity and friendship confirmed. "You're free to go," I said to Bradley.

"Officer Roundtree helped me find you," Brad said to Kevin as he took him by the elbow and urged him out of my presence before I could respond.

I watched Bradley and Kevin for a moment, two young men so uniform in looks and style it would have been easy to confuse them. With willowy, blonde, blue-eyed Gretchen Holland holding hands with Kevin and laughing at something Bradley had said, they'd have made a terrific recruiting poster for UGA. I looked around for new worlds to conquer. That's when I noticed Shawna. She was ignoring Frank, who was holding the hand of a squirming Tommy and dragging him toward the Anderson Hotel while futilely gesturing to get Shawna to join them. Instead of paying any attention to her husband and son, Shawna was laughing seductively up at a medium-sized, sandy-haired man with a camera hanging around his neck. He was smiling fatuously at her and fiddling with the earpieces of his glasses. Phil Pittman.

Seeing me, Phil waved in my direction. Shawna spared me a glance before she leaned over to whisper something in his ear.

Then she, too, waved at me, smiling wickedly.

I squelched a murderous impulse. As I've already said, Shawna doesn't always bring out my best side. Luckily for her, when she hurried to catch up with Frank and Tommy, her path didn't bring her in my direction.

CHAPTER 5

As I drove past the Stubbs house later that evening, revisiting the scene of Bradley Booth's non-crime, my eyes were drawn to the side porch again. This time instead of seeing a young man behaving in a suspicious manner, I saw two glowing red spots dancing in the darkness.

On closer inspection, the spots resolved into the tips of cigarettes in the hands of two women who were gently rocking, draped in blankets against the evening chill. They looked like something you'd see at a theme park devoted to depicting life in the rural South, or character dolls available at a place like Cracker Barrel. The red spots dipped and weaved as the rocking chairs creaked and the women gestured.

"Evenin', Trudy." The voice came from the shape on my left. Squinting into the darkness, I recognized Annie Stubbs, Shawna's grandmother.

"Evenin', Miz Stubbs," I said. Good manners in Ogeechee still dictate using a respectful title when speaking to one's elders. I interpret "my elders" loosely, to mean anybody Aunt Lulu's generation or older. These two certainly qualified.

"Vera, this is Ogeechee's nod to equal opportunities for women, Officer Trudy Roundtree. You know Vera?" Annie asked me.

"Just from a distance," I said. "I know who you are, Miz Stubbs. You're the wife of the oldest living ex-mayor."

Her cigarette flared. "That's us all right, come to revisit the scene of past glories." Her tone was slightly sardonic. I didn't know what to make of it.

"I got to the courthouse this afternoon just in time to hear the end of Mr. Stubbs's speech," I said. "He was mayor before I was born."

"Long time ago," Annie teased.

"Long time ago," Vera echoed, but I sensed she wasn't teasing. "This was his last hurrah. Just about finished him off, but there was no power in heaven, earth, or hell that could have kept him away from this Bicentennial thing once Della started in on him."

"Watch your language, now, Vera," Annie said.

"I've heard Della can be hard to resist," I said.

Annie snorted.

"What're y'all doing out here?" I asked. "Isn't it a little chilly?"

"Not too chilly," Annie said with a laugh, pulling her blanket closer around her shoulders.

Vera picked up the thread. "Gives us a little peace and quiet."

Annie continued, "And we don't have any choice. Della's turned the place into a—what did she call it?—a smoke-free environment."

"She says people have allergies," Vera said.

"And she doesn't want smoke damage," Annie said.

"And she'll be able to tell if we smoke in the bathrooms because it'll set off the smoke alarms," Vera said.

"Like we're on an airplane," Annie said, beginning to giggle.

"And her insurance will go up." Vera barely got this out before she joined Annie in her giggle.

Annie recovered first. "I think she made all that up and Willie just goes along because she can't stand up to her. Della always was the ringleader."

"Amen to that." This came from Vera. "Don't think we're awful for talking about our family like this. Since we just married in, we have a little perspective and don't have to be so protective. You understand."

Actually, I did.

"Vera and I sort of grafted onto this family tree," Annie said, knocking some ash into a saucer she held in her lap. "We married brothers."

"A family tree's a funny notion, isn't it?" Vera asked, knocking ash into her saucer.

Annie laughed. "Gordon and I used to have a pecan orchard, so our children claimed the family tree was a nut tree."

"Hard to argue with that," Vera said. "One with a few rotten branches."

"And a few squirrels," Annie added.

"If you think of it that way," I contributed when we'd all quit giggling, "my family tree—trees—would have to be the magnolias in my front yard." But that observation set off a train of thought I didn't much like. One of those trees was looking unhealthy and might have to come down.

"So, anyway, that's what we're doin' out here," Annie said. "What're you doing here? Like they say on the cop shows on TV, there's nothing here to see. It's all over. Hen didn't call for backup, did he? Or did somebody else call the cops? Don't tell me it's illegal to smoke outside, too."

"No, ma'am, none of the above. I was just driving by." I couldn't explain even to myself why I'd been drawn back to the Stubbs house. Surely it wasn't because I wanted to t.p. Shawna's porch because she'd been flirting with my guy. Surely not. I shook off that thought. "What kind of backup did Hen need? Did the party get wild?"

"Not by Stubbs standards. We're usually fairly lively, but things did get a mite livelier than usual a little while ago."

"That sounds interesting," I said. "What happened? Too

much togetherness?"

"Not enough," Annie said and Vera joined her in a quiet giggle. I waited for an explanation.

"You met that friend of my grandson Kevin's?" Annie asked.

"Yes, ma'am. I almost arrested him for trying to break into this very house."

"Oh, that's right. He told us about that. Didn't put it quite that way, but that was more or less his story," Annie said.

"Well, he is staying here, so that's all right," Vera contributed.

"So what did he do besides bad-mouth me?"

Back to Annie. "Well, we all came over here after the doin's at the courthouse were over, for coffee and goodbyes before everybody starts going back under whatever rock they crawled out from, and somebody noticed that Kevin hadn't turned up. That's when Bradley, Kevin's friend, up and announced that Kevin had asked him to tell us that Kevin and Gretchen Holland had gotten married and were off on their honeymoon. Said it was his last official duty as best man."

"I'd been wondering why he came to your family reunion," I said.

"I wondered the same thing about Jean and Roddy Holland," Annie said. "Not that I have anything against them."

"Hindsight says Kevin and Gretchen wanted them at the party so they'd get the news with everybody else," Vera suggested.

"But why didn't Kevin and Gretchen want to make the big announcement themselves, and accept congratulations?"

"Kevin knew perfectly well that we all think he's too young to get married," his grandmother said. "Nothing against Gretchen, but both of them are just kids. Sounded like Gretchen's mother has something against Kev, though. She carried on like it was the end of the world. Kind of got my back up, I'll tell you."

"You yourself just said they were too young, Annie," Vera said.

"Yes, I know I did, but Jean made it sound more personal."

A squeak from overhead made me look up. Even if we weren't talking about anything private, it was uncomfortable to think somebody might be eavesdropping.

"Ghosts," Annie said, following my glance.

"Really?"

"Uh huh," Vera said. "The house is haunted. Don't know when it started."

"Shawna left that out when she gave me the ten-cent tour," I said. "Who haunts it?"

Annie laughed. "Depends on who's telling it."

"And who they're telling it to," Vera added. "Julian always said it was his brother Franklin, who fell down the stairs when he was two and died from it. Not a mean ghost, though, so nobody worries about it. Matter of fact, it's kind of nice to have something—or would it be somebody?—like that to blame things on. An old house like this is full of noises, especially at night."

"Could be," Annie agreed. "Or if it really is haunted, maybe it's Letha, haunting Della and Willie for what they did to her house."

"Surely not," I protested, buying into the ghost theory. "She couldn't be upset about that. The house is gorgeous."

"Who knows how a ghost thinks?" Annie asked, taking a long pull on her cigarette.

"I certainly don't," Vera said.

"You two work well together," I said.

"Always have," Annie said.

"Born the same week," Vera said. "Grew up together. Wanted to be sisters so bad we wound up marrying brothers."

The way they laughed at that told me they'd used the line

before. I envied them the friendship that had lasted, I guessed, for eighty years, give or take.

Simultaneously, the winking lights were stubbed out. I took the hint. "Guess I'll go on. I hadn't realized how late it was when I came by. Good night."

"Night."

"Night, Trudy."

As I started back to the car I heard Annie's voice. "Ready to go in?"

And Vera. "Not yet. This is the first minute's peace I've had in I don't know when. Let somebody else worry about him for a few minutes. Annie, I don't know if I'm strong enough for the long goodbye. It's hard enough when he's still himself once in a while, but . . . Sometimes, I don't know, I just wish I'd wake up one morning and not have to deal with it anymore. Or not wake up."

"You'll find the strength," Annie said. "The Bible says the Lord doesn't give us more than we can bear."

"Easy for you to say," Vera said, a bit snappishly. "One of these days I may just . . ."

I went on my way thinking about old friendships, unhealthy family trees, ghosts, and an ex-mayor who might be turning into the ghost of himself.

CHAPTER 6

It is so easy to let Aunt Lulu and Teri be hostess at family gatherings that I have to remind myself every now and then to do my share. We all suffer when I do that, since they are both much better at hostessing than I am, and enjoy it more, but we all understand the necessity. For one thing, there's the house.

It's the house Aunt Lulu and my daddy grew up in, and Aunt Lulu herself might have liked to have it, or liked for Hen and Teri to have it. Teri, less diplomatic than Aunt Lulu, frankly had her nose out of joint for a while after Grandma left the house to me. I could understand everybody's feeling that they needed more room than I did. I'm happy to say, though, that they finally seemed to understand my need for a home, too.

If I didn't make a point of inviting them over once in a while, they'd be cut off from the memories that are such an important part of all our lives.

Besides that, I suffer because I feel a higher standard of housekeeping than usual is called for when they come because Aunt Lulu, who grew up there, and Teri have what you might call an understandable special interest. I wouldn't want them to think I'm not taking care of it. Since nobody has ever accused me of being a domestic goddess, I know my efforts to excel in that area are doomed.

All of which explains, more or less, why they were coming for Sunday dinner and why I'd insisted I would do everything. I'd put one of Grandma's embroidered tablecloths on the big table in the dining room instead of using the smaller table on the porch, although that one was big enough for the six of us—Aunt Lulu, Hen, Teri, Delcie, Phil, and me. I'd even hunted up six sets of matching dishes, silverware, and glasses.

"Who're you trying to impress?" Phil asked when I corrected his table setting, insisting that the napkins—yes, cloth napkins!—go next to the forks and on the left side of the plate instead of all in a pile on the plates.

"Nobody."

"Okay. You want me to make bishop's hats or swans or something out of the napkins?"

"Would you?"

"Sure," he said.

"Could you?"

"Not without some research."

"Skip it, then. No time. They'll be here any minute."

"And you're not trying to impress anybody?"

"No. When you're through with that, put the chicken on the big platter that matches the rest of the dishes."

"Why not leave it in the boxes? Won't it stay warmer?" Phil asked. He'd brought the chicken from our favorite take-out place and was feeling proprietary.

"I'm not trying to fool anybody," I said, although he hadn't suggested I was crazy enough to think I could. I tried to cover my blatant lie with something truthful. "It'll make a prettier table."

"I get it," he said. I'm embarrassed to admit he probably did. One of the things I don't always appreciate about Phil is that he's so accommodating it's hard to pick a fight with him.

Between the stresses of watching Shawna making goo-goo eyes at Phil while he smiled at her like an idiot on Saturday and having guests for Sunday dinner, I was spoiling for a fight.

I continued, defensively, "Who in their right mind would

want to mess up the kitchen frying chicken when Miz Smith can do it for you?"

"Nobody," Phil wisely said.

I had made most of the rest of the meal myself, if you count thawing frozen vegetables. I can make decent biscuits, and anybody can chop up lettuce and tomatoes and pour salad dressing on top, so that was okay. I can make pound cake, too, and nobody looks down on you if you use frozen strawberries, so that and store-bought ice cream, all in a pile or separately if you were choosy, as Delcie was apt to be, had dessert covered.

"Mashed potatoes?" Phil asked, unwisely.

"Oh, shoot!"

"Maybe nobody will notice because the table looks so good," Phil suggested. He grinned. "Or you could say with all the food at the Old South Dinner yesterday nobody needs potatoes. You could say it's to keep Hen from eating too much that's bad for him."

"I'm thinking of putting red highlights in my hair," I said.

Phil looked startled, possibly from the rapid change of subject. "Why would you do that?"

"Seems to be the thing these days."

"If you want my opinion—"

"Who said I did?"

"I was just going to suggest you don't do that cranberry juice color your Aunt Lulu has."

"What about the fire-brick color—"

"Here they are."

If I was going to pick a fight with Phil, it would have to wait. First I had to hug Delcie and look at some pictures she'd drawn, and modestly listen to Aunt Lulu and Teri brag on how pretty the table looked, and fix Hen up with a glass of iced tea, which I had not forgotten to make.

"What did you think of the Stubbs house?" I asked Teri, once we were settled at the table and the food was being passed. In all the flurry, nobody got around to mentioning the absence of mashed potatoes or gravy.

"I don't like it as well as this one," she said. "It's nice, but doesn't have nearly the personality. Goodness only knows how much money they've put into it. Delcie, take a few beans, please."

"Yes, ma'am," Delcie said. I watched her count. "Is four a few?"

Teri pierced her with a stare. Delcie added two more, smiling angelically.

"The bathrooms alone!" Aunt Lulu said.

"One of these days, if you'd be willing to do it, I'd like to get together and get your ideas about some of the things that need to be done here," I said.

"You got a fortune we don't know about?" Hen asked.

"Della and Willie could claim a lot of it as business expenses," Phil said. "Della's pretty sharp with finances. She wouldn't have missed that angle."

"It wouldn't all have to be expensive," Teri said. "The hard part might be finding somebody to do it, but Heather Arnold got a man from Glennville who's really good. Anyway, I'd love to help, Trudy."

"I know some things are overdue. Keep after me, Teri, and maybe this time I'll follow through." It has become a family joke that there are things I need to do to the house but don't get around to. Even aside from the expense, there's the cost in energy and emotion. I really want the house to be just like it's always been, so how can I get interested in looking at "updated" fixtures and faucets and cabinets? Even paint? I had to admire Teri's restraint, since I knew she'd love to get her hands on the place, even if it is mine.

"I hear there was quite a ruckus at the party at the Stubbs

house last night," I said.

Hen put down the chicken thigh he'd been working over and grinned in Teri's direction. "Teri's family's a lot more colorful than yours and mine, Trudy. Lordy, I'm glad our family tree doesn't have all those branches. With Shawna Kersey sniping at her husband and screaming at her kid, and Inez Rankin trying to make everybody mad about Della and Willie having all the family stuff, and Julian Stubbs not hitting on all cylinders . . . I thought he was rambling a little bit during his speech, but I put it down to his being very relaxed and knowing he was among friends, but it's worse than that—it was more or less a—yep, a three-ring circus." He'd been raising fingers as he named Shawna, Inez, and Julian, and seemed very pleased that he'd ended up with three.

"Don't let it get you down, Hen," I said. "I'm sure if we shook as many branches as they do, we'd be in their league. I seem to remember a story about a great-uncle, something about a horse race and heavy betting and a gate that wasn't big enough for his wagon to go through."

"Well, yeah." Hen grinned at me. "Grandma liked to tell it from the point of view of the old boy who'd bet against him, the one who fell off the fence laughing and broke his arm when the wagon hit the gateposts and broke into a big pile of match-sticks. Lordy, I wish I'da been there to see that."

"The stories about that great-uncle always centered on what a sport he was, and somehow or other I always knew that didn't mean sportsman, like in athlete or hunter," I explained to Phil. "I have a feeling he was a mean old rascal."

"Oh, he was a sportsman like in gambler," Aunt Lulu contributed, "like somebody who lived dangerously and skirted the law, as in 'the sportin' life.' I've never been exactly sure what that means, but with Uncle Crowell I thought it meant dangerous. He scared me. As a child, I always avoided him as much as possible. Mama liked this story, where he got his come-uppance."

Hen smiled and picked up his chicken again, but instead of eating, he waved it to underscore this afterthought. "With all the general uproar, and then the way Jean Holland carried on when that Bradley character announced Kevin and Gretchen had gotten married and taken off on their honeymoon, you'd have thought the rapture had happened and she'd been left behind. It was more like a four-ring circus. Way more stress and strain than I'd bargained for on my day off."

"Even the embodiment of law and order ought to be able to relax once in a while," Phil said, forgetting that he never lets himself go off duty, either.

"Well, it isn't like anybody was expecting you to keep the peace at a family gathering," Aunt Lulu said.

"I almost waded in, in spite of myself, from force of habit," Hen said, "but I was waiting to see if anybody started breaking out weapons."

"At least Delcie and Tommy Kersey got along," Teri said. "Pretty much entertained themselves the whole time. Who'd have thought the kids would behave better than the adults?"

"I heard the ruckus about Kevin and Gretchen upstaged whatever else was going on," I said.

"Well, it would," Teri said. "The surprise of it and all."

"Yep," Hen contributed. "Seemed like it gave everybody something to focus on and get upset about together, since it was at least halfway out of the family and the kids weren't there to defend themselves. Then, some of 'em starting takin' up for Kevin and—"

"Honestly, Trudy, emotions were running so high he had to go get another helping of pecan pie to settle himself down." Teri is usually content to let Hen do the talking, but when she does talk, and especially if she interrupts Hen to do it, she's worth listening to.

"It wasn't very smart of Jean to have a fit about it right there with all of Kevin's family, was it?" Aunt Lulu asked nobody in particular. "How would she expect them to take it?"

"Beats me. Women don't always think straight where their young'uns are concerned." Hen, secure in his own position as favored son and husband, grinned from his mother to his wife.

"Gretchen's being adopted might make it worse," Aunt Lulu said.

"I heard something about that," I said. "Jean is Gretchen's aunt as well as her mother? Is that right?"

"That's right," Aunt Lulu said. "That girl has been the center of Jean's life. Sort of took the place of her sister. You know about that?"

"Just a little," I answered.

"It was a sad story. Not that anybody knew the whole story, mind you. Maybe not even Jean knows the whole story. Jean was a few years older than her sister, Karen, Gretchen's mother, and when their mother died and their daddy married a woman with children of her own, a woman who didn't take to her stepchildren, Jean turned into a real mother hen."

"Cinderella with a younger sister?" Phil suggested.

"Cinderella?" Delcie asked, looking up from the modern-art composition she'd been making out of her six green beans.

"Take one more bite of beans and you can be excused if you want to," Teri said. "We'll call you when we get to dessert."

Delcie scooped out the middle of her composition and smiled at her mother.

"Delcie, come with me! There's something I forgot to do before y'all got here," I said.

"What?"

"Come on. It's something I used to do, and your daddy used to do, and your grandmother used to do, right here in this house and especially at Christmas."

"What? What?"

"You go clear off the table on the porch and when you get back, I'll show you," I said.

She dashed away, on task. If my childhood memories served me, I'd find the jigsaw puzzles in the cupboard outside the bathroom, one of the many things about the house that hadn't been changed in years—certainly not since I'd inherited it. By the time Delcie got back to me, I had spread a dozen puzzles on the floor.

"Let's pick a Christmas one," I suggested.

There were three Christmas puzzles: a tranquil Currier and Ives print, a collage of chocolate candy wrappers, and a robust Santa with a can of Coca Cola and a bulging pack on his back. No contest. Delcie reached for Santa Claus.

We poured it out onto the table. I leaned the box against the wall so that the picture was in view, and she began turning the pieces face up, methodically setting aside the straight-edged pieces.

When I got back to the dining room, having rescued Delcie from the sordid story of Gretchen Holland Purvis's family tree, Aunt Lulu was still on the Cinderella theme.

"It might have been something of a Cinderella story, but without the happily ever after. Whatever the truth of it is, Jean took care of Karen like a mother, and then when Karen started running wild, Jean felt like it was her fault for not being a good mother. When Karen turned up 'in trouble,' as we used say, Jean had seven kinds of hissy fits. Right after Gretchen was born, Karen threw herself off that bridge in Savannah that goes over to South Carolina. She didn't even try to make it look like an accident. Wanted people to feel sorry for her. Spoiled. I never did like her very much, anyway, and here she went and did that, leaving Jean with a load of guilt for not being a good enough mother to her sister."

"Who was the father?" I asked. "Somebody from around here? Somebody who had to leave town when he wouldn't do the right thing?"

"She's so naive," Phil said to everybody but me.

"That's a part of the story I don't know," Aunt Lulu said. "Jean might not even know for sure. Or maybe she knew all along and didn't say anything so the boy wouldn't have any claim on Gretchen."

"Wow."

"So you can see why Jean might take it so hard that Gretchen eloped instead of giving her a shot at a big church wedding. I think Jean felt like Gretchen was her second chance, a way to make up for failing her sister."

"You don't think it has anything to do with Kevin or the Purvises?" Teri asked.

Aunt Lulu shook her head. "Why would Jean object to Kevin?"

Except that he was Shawna's brother and Shawna's stock with me was pretty low, I couldn't find anything especially wrong with Kevin, either.

"So, Mama," Hen said, taking a breather between chicken and dessert, "I hear you and the Geezerettes are planning some Super Bowl hijinks now that the Bicentennial's behind us and most of Christmas is under control."

"Who told you that?" Aunt Lulu said, looking at me.

"The eyes and ears of the Ogeechee Police Department are everywhere," he answered.

"This isn't police business," she said.

"No, ma'am, I didn't mean to say it was. So what's up?"

"It's still in the planning stages."

"Something for *The Beacon?*" Phil asked.

It seemed that Aunt Lulu turned to him with relief. "It might be, Phil, thank you, once we get it all ironed out. We're still researching it."

"Idle minds are the devil's workshop?" Hen suggested.

I thought that was kind of clever, but Aunt Lulu bristled. "Our minds aren't idle, and what makes you think the devil has anything to do with it?"

I put her short temper down to overwork and the stress of the recent festivities right at the Christmas season.

"I think everything went well at the Bicentennial on Saturday," Phil said.

"If you don't count that poor excuse for banana pudding they served," Aunt Lulu said, recovering her usual good humor. I was glad I'd decided to offer pound cake and strawberries, which I now brought to the table.

"Dessert, Delcie," I called.

"Just a minute," she called back.

"I got there right at the end of Julian Stubbs's speech," I said to those at the table.

"People around here still have a lot of respect for Mr. Stubbs," Phil said. "Next week's paper will have a story about some of the things he did for the town, sort of a testimonial."

"He did do a lot for the town, no two ways about it," Aunt Lulu said, "but don't you go and try to make him out to be a saint."

"Wasn't he a saint?" Phil asked, giving me a wink, which I ignored. He has a way of being mildly provocative in interviews that brings out good stories.

"Watch out, Mama," Hen said. "I have a feeling he's working, not just making conversation."

"Oh, I'm not worried," Aunt Lulu said. "I know Phil well enough to know he wouldn't want to stir up muck just for the sake of it."

"Muck's my business," Hen said, spooning extra strawberry

juice over his ice cream. "What kind of muck is there to stir up?"

"Not muck. Not real muck, and y'all can't make me say there is," Aunt Lulu huffed. "But some people said Julian didn't always walk the straight and narrow."

"Graft? Corruption? Right here in Ogeechee?" Phil asked.

"That was before the present law enforcement regime," Hen said.

"What do you mean, Aunt Lulu? What kind of straying from the straight and narrow?"

"I don't want to gossip," she claimed. "I just don't think Phil ought to make out like Julian was a saint, that's all. He was in politics around here for a good while, and nobody can do that without making some people mad."

"I'll try not to give him a halo," Phil said.

"And you'd better check anything he tells you," Hen said.

"Yes," Teri said. "Jean Holland was annoyed even before Bradley told about Kevin and Gretchen because Uncle Julian kept calling her Karen."

"Poor old Julian," Aunt Lulu said. "He's probably living in the past. Karen worked for him for a while, so he knew her better than he did Jean."

"Did you get that puzzle finished?" Hen asked Delcie.

"I finished turning the pieces right-side-up," she said.

"Need some help?" he asked.

She nodded.

We all took our bowls of dessert to the porch, where we let Aunt Lulu and Delcie have chairs around the table while the rest of us jockeyed for a spot.

Many hands do make light work, even when it's something like a jigsaw puzzle, where it's easier to get in each other's way than to be helpful. Before they left, we'd pieced together the entire border and Phil had assembled most of the Coca-Cola bottle. Delcie concentrated on the various toys that were sticking out of Santa's pack.

All in all, it was such a successful and entertaining dinner party I forgot about quarrelling with Phil until after he'd already gone home. That's just as well, because he fights dirty. He doesn't fight back with the universally accepted weapons of warfare between the sexes. He usually seems to think it's funny when I get riled up and go on a tear, and more often than not I wind up laughing at myself right along with him. Even when I'm upset with him, which doesn't happen very often, he thinks it's funny. Either he is seriously defective in some important way, or he is the best balanced, most secure person I've ever known.

CHAPTER 7

"How come you knew so much about the goin's-on Saturday night?" Hen asked the next morning when I met him at the official station house coffeepot.

"Informants," I said.

"Glad to know you've got informants," Hen said. "That's a real asset in police work."

I thought of my informants, two elderly women banished with their cigarettes to a chilly porch. "Oh, yeah. My network is vast and comprehensive. It never sleeps. Nothing happens on my turf without my knowledge."

"Yeah. And you're a one-woman anticrime unit." The expression on his face should have warned me not to ask, but I asked.

"What do you mean?" I took a sip of coffee and decided to use it to unclog the sink instead of drinking it.

"When Bradley Booth didn't think I was within earshot, he was regaling the assembly with a hair-raisin' tale of his encounter with a hard-nosed, ball-bustin', gun-totin' female impersonator who's gonna give the whole field of law enforcement a bad name on accounta her mistreatment of an innocent visitor to our fair city." Hen paused. "Or words to that effect."

"That would be me," I admitted.

"Made me plumb proud, Trudy, plumb proud."

"I'm plumb grateful," I responded, and hastened to change the subject. "Anything else you want to say about the party out of Teri's hearing?"

He shook his head and watched his coffee follow mine down the drain. "Being the in-law, I do my best to be a wallflower at her family gatherings. Yeah, it's a strain," he added without looking up, just as though he could see those words forming in my mind.

"Teri wanted to go see the house they're all so proud of, and I thought that's all we were going to do—that and have a cup of coffee—" he looked at the coffee grounds in the sink and shuddered "—and to say goodbye to the out-of-towners. Whoo!"

"Did that 'whoo' refer to the coffee, the house, or the out-of-towners?"

"Uh huh."

"It surprised me that not even Aunt Lulu had the scoop on who Gretchen's father was," I said, unwilling to get to work.

"Maybe he wasn't from around here and they were just two star-crossed lovers that passed in the night."

If Hen was going to start mixing his metaphors, and sappy metaphors at that, it was time to bring him down to earth. "Did you think Aunt Lulu was acting peculiar about the Super Bowl party the Geezerettes are working on?"

"No telling what that buncha women will get up to. Maybe she was afraid we'd laugh at her."

"Us?"

"Yeah, us," he said.

"Well, I did tease her about its not being a real Super Bowl party without beer, men, and gambling. I'm not sure she took it in the spirit I meant it."

He did laugh then. "Matter of fact, even when I'm laughing at 'em, I'm getting a kick out of what they come up with. Sometimes I wonder if they keep pushing the envelope, the way kids will, to see what kind of reaction they'll provoke from people."

"Anything to keep from being written off as harmless old

ladies? I hope I'm that kind of old lady. I mean, mature woman."

"Yeah, Trudy, I hope so, too."

"At least they gave up trying to be detectives," I said.

"Thank good merciful heavens for that!" Hen said. "I gotta admit it's a stretch for me to picture them stocking up on beer and cheese dip and watching the Super Bowl."

"Whatever shape their party takes—and did I tell you it's supposed to be a fund-raiser of some kind?—it probably won't look much like it would if you planned it."

"A fund-raiser, huh? Hmm."

I was turning back to my paperwork when Dawn, the dispatcher, interrupted to tell us that Willie Lanier had called to report a theft or a burglary or a robbery. Willie wasn't clear on the nuance and didn't appreciate Dawn's well-meaning attempts to clarify whether it was burglary (Did somebody break in? At night?) or robbery (Was it face to face? Was the perpetrator armed?), but was clear that she needed somebody to come investigate.

"I've had just about all of that bunch I can stomach," said the Chief of Police. "You go see about it, Trudy."

"Yes, sir," I said cheerfully, grateful for the distraction. Paperwork can always wait.

CHAPTER 8

When I got to the Stubbs house, the parking area at the side held two cars. The tan Saturn I now recognized as Bradley Booth's seemed to cower at one end, as far as it could get from the silver Lincoln that was parked at an angle near the opposite end. Graciously leaving room for the guest who had obviously occupied the middle of the space, I circled the block and parked on Main Street, in front of the house. Since I was on official business, not coming as a friend or a guest, it was probably more fitting that I come in the front door, anyway.

Noting the Bicentennial Committee's yard sign, "Stubbs House, circa 1900," it occurred to me that it would help customers find the bed and breakfast establishment. It amused me to think the sign in my yard might make people think the Roundtree house was a business establishment, as well. Boy, would they be in for a surprise if they came to my door.

Willie Lanier answered the door wearing an apron. Central casting got it backwards. Willie's dumpling-like, business-savvy sister, Della, looked like everybody's idea of a homemaker; Willie, the real wife, mother, and homemaker, was tall and angular. Put her in a business suit and she'd command respect in any board room. Her short hair looked barbered, rather than coiffed. If she patronized the Cut-n-Curl, she wasn't a very good advertisement.

"Come on in," she said, wiping her hands on the apron. "You caught me in the middle of cleaning up from breakfast. I might as well tell you right now I didn't want to call you."

"If there's been a crime, you were right to call the police." My conversation with Hen had me wary and neutral.

She glanced heavenward, or maybe merely upstairs. "Well, Inez said she'd call if I didn't."

I pulled out my notepad and tried to look official. "Inez? That would be your cousin Inez Rankin?"

"You know her?"

"We haven't met, but I know who she is." I wrote down the name. "What's the problem?"

"Inez says somebody stole her diamond earrings—those tacky monstrosities she wore to the mayors' speeches yesterday. You were there. You must have seen them."

Yes, I remembered the earrings. Willie's careful disassociation from the crime, the alleged crime—"Inez says"—strengthened my impression that she had her doubts about a theft.

Considering what I knew of Inez, it wouldn't be too much of a stretch to believe she was just bent on making trouble for her cousins. "Is she here? I ought to talk to her."

"She was here a few minutes ago, stomping around, threatening me with everything from lawsuits to physical abuse if I didn't report the crime."

"You want me to arrest her for intimidation?"

The furrow on Willie's brow eased and a smile told me how much she liked the idea, but all she said was, "I'll get her."

She went to the bottom of the stairs and yelled, "Inez? The police are here." The system lacked the gentility I'd have expected from such a high-toned bed and breakfast establishment, but it worked.

"I'll be there in a minute," Inez called back in that grating voice I remembered.

"She'll be here in a minute," Willie repeated with a slight smile.

Linda Berry

"Is there anything you can tell me while we wait for her?" I asked, pencil poised.

Willie gestured impatiently toward the dining room. "I can tell you I've got work to do and this nonsense isn't getting it done."

It was obvious that the housekeeping staff—Willie—had work to do before the room was the pristine showplace I'd seen the day before. The carefully arranged display I'd seen on the sideboard had been pushed aside as if to make room to set something down. The porcelain hand that had held up an amber necklace seemed oddly frozen in mid-gesture, Queen Elizabeth without a fawning crowd. I could imagine Inez Rankin pushing things aside to make room for her pocketbook, or just for the sake of messing it up. I followed Willie into the dining room, where the remnants of breakfast waited. A pitcher with some orange juice in it, glasses, a cereal box, crumpled napkins, dirty plates, cups, saucers, showed the effect of real life on the artificially beautiful scene of the day before.

"Did your bunch of guinea pigs eat and run off?" I asked.

"Well, more or less. Some of them tried to be nice about it— Julian and Frank, anyway—but no matter when you serve a meal, it's too early for some people and too late for others, and they all had plans and took off as soon as they could. Dennis was so impatient to get out and start fishing that he couldn't even wait and eat with everybody else. He sat in the kitchen and gobbled it down as soon as it was off the stove. Not quite what Della and I had in mind for our genteel breakfasts. The others weren't in that big a hurry, but they didn't hang around."

"Fleeing the scene of the crime?" I suggested.

She made an unladylike noise and gestured toward the messy table. "Uh huh. Every last one of them."

"Do you know where they went?"

"I'm just the chief cook and bottle-washer, not the activity

70

director." But she smiled and relented. "I don't know who's actually here and who isn't, but Inez will probably want you to give the whole bunch the third degree." Willie seemed to be taking roll as she circled the table, putting silverware into a shallow pan, throwing napkins into a pile on the floor.

"Della left before breakfast so she could get to Savannah early and take care of some business she'd been putting off till the Bicentennial was over. All this came up after she left, so she doesn't even know about it. Too bad. She can usually stand up to Inez better than I can, and we might not have had to bother you."

I shrugged. "It's my job. What about the rest of them?"

She tossed another napkin. "Well, Bradley said he was going running, so you'll have to talk to him later. I kind of feel sorry for the boy."

"Why's that?"

She gave me a sidelong glance. "Kevin Purvis invited him, and then left him stuck here with a bunch of strangers old enough to be his parents or grandparents. Not much fun for a young man like him. Give him credit, he tried to make the most of it, entered into the conversations, acted interested in our family stories. Even seemed to enjoy looking at all the antiques. He's going back to Columbus today, but he's not in any hurry about it. He asked if he could leave his things in the room till a little later, so he could clean up before he leaves. Suited me. I won't get to the upstairs for a while, anyway."

She moved on around the table. "Frank and Shawna have already cleared out. Left right after breakfast. They're going over to stay with her folks, since Kevin took off and doesn't need that room."

"I heard about Kevin."

"And the uproar, too, I'll bet."

"A little bit. What did you think about it?"

71

"Maybe it's easy for me to say because my kids married people I like, but I don't see any point in getting into a swivet about it. Especially since it's already done and all. Yes, Kevin and Gretchen are both young, but that doesn't have to mean they don't know what they're doing. If I was the Purvises and the Hollands, I'd put a big smile on my face and help the kids as much as I could and hope for the best. Don't see any point in making the in-laws think you've got something against them."

"From what I hear, it's too late for your good-sense advice."

"There's never a good time for unasked-for advice, no matter how much sense it makes," she said, then continued taking roll. "Julian and Vera are still here. They're upstairs. And Inez, of course." She glanced toward the stairs. "Inez's sure taking her time for somebody who was all het up about getting you over here."

"That's all right. No hurry. Anything that gets me away from the paperwork waiting for me at the station house is fine with me. Besides, I'm enjoying talking to you. Tell me about the bed and breakfast angle. Looks like you go all out for your guests. I hope they appreciate it."

"Some do. Actually, we haven't had many guests yet, real guests, I mean. We're kind of practicing on the family bunch to see what works and what doesn't."

"So all this—" I gestured at the messy table "—was a practice breakfast?"

"You could say so." She circled the table again, stacking coffee cups and saucers.

"How'd it go?"

"Not too bad, considering everybody's tired of each other and itching to be somewhere else. But I told them if they wanted the breakfast part of the bed and breakfast, they'd do it my way."

"Good for you. Your real guests will all have breakfast together?"

"It may not be a good idea, and we may have to change our minds about it, but that's what I told them. Della and I are still working on it. I have enough else to do that I don't want to be in the kitchen doing short orders to suit everybody's whim. We've thought about putting out a continental breakfast that they could pick up whenever they wanted it, but I don't want to do it that way. I like cooking and setting a pretty table and all."

"Even if it's a lot of extra work?"

She shrugged and began removing the tablecloth. "We think of it as an added attraction, something that will feel special to most people."

"You could be right," I said, thinking of the carton of yogurt I had eaten in the car on my way to work and the terrible coffee I found once I got there. "Will you always have the same breakfast menu?"

"Well, now." She stopped wadding up linen while she thought about it. "We're still working on that, too, but we thought three different breakfast menus would be about right. Mostly, people won't stay more than a night or two, and it would be nice to give them some variety. Today we had sausage and eggs and grits and biscuits—" she pointed disdainfully at the remnants on various plates "—since I know Julian and Vera are partial to that sausage Junior Wilcox makes in spite of all the jokes about him using road kill to fill it out. We'll always have cereal and fruit, for people who don't want a big breakfast. That's what Shawna's boy had. It seemed to work out pretty well today, in spite of everything. Not even Inez and Shawna found much to complain about."

"What other menus have you worked out?" Breakfast is one of my favorite meals, maybe because I don't usually have time for it, and I was torturing myself.

"We were thinking French toast with bacon and homemade jelly and then, anytime we had somebody three mornings in a row, maybe an egg-and-cheese casserole with ham and toast to go with it. What do you think?"

"Sounds great." I tried not to, but I must have sounded hungry.

"The eggs are all gone, but how do you feel about sausage and grits?"

"I feel very friendly toward sausage and grits," I said.

"Come on back, then," Willie said, handing me the cereal box and picking up her tray, kicking aside the pile of laundry as she led the way to the back of the house. "One of the things we've got to figure out is how much to make. Waste not, want not, you know. We don't want to be eating leftovers all week long."

A minute later I was sitting in front of a plate full of grits and sausage, with a glass of orange juice on the side, watching Willie pour me a cup of coffee. I could learn to live like that.

While I ate, I watched Willie work. She was efficient and careful, obviously respecting the good old dishes and silver she'd used to serve her family. She refilled my coffee cup and looked at my empty plate.

"There's more," she said.

"That was plenty. Plenty and delicious. Thank you." I heaved the biggest sigh I could get around the belly full of breakfast. "I could be working while we wait," I said, taking out my notepad and pencil again. "Is anything missing besides the earrings?"

"If they're missing," she said. Then she turned thoughtful. "I don't know. I don't think so. It never occurred to me to look."

"Maybe we should look around while we wait for Inez."

"Okay." She looked around the kitchen. "Nothing of much value in here, if you don't count the stuff that's nailed down."

"What about the dining room? Anything valuable in there?"

"Some of the dishes, maybe. But, really, Trudy, I think Inez just likes to be the center of attention. I don't even believe anybody took her earrings."

"Might as well look like we're taking her seriously, though, as long as I'm here."

"All right. If you say so." She led the way back to the dining room and looked around, obviously humoring me. Then her attention came to rest on the china cabinet. "Most of what's here is just knickknacks, pretty, but not especially valuable. There's a pair of vases we've always thought was special. I think they're ugly, sort of a muddy brown color with some muddy-looking flowers on them, so I don't put them right out where everybody can see them. The story is they came from somebody famous, but we've never had them appraised or anything. They're right—"

She stopped in the act of opening the glass door and looked at me in surprise. "They're supposed to be right here, behind this platter, but they're not."

"Are you sure you haven't moved them?"

"No. This is where they always are."

"Might Della have moved them?"

"To where? I'm completely fuzzled."

"How big are they?"

"Oh, about a foot tall. Maybe a little taller."

I made a note. "You let me know if they turn up, will you?"

"Sure. Yes. I don't know what to think."

"Let's see if there's anything else," I suggested.

As Willie was closing the door to the china cabinet, creaking from overhead reminded me of the ghost stories of the night before. I was just about to ask Willie's position on the haunting question when calamity struck.

The sounds from overhead gained in decibels and confusion and were followed by a strangled cry—words that sounded like "No! Don't!" Ghostly overhead creaking was drowned out by the unmistakable sound of something tumbling down the stairs—chaotic *thumps,* interrupted by a louder *thunk,* a human-sounding airy grunt, and then silence.

Willie and I reached the foot of the stairs at the same time and barely avoided stumbling over the still form of Julian Stubbs. Instead of grabbing the banister, which might have saved him, it looked as if the poor man had reached for the framed family tree I'd last seen hanging on the wall at the top of the stairs. He lay on his side, clutching the heavy frame.

There were no protruding bones, no part of him at an unnatural angle, but I could see a slight wound on his head, hardly more than a scrape, as though he'd hit something on his way down, poor man. For a moment it seemed possible that he would stand up and smile at us, deprecating his clumsiness, but the moment stretched on, and he didn't move.

Did I hear ghostly footsteps retreating?

CHAPTER 9

"Julian? Julian?" Vera Stubbs, both hands holding tightly to the handrail as she awkwardly descended, looked pale and shaken, as if she might actually have seen a ghost. "Is he all right?"

"What happened? What's going on?" This was Inez Rankin, close behind Vera. Even in the stress of the moment, I noticed that Inez appeared to be completely dressed, ornamented, and cosmeticized. Why had she delayed coming down to make her report after being so insistent that Willie call the police? Had she been playing some infantile power game with me, for goodness' sake, or with Willie?

"Don't ask me what happened. You were with him."

Vera paused in her downward journey to turn and look up at her cousin. Inez nearly tripped over her. "Why would you say a crazy thing like that?" she snapped back, grabbing at the handrail. "I was in my room. You were the one out there talking to him."

"I was not, either! What . . ."

"Hold it," I said, trying to forestall further injury. "The first thing we need to do is take care of Mr. Stubbs."

Vera hurried down the few remaining steps and knelt at her husband's side. "Julian?" She patted the wound on his forehead and seemed to be talking to herself, reciting an old story. "He bleeds so easy. I think it's his blood pressure medicine. He didn't used to be so thin-skinned."

"Don't move him," I cautioned, even though his absolute

stillness made me fear it wouldn't make a bit of difference to him.

I reached for my belt radio, but Willie was already on the phone to the 911 operator. I took the phone from her and identified myself. "I'm on the scene. Can you get an ambulance rolling?" We could expect quick service. The hospital is on Main Street, only a few blocks from the Stubbs house.

"I don't know why you want to pretend you weren't talking to him." Inez wouldn't let the quarrel die. "No law I know of against talking to your husband, is there, Officer?"

As I looked down at Julian and Vera Stubbs, my imagination supplied ghostly footsteps retreating from the top of the staircase. "What? Oh, no. Most people think it's a good idea for married couples to talk to each other."

My mind was racing. I'd come to the Stubbs house to investigate the theft of a pair of earrings. Now, with Julian Stubbs tumbling down the stairs and Vera and Inez sniping at each other over which one of them had been talking to him, the house had suddenly become more interesting. No, I had no real reason to think he'd been pushed, but I wanted to know why he fell. Everybody's priorities are clear in a situation like this, no matter how ambiguous the circumstances. Preservation of life comes first, and the interest of the paramedics would be in seeing to Julian Stubbs. That would take precedence over investigation of a crime scene, if there was a crime scene, which there probably wasn't, but my job was to do the best I could to preserve evidence, if any. I reached to take the framed Stubbs family tree from Julian's hand, lifting it by the wire.

The awkwardness did not go unnoticed.

"My fingerprints will be all over that," Willie said. "I live here and do the housecleaning, after all."

"What?" Inez squawked. "What did that mean, Willie? What's that got to do with . . . oh." She turned to me. "You don't mean to say you think somebody pushed him?"

Vera, her hand on her husband's chest, gave me a stricken look.

I could hear the ambulance pulling up outside. "We'll talk about that later," I said. "Right now, y'all need to get out of the way." I gestured toward the library as I opened the front door for the paramedics.

"Come on, Aunt Vera," Willie said. She helped Vera to her feet and led the way into the library. Inez shot me an evil look as I shooed her in after them.

I got myself out of the way, too, stepping into the doorway of the living room, a vantage point from which I could see the women dithering in the room across the hall and the paramedics bent over Juilian at the foot of the stairs. As the paramedics moved into the intricate but carefully choreographed ballet that so often means the difference between life and death, I leaned the family tree against the inside wall of the living room and used my belt radio to call for a different kind of help, keeping my voice low.

"Hen? I need you at the Stubbs house. Julian Stubbs just fell down the stairs. The paramedics are here, but I'm pretty sure he's dead."

Even if Hen does outweigh Aunt Lulu by about a hundred pounds, I'm sure she would have tried to wash his mouth out with soap if she'd heard the very next word he uttered, but he said he was on his way.

When the gurney holding Julian Stubbs passed my doorway on the way out of the house, I stepped across the hall.

"Can't I go with him?" Vera was asking.

"No, it's better if you don't do that," I said.

Willie was quick to support me. "You don't want to get in the way in the ambulance, Aunt Vera. I'll drive us over there. We'll be right behind them. You want to go, Inez?"

Inez caught my eye as she shrugged.

"We can talk later," I said. "Y'all go on to the hospital. Don't worry about the house, Willie. I want to look around, anyway, and see if I can figure out what made him fall, and I'll lock up when I leave."

"Look around?" This was Inez, naturally. "Is that police jargon for searching the place? Don't you need a search warrant for that?"

"Not if I have permission to look around. It's what's called a 'consent search.'" I raised my eyebrows in Willie's direction.

"By all means," she said. "Make yourself at home."

"He probably just stumbled," Inez said. "Old people do that, don't they? She's just trying to impress us with her gun and all." She turned to me. "You can't intimidate us."

"Willie, can we go?" It was Vera Stubbs.

"Yes, Aunt Vera. Let's go. You comin', Inez?"

"Shouldn't somebody stay here to keep an eye on her to keep her from planting evidence?"

This suggestion earned Inez a stare from each of us. Vera's conveyed puzzlement. Willie's held mild surprise. I'm sure mine held exasperation.

Inez abandoned that position. "Okay, I'll come with you. Just let me get my purse."

"Not if it's upstairs," I said. "Until we find out why Mr. Stubbs fell, I'm treating the house, especially the upstairs, as a crime scene. It's off limits. Besides Mr. Stubbs's fall, there's also the issue of the missing earrings. That's why I'm here in the first place, you may remember. I'll keep my eyes open for them, too." We'd see about intimidation.

Willie Lanier, from the secure position of one who was with me when her uncle fell and could not therefore be suspected of contributing to his fall, smiled at me, then at her cousin, Inez. "Let's go, then."

As soon as the three of them were out the door, I got the roll of crime-scene tape from my car and strung it from the sideboard around the end of the stairs. Then I got evidence bags from my cruiser and bagged the framed family tree. I donned the gloves that would keep me from contaminating evidence and headed up the stairs, studying each step as I climbed.

Feeling like Sherlock Holmes, I used a large magnifying glass, peering at the handrail and each of the turned spindles along the banister for any bit of hair or skin or blood that would indicate Julian had hit it on his way down. I found nothing that showed signs of having come into contact with anything more than Willie Lanier's feather duster.

There was nothing obviously amiss, nothing I could see to account for the old man's fall. Of course, since I was determined to be suspicious, I remembered that Inez had been the last one down the stairs. If she'd put something there to trip Julian, she could have removed it. But why would she have done it? And would even Inez have had the gall to be so obnoxious afterwards? Vera? At the moment, discounting ghosts, they were the only two possibilities. Would I be able to find something to account for Julian Stubbs's fall, something that would incriminate or clear his niece or his wife of sixty-something years?

"Anybody up here?" I called. No answer. I knocked on each of the closed bedroom doors and called again. Nothing.

Sunlight filtered into the hallway from Willie's sitting room at the front of the house, and the chandelier that hung in the center of the ceiling was on, but even so, with all the bedroom doors closed, the light in the hallway was dim. Had Julian taken the framed family tree from the wall in order to see it better? To move to better light? Had the dim light caused him to make a misstep?

I examined the carpet and posts at the top of the stairs. No loose carpet. No trip wire or other impediment and no holes for tacks, nails, or screws; no scratches, no obvious sign that anything had been attached. Inconclusive. I stood in front of the spot where the family tree had hung and went through the motions of taking it from the wall. If Julian had, for some reason, removed it and turned quickly, might he have lost his balance? No. Even if he had, it was too far from the head of the stairs for him to have fallen down them.

Could he have banged his head into the wall with such force that a staggering recoil would have sent him down the stairs?

Highly unlikely. A careful examination of wall and door frames within a reasonable distance of the head of the stairs revealed nothing.

Could he have started down the stairs and simply stumbled, as Inez suggested? Not unlikely. He was an old man, after all, and his vision and balance might have been impeded by the frame. That was probably what happened.

Sometimes being a police officer involves more judgment calls than hard science, and my judgment told me I was fishing in a dry hole, as Hen might have said. If somebody had pushed Julian or otherwise contributed to his death, what kind of evidence could I expect to find? Stubborn to the core, I kept looking. Willie Lanier's casual "Make yourself at home," constituted legal permission for me to search her areas of the house, the common areas, but that permission did not extend to the private rooms the others inhabited, and with the doors closed, they were off limits to a legal search.

But Willie had said Shawna and Frank were already gone. I opened the door to the Brewton Suite.

Willie hadn't gotten around to cleaning the room and putting it back into the beautiful order I'd seen on my tour with Shawna, but I scarcely paid attention to the disorder.

If there had been a person, and not a ghost, making the floor creak while I was downstairs with Willie, the most likely means of retreat would have been through the Brewton Suite, out onto the porch, and down the back stairs. Anyone, even a being far more substantial than a ghost, who used that means to flee the upstairs of the Stubbs house, stood a good chance of being unobserved. Like the door to the suite itself, the door leading to the upstairs porch was also shut, but unlocked. Anyone could have left that way. Inconclusive. I pushed the button that locked the door to the porch, making sure nobody—nobody without a key, anyway—would come back in that way. I'd need to string crime-scene tape to keep people away until I'd had a chance to take a close look at those stairs—for evidence of what? That's not where Julian Stubbs fell. Egad. Was I hoping to find a bloody footprint? Still.

As I reached the top step of the inside stairs on my way down to string more tape, listening in spite of myself for any sound that would tell me there was somebody who didn't want to be found hiding in one of the rooms, I heard the unmistakable sound of footsteps, solid, deliberate, coming from below.

CHAPTER 10

The footsteps were not ghostly at all, I realized almost immediately. They were far too substantial.

"Hen? I'm up here," I called.

"Who's securing the downstairs?" he called back. His question was designed to disguise the fact that he doesn't like stairs. Teri, Aunt Lulu, and I are all free with our opinion that he wouldn't mind stairs so much if he'd lose a few pounds, but he ignores us as freely as I ignored his question. If somebody caused Julian Stubbs to fall down the stairs, the crime scene would be upstairs, and Hen knew that. More to the point, he knew that I knew it. Nobody was fooling anybody here.

"I'll be right there." I scampered lithely down the stairs and was disappointed to see that Hen wasn't there to see the performance. He'd wandered into the library.

"Come on in and bring me up to speed," he said.

Hen pulled one of the easy chairs forward a bit so that we could sit and look at each other around the Christmas tree while I explained what had happened and told him what I'd done so far. "Most likely he just stumbled and fell. Foul play is not necessarily in the picture," I said in summary.

"But?"

Yeah. But. "Both Vera and Inez seemed sure there'd been somebody out in the hall talking with Julian before he fell, and I thought I heard him, too, saying something like 'No! Don't!' But both of them denied being that somebody. And I did have the impression, so faint it could have been imagination, that I heard somebody walking around upstairs just before he fell." I didn't see any reason to go into the ghost business.

"Ah. Well, it's a good thing you kept everybody out. We get one crack at investigating an uncontaminated scene. Heaven help us if we let a bunch of hysterical women loose."

While I was basking in that rare, if faint, praise, I gazed in admiration at the Christmas tree, impressed by the dazzle that is possible if you can manage to stick to a theme, instead of decorating haphazardly, miscellaneously, the way I always do— hanging anything that will hang, everything from Delcie's homemade ornaments to souvenirs from vacation trips, seashells, feathers, birds' nests. But wait! A break in theme! Among the beautiful burgundy bows and crystal ornaments, there was an ornament unlike the others. I squinted, delighted by this departure from the theme, prepared to feel if not superior, then at least on a more equal footing. Then I realized the renegade ornament wasn't unique. It was unlike almost all the others.

Yes, there was one other ornament that matched it.

"Look here," I invited Hen. "Behind that bow. What do you see?"

"That bow? Which bow?" He squinted, too, and smiled hugely when he saw where I was directing his attention. "Right nice little dingle-dangles," he said. "Looks like whoever took Inez Rankin's diamond earbobs has a sense of humor and an acquaintance with Edgar Allen Poe."

"And the good sense not to stash the purloined jewelry among his or her own belongings," I added.

"I'm assuming they fit the description of Inez's missing valuables?"

"Based on Willie's description, yes," I said. "The first I saw of Inez Rankin this morning was when she followed Vera Stubbs down the stairs after Julian took his header. Had his mishap."

"Mishap. Yeah. Mishap."

"Then they all left for the hospital. So I haven't talked to Inez about the earrings at all. But they do look like the ones she was wearing at the speeches yesterday. Shall we leave them there for now?" I asked, leaning back in my comfortable chair, happy to leave the decision-making to Hen.

"Nah. Be our luck to have them disappear again, and we'd wind up looking about as smart as that fella who showed up to a job interview out at the prison driving a stolen car." He removed the earrings from the tree and slipped them into one of my small evidence bags. "This way we get credit for returning the stolen property only a couple of hours after it was reported stolen."

Had it really been only that long? "I'm sure Inez will be happy to get the earrings back," I said. "But I don't think she'll be completely happy unless we clap somebody in irons for the crime. Preferably one of her relatives, unless I read her wrong."

"We'll keep that on our agenda, especially since there's this business with Julian Stubbs in the mix. Be something if the two things were connected, now wouldn't it?"

"Yes, sir, it would. Seems like a stretch, though."

"Wouldn't be the strangest thing's ever happened around here, though. Remember Miz What's Her Name and the aliens who took her telephone? And our esteemed high sheriff giving a one-way ticket out of town to the wrong felon?"

We paused for a moment in fond remembrance before Hen broke the spell. "Let's us do a little armchair detectivin'," he said.

"Okay."

"These dingle-dangles turning up here pretty much makes it an inside crime, wouldn't you say?"

"I would say. Except that, to be completely accurate, I would quibble with the word 'crime,' since if somebody really meant to steal them, they wouldn't be hanging on the tree."

"A joke?" Hen suggested. "Some kind of a leg-pull?"

I thought about it. "Maybe. Somebody with access to Inez's jewelry box—or wherever she kept them—who wanted to get a rise out of her."

"But who wasn't around to keep her from reporting a theft," Hen added, still gazing at the tree.

"Unless whoever it was didn't mind if she humiliated herself."

Hen grunted.

I continued. "Not Willie, then, I'd say, since practical jokes don't seem like the kind of thing she'd do, and especially not if it would reflect badly on her business. And she was the one who called to report the theft. No, not Willie." I was thinking out loud. "Not Shawna. She'd have kept the earrings. Not . . . what about Julian?"

"Maybe," Hen said after a minute's thought. "If for some reason Julian picked 'em up, which I would not rule out. The general opinion seems to be that, while he used to run as smooth as a new Cadillac, his engine's been cuttin' out on him a lot lately. He might have had his own reasons for putting 'em here, reasons that wouldn't make sense to anybody else. They weren't family heirlooms, were they? Something that would have meant something to him?"

"I'll ask that when I ask Inez where she kept the earrings." I made a note. "There's still everybody else who was here Saturday night."

"Right. We can't do it all from our armchairs. Gotta do some actual footwork. Okay, then, Officer Roundtree, if you're gonna take that attitude, I guess we've admired the Christmas decorations down here long enough. Reckon we'd better start lookin' busy, maybe go put some tape up around the back stairs. If somebody did push Julian Stubbs, unless whoever it was is still upstairs, he or she musta left that way. Mighta left a trace."

"Yes, sir." I got to my feet.

"Let's go do that, then." Hen locked the front door and led the way toward the back of the house, pausing briefly in the kitchen. He sniffed. "Sausage," he said. "Umm umm." He swiped at his mouth with the back of his hand as though to block any wayward flow of saliva. I wasn't especially impressed with his detective abilities. The spicy, mouthwatering fragrance of Junior Wilcox's sausage is easily distinguishable from bacon and ham, after all. Even so, for some reason I was glad he hadn't detected it on my breath.

We left the house through the kitchen door, and I noted that the tan Saturn and silver Lincoln which had been parked there when I arrived were still there, apparently unmoved.

"Willie keeps her car in the garage back here," Hen said, waving a casual arm in the direction of the empty garage at the edge of the parking area handy to the steps at the back end of the porch. He has an irritating habit of reading my thoughts before they're fully formed.

"Let's mark off this area, too," he said, oblivious, as usual, to my irritation. "If somebody did come down the stairs, whoever it was might have cut this way."

"Yes, sir," I said. "Or that way, through the driveway next door and then out onto Main Street, or on through the back way to Short Street." Short Street is a mere four blocks long, running between Court Street and Stubbs Street just west of Main.

"You can ask around, see if you can find anybody who saw somebody leavin' by any of those routes."

"Right."

We taped off a generous area for our scrutiny, including the lower porch and rocking chairs and the ground- level approach to the stairs leading to the upper porch. We scrutinized. It seemed to be my day for inconclusive investigation. The mix of gravel and patchy grass in our area of scrutiny would be unlikely to show evidence of merely having been trod upon. If we'd been looking for body parts, evidence of fire or explosion, signs of a scuffle, oil drips, marks that something had been dragged, then the gravel and grass might have had something to tell us. As it was, we could find nothing at all to draw our attention.

"Here's a calling card from a good-sized dog," Hen said, "but nobody stepped in it, so that doesn't help."

"I give up," I said.

"Let's check the stairs."

We slowly climbed the stairs. No muddy or bloody footprints, no fresh damage to the stairs or any of the banisters or handrails, no damp clumps of vegetation, no errant credit card receipts.

"Unless we get a big fat identifiable print from somebody who had a grudge against Julian Stubbs but had no business at this house, we're not gonna be doing ourselves much good here," Hen said.

He'd done it again, but I expressed my thought anyway.

"If we hope to prove any wrongdoing, we'll have to hope for something like that. Practically all our suspects have the right to be here. A stray fingerprint anywhere in the house wouldn't necessarily prove anything."

I was behind Hen going up the stairs. Otherwise, I'd have been the one to spot the bag. As it was—

"Funny place for this," Hen said.

The battered leather bag I had last seen in the upstairs hall filled with magazines now huddled near the door to the Brewton Suite, in the corner where the porch joined the house.

The door would have screened it from anyone coming onto the porch from inside.

Hen hefted the bag. It rattled. Definitely not magazines.

"Let's take this inside where we can have a look," he said. He tried the door into the Brewton Suite.

"I locked this door from the inside, to make sure nobody could sneak back in. You want to wait here while I go open it?" It was petty, I know, but it did force him to think of some reason not to come down the outside stairs and back up the inside stairs, carrying the bag. He rose to the occasion.

"I'll take another look around here. You go ahead." He frowned and pursed his lips, staring off down the stairs, the very picture of the great detective exercising his little gray cells. He was still—or maybe again—in that pose when I opened the door from the Brewton Suite to let him in. Once we were both inside, he became less dramatic, more businesslike. But he didn't open the bag right away as any normal person would have.

"Let's finish checking the house before we see what we've got in the bag," he said. "You were up here before, with Shawna, you said. You notice anything different?"

"It's a lot messier than it was yesterday."

"Just the three of them in here—Shawna, Frank, and the young'un?"

He was looking at the jumbled beds, all three of them, the towels flung all around the room. Again, Hen echoed my thoughts.

"Reckon they're always this messy? Unless they had a bunch of monkeys in for a sleepover, it looks like they went out of their way to make as big a mess as possible."

"And take everything, too," I added. "No little soaps or shampoos or anything like that left behind."

"We may need to get Willie in to see if they took anything they weren't entitled to," he said.

"Like earrings?"

"Uh huh," Hen said again.

"Knowing Shawna," I said, "she might have been just making the most of the opportunity to have somebody else clean up behind them." I couldn't squelch the self-righteous feeling that I would instinctively behave better than this.

"Uh huh."

Having no particular object in our search, once we'd assured ourselves there was nobody hiding under any of the beds, in the shower, in a cabinet, the search felt aimless. I picked up towels, shook them, and piled them together. Hen shook the bedding. Nothing fell out. Knowing that the thoroughness of our search was completely unwarranted by the circumstances, prompted instead by Hen's perverse pleasure in thwarting my curiosity about the bag, I retaliated by insisting that we pull out all the drawers and check the backs and bottoms, as well as the cavity behind them. Nothing but dust, and not much of that.

Finally, we took the bag to the conversational area in the upstairs hall and opened it.

Knowing he was trying to get a rise out of me helped me be patient as Hen slowly, with totally unnecessary flourishes, drew the following items from the bag, setting each one on the chest in front of the couch: the amber necklace I remembered seeing on the sideboard downstairs; a battered brassy bugle (It looked familiar. Had it been part of the Christmas decor?); a book; not one but (ta-da!) two silver candlesticks; an ornate pocket watch on a gold chain.

"What in the name of speckled peas do you make of this?" Hen asked.

"A pack rat with a taste for old things?" I suggested. "Or maybe a robber so incompetent he forgot where he put the swag?"

Hen snorted. "Hid it from himself behind the outside door?" Hen picked up the book. "*My Life in Baseball: The True Story,* by Ty Cobb, with Al Stump," he read. "Is that a clue?"

"Probably. The other things look like they might be valuable. Do you suppose the book is?"

He carefully replaced the items in the bag. "Might be able to get a good fingerprint or two off some of this. I got to hand it to you, Trudy, you managed to make this a lot more interesting than it sounded like it was gonna be when I sent you over here to talk to Inez Rankin about a pair of missing earbobs."

"I can't take all the credit," I said modestly. "I didn't put that stuff there."

"Here I was all set to declare a lack of police interest in the Stubbs house. We've recovered the earbobs and found no evidence whatsoever of any kind at all that there was foul play involved in Julian's fall—"

I nodded sympathetically.

"—and then we find this mess. I reckon we've got to keep on investigating."

"Yes, sir, but what are we looking for? And where?"

"You got me there, Officer Roundtree. Let's us think about that."

"Maybe we should get Willie to go through the house with us," I suggested. "We'll have to do that, anyway, to see what she can tell us about this collection. She can tell us if anything else is missing. She already mentioned a couple of vases that have wandered away."

"Vases?"

"Ugly. Muddy brown. Should have been in the china cabinet in the dining room."

"Who'd steal ugly—"

That's when the front doorbell rang.

"You want to get that since you're so much lighter on your feet than I am?" Hen asked with a smirk. "I'll meet you downstairs."

"Yes, sir," I said smartly.

The doorbell was ringing again by the time I got downstairs and opened to door to face Dennis Rankin. He looked irritated.

"Why's everything all locked up? And what's all that yellow tape about?"

"Come on in, Mr. Rankin."

"You're the police. What's happened? What's goin' on? Where's Inez?"

"Inez and Willie and Vera went to the hospital," Hen said from behind me. He can be quick and quiet when it suits him.

"The hospital! What—"

"Julian had an accident," Hen said.

"Oh." The irritation disappeared from Dennis Rankin's face. "But his car's right out here. And Vera doesn't let him drive, anyway."

"It wasn't an automobile accident," Hen said.

I waited for some expression of guilty knowledge, but Dennis let me down, so I added, "He fell."

"Hmm," he said. "Must not have much going on here in Ogeechee if the police investigate any time a senior citizen takes a fall."

"Just a sleepy little place where we still keep an eye out for our citizens," Hen said amiably. "Not a cesspool of depravity like Augusta."

Before Dennis could formulate a response to this, I added, "I was here when it happened. Mrs. Rankin reported a theft. She's missing a pair of earrings."

"Oh, shi—shoot."

"Maybe you'd already gone fishing before she missed them?" I suggested.

"Uh. Yeah. I guess so. Listen, I wouldn't take that too seriously. Inez's always losing track of things. They'll turn up. Well, if you'll excuse me, I'll go get cleaned up and go on over to the hospital. Oh, for Pete's sake! You've got that tape around the stairs in here, too!"

"That's right. You can't go get cleaned up right now, Dennis," Hen said. "Not here, anyway. We've closed off the upstairs while we investigate Julian's fall."

"You're not serious?"

"Serious as sin," Hen assured him.

Dennis was beginning to look irritated again. "I thought you said you were here about the earrings."

Hen nodded. "That, too, so we've got lots of investigatin' to do. You remember what time you left here this morning?"

"I didn't pay attention. I know it was while the rest of 'em were eating. No sense in going fishing if you don't get out there pretty early."

"Where'd you fish? Over at Tom's?"

"Uh huh. The weather's been nice enough he's having a fish fry this evenin', and I offered to help him with the fish. He goes out and feeds those catfish every day. They got no judgment. They'll bite at anything."

"He fishing with you?"

"You interrogating me?"

"Uh huh. Tom fishing with you?"

"You bet he was fishing with me. Nancy wasn't fit to be around, upset over her precious boy keeping secrets from her, I guess, and it was nice and peaceful out at the pond. Tom's got the fish to prove it. Can I go now?"

"Sure, as long as you don't go upstairs."

Dennis Rankin turned and went back out the front door. I'm sure a flimsier door would have slammed behind him.

"Well, that was productive," I said.

"You never know what'll turn out to be helpful, Officer Roundtree, and this whole situation looks stranger by the minute. We've got earrings in the Christmas tree, the family silver hidden in a ratty old valise, and a man taking a header down a flight of stairs. We're gonna need to talk to all of 'em, including Dennis again, see what we can find out. For instance, one of 'em might know if there's a ravin' lunatic in the attic, which wouldn't come as all that much of a surprise."

"You want to interview them yourself?" I asked.

"We'll split 'em up."

"You want Inez?"

He snorted. "No, you can have her. After all, you're the one who came to see about those earrings. And you're the one who found 'em. I think you deserve to be the one to tell her. Think of it as a reward for your good work."

"I'll try to look at it that way," I said.

"Let's go by the hospital," Hen said.

CHAPTER 11

We found Inez Rankin and Willie Lanier in the waiting room. "He's gone," Willie told us. "Aunt Vera's with him."

The pronouncement of Julian's death did not come as a surprise to me and probably had not come as much of a surprise to the women who had seen that pitiful crumpled heap lying at the bottom of the stairs.

Hen stopped briefly to offer his condolences, then went off to talk to the doctor. That left me with the tricky task of showing that I was sympathetic to their loss while being alert to anything that would give me an insight into what had been going on at the Stubbs house.

"Is Miz Stubbs all right?" I asked.

"She'll be all right," Willie said. "We're all in shock right now."

"When she thinks about it, she'll probably realize it's a good thing he went fast," Inez said.

"I wouldn't mention that right now, if I were you, Inez," Willie said.

"Well, it's the truth." But Inez didn't expand on her theories on life and death. Instead, she turned to me. "Why aren't you looking for my earrings?"

"We never did have a chance to talk about your earrings," I said, pulling out a pad and pencil. "I need to get some information from you." In light of all the unanswered questions about what had happened at the Stubbs house I saw no reason to tell her we'd already found the earrings. Besides, talking about the earrings would be a screen for questions about Julian Stubbs's fall and the odd collection of items we'd found in the bag outside the Brewton Suite.

"All I know is I was wearing them yesterday."

"The ones like chandeliers?" I asked.

She nodded. "Real diamonds, I want you to know."

"When did you take them off?"

"When we got home from the courthouse I changed clothes into something more suitable for the family party. I took them off then."

"What did you do with them when you took them off?"

"I put them on the dresser in our room."

"You're sure of that?" I paused before writing that down, giving her a chance to think. "Not in a jewel case or bag or anything? Just on the dresser?"

"That's what I said. Right there in plain sight." Her defensiveness made me think she wasn't all that sure. "It had to be an inside job," she continued. "There was a lot of confusion last night with everybody comin' and goin' and all the uproar about Kevin Purvis and that Gretchen. Anybody could have gone upstairs and seen them lying there and taken them. We couldn't lock our doors, you know, like you'd expect to be able to do in a public hotel."

Inez gave Willie a sidelong look, but Willie had developed an acute interest in the art on the nearby wall, a series of pastel watercolors of Victorian houses, and didn't react.

"Not to speak ill of the dead," Inez continued, doing just that, "but maybe it was Uncle Julian. With his mind so far gone, there's no telling what he might have done, or what he might have thought he was doing when he did it. Maybe it was that little boy of Shawna's. Nothing he'd do would surprise me. Or that friend of Kevin's. Nobody knows anything about him."

97

"Do you remember if they were still on the dresser when you went to bed?"

She squinched up her eyes, the very picture of deep thought. I surmised she was trying to figure which answer would cause the most trouble. "No" could mean anybody at the party had taken them; "yes" would narrow it to the people who were staying there. But then another exciting thought occurred to her.

"You mean did somebody sneak in while we were asleep and take them? Ooh! How awful! We could have been killed in our beds."

The look Willie shot her cousin suggested she liked that idea, but she said, "Della and I locked up the house after everybody went home, Inez."

"So it had to be somebody in the family!"

"Let's be careful here," I said. "Can you swear the earrings were there when you went to bed?"

"No. I can't honestly say I noticed for sure. But they were missing when I got up this morning. I do know that."

"Okay. That's a starting place, then." I took my time writing a few notes on this irritating conversation. Both women watched me write. Apparently, small talk was out of the question, so I continued my police work, again addressing Inez. "You were upstairs when Mr. Stubbs fell this morning," I said. "What can you tell us about that?"

"Nothing. I . . . I was in my room. I could hear you and Willie talking, and I was just about to come downstairs when . . . when . . ."

"Yes?"

"When . . . you know. When I heard Uncle Julian."

"When you heard your Uncle Julian what?"

"Fall. I heard him fall."

"Back at the house you said you heard him talking to somebody. Who was he talking to?"

"How would I know?"

"You didn't hear the voice well enough to identify it? Could you tell if it was a man or a woman?"

"I didn't hear it very well. I just assumed it was Aunt Vera." Inez looked bored and disgusted.

"Let's try this another way. Tell me again what happened just before Julian fell," I said.

"There's nothing else. Do you mean why he fell? I have no idea. I told you. I thought I heard him talking to somebody. I didn't pay any attention. The next thing I knew there was this noise from him falling down the stairs."

"Maybe he was talking to himself and wasn't paying attention to where he stepped," Willie suggested.

"Did he do that a lot, talk to himself?" I asked.

That suggestion was met with shrugs and shaking heads.

"I hadn't been around him all that much lately," Willie said, "but I got the notion he liked having an audience when he talked."

"Guess you'll have to ask Aunt Vera," Inez said. "There she is."

Hen and Vera Stubbs were coming down the hall in our direction. Hen was talking; Mrs. Stubbs was dabbing at her eyes as she listened, nodding. Willie stood and took her aunt's hand, guiding her to the chair next to Inez.

"I was just explaining to Miz Stubbs that I've made arrangements for an autopsy," Hen said.

Willie looked bewildered. "An autopsy? What does that mean?"

"It means they're going to cut him up," Inez said, perking up.

"It means y'all shouldn't set up funeral arrangements for the next few days, till we've found out the cause of death," Hen said neutrally.

"He says we have to have the autopsy," Vera explained to Inez

and Willie. "Julian had a lot of problems, was on a lot of medica-
tion. Any one of half a dozen things might have made him fall."

"Yes, ma'am, that's right. He might even have been dead
before he fell," Hen amplified. "The thing is, no doctor worth
his Hippocratic Oath would sign a death certificate without a
little more to go on. We want to be sure what killed Julian."

"What difference does it make?" Inez asked.

Hen turned to her. "It might make a whole heap of difference. If there was anything wrong with the way he died, for
instance if somebody pushed him down those stairs, we'd like
to know it." He turned back to Vera. "Isn't that right?"

Vera nodded slowly, as if she was having to translate his words
from a foreign language. "Y'all have to excuse me," she said.
"I'm still not sure which end is up. Yesterday he was giving a
speech there at the courthouse and this morning—"

"We're all in shock, Aunt Vera," Willie said. "Don't you worry
about anything. We'll help you take care of things."

"We've got the plot out there with his folks," Vera continued,
"and we'll want Carlisle to take care of arrangements. He is still
running the funeral home, isn't he?"

"Yes, ma'am," Hen said.

"Do you think Brother Avery would come back and do the
service? Julian always thought a lot of Brother Avery."

"I'll talk to him about it," Willie said. "I'm sure he will if he
can. But you don't have to—"

"Maybe a memorial service in Kennesaw, there at Park
Meadows. He made a lot of friends after we moved up there."

"We'll work it out, Aunt Vera," Willie said.

"I resent the way you're acting about this, treating us all like
a bunch of criminals when we're in mourning," Inez said to
Hen, narrowing her eyes as she gave him a look that would
curdle cream.

"Resent to your heart's content," Hen told her. "That won't

keep us from doing our job."

He sat and added conversationally, "If somebody helped that old man on to his eternal reward a little bit ahead of schedule, we want to know that and we want to know who it was. Okay, now, we all clear on that? One more thing. We don't want to add to your troubles any more than we have to, but we need to finish going over the house before we let y'all back in."

"We can't go back to the house?" Inez asked. "But . . ."

"It'll be better if we can look at things without people running around all over the place. You could stay here." He looked around at the stiff, square wooden chairs, the square coffee table, the bland colors. "But I think you'll be more comfortable somewhere else. And there's nothing else for you to do here," he added gently.

"You could go to Mama's," Inez said. "I think she got her nose out of joint when we all wanted to stay at the bed and breakfast. She'll be glad to have you."

"Yes, Annie's," Vera said. "Has anybody told Annie?" She sniffled into a wad of tissues.

Willie pulled a phone from her purse. "Let me see if she's home."

We waited during Willie's brief conversation with Annie Stubbs. "No, don't. There's no reason for you to come over here. We'll come over there," she concluded.

"I want you to come back to the house with us," Hen said to Willie, "to tell us if you see anything out of place. Somebody else can take them over to Gordon and Annie's."

"Willie, would you pack up our things and bring them to Annie's?" Vera asked. "I don't think I could go back to your house, even as nice as y'all have it fixed up. I'd always see him lying in a pile, dying right there where he grew up."

"Of course I will, Aunt Vera. Just as soon as I can," Willie said.

"Just as soon as the police will let you, you mean?" Inez asked.

"You run them over to Gordon and Annie's," Hen told me, ignoring Inez. "I'll go on back to the house with Willie."

We made our slow way outside. I had just opened the car door when Dennis Rankin drove up.

"Where have you been?" Inez demanded.

"Over at Tom's. Didn't want to come down here smelling like catfish, and they wouldn't let me in the house, so I went back over there and cleaned up. They said if there's anything they can do . . . How is Julian?"

"He's gone, Dennis," Vera said.

Dennis folded her in his arms. "I am so sorry, Aunt Vera. So sorry."

"I never knew what he'd do," she said. "I never should have taken my eyes off him."

"That's just not reasonable, Aunt Vera," Willie said. "It's not your fault he fell down those stairs, and don't you start thinking it was. Isn't that right, Inez?"

"Of course it's not your fault," Inez said, for once saying the right thing.

"Where y'all headed?" Dennis asked, still patting Vera on the shoulder.

"Mama and Daddy's," Inez said. "At least Aunt Vera and I are. We were about to have to ride in a police car, but you can take us."

"We'll want to talk to you again, too, Dennis," Hen said, "but we can do that later."

An odd look—Surprise? Panic? Guilt?—crossed Dennis Rankin's face. I caught just a glimpse and didn't have time to analyze it before he quickly turned to help the women into his car.

I'm almost sure I heard Vera Stubbs saying, "I could sure use a cigarette."

CHAPTER 12

As we turned the corner onto Stubbs Street—Hen, Willie Lanier, and I—there was Bradley Booth on the kitchen porch, inside the crime-scene tape, turning away from the window.

Hadn't I already seen this movie? He knew he was in the wrong, and he started on the offensive. Definitely a re-run.

"What's goin' on here?" he asked. "Why's everything all locked up? Oh, Miz Lanier, I thought you'd be here to let me in. I've got to get cleaned up and hit the road."

"It ain't all that far to Columbus," Hen told him, swaggering a bit as he approached Bradley. Hen does love his job. "And you might not get to leave today at all if you don't start showing a little more respect for the law. Columbus such a backwoods place you don't know what that yellow tape means?"

Bradley pretended to notice the tape for the first time. "Oh." He looked around at Willie and me as if expecting us to help him out. We didn't. "It means, I guess, that I'm not supposed to go in the house."

"It means you're not supposed to be on that side of the tape at all, not even on the porch."

"But—"

"Don't but me, son. That tape advertises the fact that we are treating the house like a crime scene. We've got us a dead man and some stolen property, and I think it's only fair to tell you you're the only person we've come across so far who's acting in a suspicious manner."

"Whoa! What? A dead man? Some kind of a crime wave hit while I was out running!"

"Uh huh. Julian Stubbs."

Bradley looked genuinely concerned. "Mr. Stubbs? He's dead?"

The looks on our faces must have convinced him.

Bradley frowned. "He was fine at breakfast. What happened to him?"

"That's what we're going to find out," Hen said.

"Don't look at me. How would I know? As soon as I finished eating, I went out running. Lots of people saw me. Several of them wanted to know if I needed help. For some reason, people in this town think there's something wrong with anybody who's running. All I'm trying to do right now is go inside and take a shower. That doesn't make me a criminal in Ogeechee, does it?"

"No, son, we like our citizens to pay attention to personal hygiene, just like they do in the big cities, but that ain't quite all you were doin'. We just now caught you in the act of flagrantly disregarding the law. Furthermore, you are presently engaged in antagonizing the police."

One of the reasons Hen enjoys being Chief of Police is that it gives him full scope for his theatrical tendencies. Sometimes he plays the hick, making it easy for smart alecks to underestimate him. Sometimes, like now, he plays the heavy-handed ponderous pontificator. I've always assumed he rummages around in his head for whatever persona he thinks will accomplish the task of the moment. He apparently chose well this time. The bluster went out of Bradley. But not the drama. He fetched a sigh from somewhere down around his toenails, held out his wrists, and said, "You got me. Take me in."

Hen shook his head in exasperation. "I'll take you in, all right, but right now we'll just go as far as inside the house here. It'll be up to you whether we take you in to the station house.

We want to take a look at your room and get a statement from you before you leave town. That all right with you?"

"You can count on my cooperation," Bradley said.

Hen stifled a snort. "We'll see how that goes before we think about the handcuffs. Or whatever else might be called for."

"Inside. Statement. Room. No handcuffs. Got it." Bradley grinned in what I'm sure he thought was an ingratiating manner. "I won't even call my lawyer or complain about you violating my civil rights."

Hen reached for his handcuffs. Bradley grimaced. His hands fell.

"You ready to settle down?" Hen asked.

"Yes, sir."

"That's more like it."

Hen lifted the tape so the rest of us could walk under it and ushered us into the house. "Trudy, you and Willie go on and pack up for Vera like she asked you to while I accompany this young gentleman upstairs. Wouldn't want you to have to look at his unmentionables."

"Yes, sir," I said, with enthusiasm. I had no interest in pawing through Bradley's underwear.

But Willie and I had just reached the bottom of the stairs when the telephone rang. I waited while she turned back to the kitchen. "I keep saying I'll get rid of the regular phone and just give everybody my cell number and keep it strapped to me," she said as she went. "Seems sort of stupid, but . . . Hello? Yes, that's right. How'd you find out so quick? Oh. Uh huh. No, she went over to Aunt Annie and Uncle Gordon's. Yes. Thanks."

"Betty Collins," she said when she got back to the stairs. "Heard about Uncle Julian from her cousin Claire who had a doctor's appointment over near the hospital while we were there and heard it from the receptionist."

"That may set a new land speed record for the Ogeechee

grapevine," I said, following her up the stairs.

Except for some clutter on the top of the chifforobe and personal toilet articles in the bathroom, the Scott Suite looked much like it had when Shawna had shown me around earlier.

Someone—presumably Vera Stubbs—had even straightened the quilt on the bed, so that the room looked neat. I couldn't help contrasting it with the rooms Shawna's family had occupied.

"When Hen ordered me to help you pack up for Miz Stubbs, he meant I'm supposed to look for anything that can help us figure out what's been going on. Do you see anything that looks wrong to you?" I asked.

Willie glanced around, then walked to the bathroom and looked inside. Returning to where I stood watching, she shrugged.

"Okay, then, you watch while I look a little deeper. Holler if you see anything that strikes you wrong." With Willie at my shoulder, I opened drawers, looked inside the chifforobe and medicine cabinet, peered under the bed. I mimicked her shrug. "Okay if I strip the bed?"

"It'll save me having to do it. Just pile the sheets on the floor."

I flipped and shook the bedcovering. Nothing fell out. I stripped the pillowcases and the sheets without revealing anything except pillows and mattress.

"Help me lift the mattress," I said. We looked underneath and saw only the satiny quilted surface of the box springs. "All right. Let's have a look at the suitcases."

We pulled two suitcases out from under the bed and placed them on top of the mattress.

"I need to check them, too," I said. "You watch."

"Why?"

"A couple of reasons. First, if it should come to that, you can testify that I didn't take anything or add anything."

"Oh, for goodness' sake. Oh, wait a minute."

At least she didn't have to go all the way back downstairs to answer the telephone when it rang this time. I followed her only as far as the hallway/sitting room. Her end of the conversation was very much like the last call.

"Odetta Crowell," she reported when she hung up. "Where were we?"

"About to go through the suitcases. You stop me if you see something that shouldn't be here."

"Like what?"

"Anything that catches your eye. Maybe something they might have packed up that doesn't belong to them."

"You sure do have a low opinion of people," she said. "You're thinking Uncle Julian was . . . collecting things?"

"It's possible. I've gathered that he's been getting unpredictable. I'm trying to be thorough."

She watched as I removed the carefully folded clothing and examined the pockets and pouches of the empty suitcases.

"Oh." Willie's voice was soft when I held up a photograph of a group of children in an oval wood frame. "Who'd have thought he'd be such an old softie?"

"Hmm?"

"Uncle Julian. That's all the Stubbs children. Must have been taken about . . . let's see . . . Uncle Julian doesn't look like he could be more than three or four, so say nineteen twenty-two or so. That's Uncle Gordon on the left with the grin. Still has that grin. Franklin's next to him. Franklin died when he was two. My daddy is the next boy, the one sitting down. The other boy is Emory, and the girl is Letha. I have a copy of this picture right next to my bed. There aren't that many pictures of my daddy when he was little. Hmm."

"What?"

"It's even the same frame."

"Maybe you'd better go see if yours is still there."

She was gone for just a minute and came back looking sad. "It's mine. I never would have thought he'd steal."

But it did look as if Julian, confused about ownership or not, had been taking things from the house. Had meant to take at least this from the house. Was he responsible for the bag swag, as well? I finished going through the pockets of the few garments, and then, piece by piece, replaced everything in the suitcases.

"I want to hold on to this photograph," I said.

"Why?"

"Check it for prints. There's enough oddball stuff going on around here, I don't want to take too much for granted. Let's not condemn the poor old man as a thief without some evidence."

"It's hard to believe, but there it was, right there in his suitcase," she said. "And I can see why he might have wanted it."

"Circumstantial," I countered. "Let's presume him innocent until he's proven guilty—and even then we can keep the secret, if you like."

"Sure, then. Take it."

I slipped the photograph into an evidence bag. "Let's go ahead and pack the rest of their things now," I said.

Willie looked around as though for inspiration about a good starting place. "This is worse than trying to clean up somebody else's kitchen," she said. "I don't stand a chance of putting things where Aunt Vera would want them."

"I think she'll be grateful not to have to do it herself."

Willie nodded. "You're right."

We worked together, with me taking the few things from hangers, checking the pockets, and handing them to Willie. Nothing else of interest turned up.

"That just leaves the bathroom," I said.

I watched as she put jars and tubes into a plastic bag decorated with red and pink poppies. A shoebox held an array of medications, ranging from aspirin and Metamucil on up to complex names I couldn't pronounce with purposes I couldn't guess at.

"I'll hold on to this," I said, "and go through it with your aunt Vera."

"Yes."

As we carried the suitcases and box full of medicines downstairs, we could hear the sound of the shower from the Durrence Suite, Bradley's room. We found Hen in the kitchen heating a cup of coffee in the microwave.

"I've satisfied myself there's nothing illegal in Bradley's room," Hen told us. "I'd like to close off the room the Rankins are in till we can look around in there with them, but you can have the rest of your house back."

"Thank you. It'll be good to try to settle back down," Willie said. "Getting after the housework will help me feel normal again, but I don't know about anybody else. What a day. Poor Uncle Julian. Poor Aunt Vera."

She surveyed the kitchen, which still hadn't been cleaned up after breakfast. "I've got a little bit of sausage left. You want a sausage biscuit to go with that coffee?"

"Don't mind if I do," Hen said, giving her a big smile.

Willie raised her eyebrows questioningly in my direction, and I shook my head.

"Won't take a minute," Willie said.

"While you're puttin' that together, let me get something to show you," Hen said. "I'll be right back. Trudy, you go tape off the Rankins' room."

Right. He wouldn't want to do the stairs again. By the time I got back he had spread out the things we'd found in the valise on the veranda, each in its own plastic bag, and Willie had spread out some breakfast.

"You recognize any of this?" he asked. He took a bite of sausage biscuit and growled with pleasure.

"Yes. Of course," Willie answered. "What is going on? That book's been in the family forever. If you'd asked me where it was, I'd have told you it was in a bookcase in the library. Where did you get it?"

Hen told her. "You got any idea why it would be with these other things?" The last bit of biscuit disappeared into his maw.

Willie shook her head. "I've got the fixin's for one more sausage biscuit, Hen," Willie said. "Can you handle that?"

Hen smiled and held out his plate.

Willie talked as she put together the sausage biscuit. "No. I don't see any connection between those things, not even any reason anybody would be interested in all of them. If anybody wanted that book, all they had to do was say so. Inez likes to make out like Della and I are some kind of greedy-guts, but we haven't been mean about holding on to family things. The necklace belonged to Grandma Stubbs. It's pretty and we like displaying it. I suppose it might have had sentimental value for somebody, but even that's a stretch. Anyway, like everything else, if anybody really wanted it, they could have asked for it. The bugle is supposed to be from one of our Civil War ancestors. Might have some interest for Civil War buffs. I don't have any idea about dollar value. We're proud of it because it's part of our history. The watch is supposed to have belonged to Granddaddy."

She paused and frowned. "Della and I thought using the old stuff to decorate would add character and make the bed and breakfast more attractive, but we may have to reconsider what we leave lying around, with strangers in the house."

I didn't point out that this was family, not strangers, even though Inez could be considered strange by some standards.

Willie tried a smile. "This watch doesn't run, of course, but I keep it in my little room upstairs because it's pretty and I like to look at it."

"What about the candlesticks?"

"Nothing special about them at all. Might be worth something to a thief. I don't know. They were wedding presents, back in the days when we all took it for granted that we'd be living elegant lives and hadn't thought about having to polish all that silver. They were in a cabinet in the dining room with a lot of other odds and ends. With those brown vases, Trudy. Did y'all find them?"

"Not yet," Hen said.

Willie explained. "No telling how long it would have taken me to miss any of this. It's a pretty miscellaneous collection, isn't it? Looks like something a pack rat might gather up."

I took a turn. "What about that family tree from the upstairs hall? Did Mr. Stubbs have some special interest in it that you know of?"

She shook her head, then continued thoughtfully, "Not that I know of. Not more than the rest of us, usually. But maybe with him getting older he was more interested, and he hadn't been down here a lot in the last few years, so everything was interesting to him. Last night we got to talking, like we always do, about family connections. Were you still here, Hen?"

"We—" Hen began, but stopped when there was a creaking overhead. This time I didn't think of ghosts but of the one person we knew was upstairs, and the room I knew was over where we sat. Hen gave me a nod to indicate he'd heard what I'd heard and had the same thought. What was Bradley doing in the Brewton Suite?

"Want me to go see what he's doin'?" I asked.

"If he's up to something, he'll be through by the time you get there," Hen said. "I'll just keep an eye out." He shifted his chair so that he could see the tan Saturn parked outside.

Willie picked up the earlier thread of conversation. "Well, somebody said it was time to update that family tree, now that all the Stubbs children have finished having children, and somebody else said maybe it was time for each family to make their own, and we got it down and passed it around. Julian and Roddy Holland took it back upstairs."

"We'll hold on to it and this other stuff till we figure out what's been going on," Hen said.

"Fine with me," Willie said. "What about Inez's earrings? You didn't find them with this?"

"No," I said, choosing my words, not looking at Hen. "No, they weren't with the rest of this."

"We'll be in touch," Hen said, daintily wiping his lips, "and you let us know if you think of anything we need to know. I don't have any reason to insist that young Bradley hang around, so we're cutting him loose. He doesn't owe you any money, does he?"

With his coffee cup, Hen gestured toward the window, through which we could see Bradley putting a suitcase into the trunk of the Saturn. He'd obviously come down the back stairs, through the Brewton Suite.

Willie smiled. "I've got his credit card number."

"I warned him he'd better hope nothing turns up missing around here or he'll be the first one on our list of suspects," Hen said, "so I don't think we need to check his suitcases again, but, Officer Roundtree, it might be a good idea for you to go remind him we're planning to lead him over to the station house where he will willingly and cheerfully give us a statement and a set of his fingerprints."

"Yes, sir," I said smartly.

I could hear the telephone ringing in the kitchen again as I stepped outside.

When I conveyed Hen's message, Bradley nodded, resigned, if not willing and cheerful. For once he wasn't chatty. Even though I didn't mention anything specific, he seemed to understand my desire to search his car. I satisfied myself that there was no place in the car that a couple of foot-tall vases could have been hidden. Hen joined us and indicated that Bradley would follow us to the station house if he knew what was good for him.

Before we could pull out, the Rankin car drew up next to us, with Dennis at the wheel. Dennis's window crept down, and Inez's irritating voice came through from the passenger's side.

"Dennis said you said we couldn't go to our room!"

Hen took his time getting out of the cruiser and going over to the Buick. He leaned down at Dennis's open window. "Not till we've had a chance to look through it."

"What for?"

"We're treating the whole house like a crime scene, ma'am," Hen said. Inez Rankin didn't know him well enough to recognize the over-respectful, over-patient tone as an insult. "Naturally, we can't search your room without your permission, so it's still off limits."

"Search!" It was a screech.

Dennis Rankin's only participation in the conversation was swiveling his head back and forth. He didn't seem to enjoy being caught in the crossfire.

"After all," Hen continued with insulting patience. "We've had a report of a crime on the premises, and we wouldn't want anybody tampering with evidence."

Dennis focused his gloomy gaze on the steering wheel.

"How long to do we have to put up with this?" Inez asked.

Instead of saying, "As long as I say so," as I hoped he would, Hen straightened and stretched his back and turned to me.

"You go on and take care of our business with Bradley. If the Rankins will give me permission, I'll go with them now and check things out so they can have their room back."

He looked at Inez.

"Oh, all right!" she said.

As I drove off, happy to be dealing with Bradley instead of the Rankins, in my rearview mirror I could see Inez, boiling out of her side of the car, giving a good impression of an infuriated monkey, and Dennis, climbing out much more slowly, more like a depressed basset hound.

CHAPTER 13

Back at the station house, I fingerprinted Bradley and took his statement, which wasn't very helpful. He might have touched just about anything in the house, he said, since the place was so interesting and he liked old things. Specifically, and with a knowing gleam in his eye, he allowed as how he had probably picked up the Ty Cobb book, since he's a baseball fan, and the necklace because it was there in the hall by the bed and breakfast brochures (clever, since there was no possible way for us to raise fingerprints off that), maybe even some of the silver, since it was an old style he admired. And, oh yes, the family tree, too, because he was interested in that kind of thing. He didn't remember seeing any ugly brownish vases.

I let him go, having no grounds stronger than general dislike for holding him. He surprised me by having the good sense not to burn rubber out of our parking lot, but he was so eager to get out of town he probably overshot Columbus and wound up in Alabama.

My next chore was to take Vera Stubbs's suitcases and the box full of medicine to her at another Stubbs house, that of Julian's brother and his wife. While not new, Gordon and Annie's house is considerably newer than the Stubbs House Bed and Breakfast. It's part of a development of brick ranch-style houses clustered around a lake north of town.

Gordon Stubbs met me at the door, his beautiful false teeth gleaming beneath a neat moustache the same pewter color as

116

his thinning hair, only his eyes showing the strain of the sudden violent loss of his brother.

"How's Miz Stubbs doin'? Miz Vera, I mean?" I asked.

"Still cushioned by shock, I think," he said. "Like all of us. We knew he was failing, but we weren't ready for this."

"No. Of course not. I'm sorry to bother y'all right now, but I brought the things over from the other house, and I need to talk to Miz Vera for a minute, if she's up to it."

"Come on in."

He reached for one of the suitcases. I handed him the pink and red toiletries bag, and followed him into the house, carrying the other suitcase and the box of medicines.

I had come to the front door. To the right I could see that the dining-room table held an assortment of pies, cakes, cookies, a deli tray, and a ham. The spread, and the discreet buzz from the living room, made clear that the grapevine in Ogeechee had done its job. The Gordon and Annie Stubbs house was established as the headquarters for condolence calls. Maybe Willie's phone wouldn't ring too many more times.

"Trudy's brought your things, Vera," Gordon said to the small group in the living room to the left of the entryway.

Vera Stubbs blinked at me, then nodded, apparently remembering where she'd seen me before. "Oh. Thank you. My goodness, the police are nice down here."

"Our motto is to serve, as well as to protect," I said, the condensed version of one of Hen's favorite speeches. I added a smile as I hefted the box of medicines. "And I wanted to make sure you have everything you need. Do you mind looking through these with me, just to make sure I got everything?"

She stubbed out her cigarette and got to her feet.

"Why don't y'all use the kitchen table?" Annie said. "You don't want everybody in town knowing what you're doctorin' for, do you, Vera?"

117

It wasn't much of a joke, but in the circumstances, it was welcomed by the small gathering of friends and family, all of whom knew—of course they did!—that Annie Stubbs wasn't accusing any of them of gossipmongering.

We spread out the contents of the medicine box on the dark pine kitchen table and Vera made short work of separating the prescription medications into his and hers, pushing the over-the-counter remedies to the side. As she sorted, I noted a spiral-bound notebook next to the telephone, where Annie Stubbs had already begun logging in telephone calls and offerings of food so that appropriate thanks could be tendered in due time.

Efficiency born of experience and old-fashioned good manners.

"I'm not smart enough to know what all this medicine is for," I said when Vera had finished separating them. "Was Mr. Stubbs suffering from anything that might have made him dizzy enough to fall down the stairs?"

She gave me a wry smile. "Not that I know of. If he was, it was something new. He had a lot of things going wrong lately, though, and they always seemed to come on all of a sudden, so I don't know."

"I'd like to hold on to his medications and see what a doctor can tell us about their purpose and side effects, if you don't mind."

"Help yourself."

"Vera, I thought you'd want to know Fred and Ione Martin are here." This came from Annie Stubbs, standing in the doorway.

"Are we finished?" Vera Stubbs asked me.

"Yes, ma'am."

Vera's exit left me with Annie, who wrote something in the spiral notebook before saying, "Why can't you just take it at face value? Accidents happen."

118

"Yes, ma'am, accidents happen. They do. But the police get involved in cases of accidental death. Besides, this case is complicated by the fact that we were called in to investigate a theft. We need to find out what happened."

Annie waved away the theft. "Knowing why he fell won't bring him back."

"No, ma'am."

"I didn't want to say it in front of Vera," she said, "but it's a blessing."

"I can see that side of it," I admitted.

"You start acting like there was something wrong, people will imagine all kinds of I-don't-know-what about Julian."

"We aren't necessarily acting like there's something wrong. But if there is something wrong, if he had an accident because of something that could have been prevented, don't you think we ought to know it?"

She gave me an exasperated look, the kind of look a thirteen-year-old girl would give her mama when denied the God-given right to get a tattoo on her forehead and date a college man, a look that said I couldn't possibly be that dumb and still manage to dress myself in the morning. But, to give her credit, she did try to explain what she meant.

"A man his age, a man in public life, he's bound to have people who don't like him and will use something like this to drag up all kinds of old business, things best left buried."

"You mean they'll think somebody murdered him because of an old grudge?" I asked, looking up from the pile of over-the-counter remedies I was listing. Rather than make Vera Stubbs tell me whether it was her or her husband who was using Compound W, Preparation H, and Metamucil, I would leave them all behind.

Annie looked scandalized. She darted a glance toward the door and lowered her voice. "I was just thinking of the way

119

people gossip. When he was younger, Julian had a roving eye. Some people might remember that."

"You're afraid somebody will think a jealous husband did him in?" However ill-judged the impulse, I'd meant to be funny, but Annie Stubbs looked horrified instead of amused.

"I am not suggesting any such thing. Just that, well, there's no reason for people to start remembering that right now, is there?"

"But you were thinking about it," I said.

"Yes, I was." She sat down beside me. "At the party the other night, Julian kept calling Jean Holland by her sister's name. Karen. Karen worked for him for a while, and there was talk."

I didn't have to ask what kind of talk. "Would that talk come as a surprise to his wife?"

She sighed. "Probably not. But it was a long time ago. History."

I put the medicines I was taking with me back in the box and stood to go. "We're investigating several things, Miz Stubbs. Don't worry. We'll try not to blacken Mr. Stubbs's good name."

Even if she suspected me of insincerity, Annie Stubbs thanked me and saw me to the door.

"Do you know when can we schedule the services?" she asked. "It would be good if we could do it while everybody's already here."

Everybody? "Julian and Vera don't have children and grandchildren?"

"No, never had children. Most of the rest of us have some young'uns around us, but not Vera. She's all by herself now, except for the rest of us old-timers, but we'll help her all we can, like with the funeral arrangements. In a way it's a good thing it happened while they were here, since he'll be buried here, and so many of us are already here. Of course, from here on out, now, we'll think of Julian dying at Christmastime."

"I'll check with Hen," I told her. "The autopsy shouldn't hold things up for long."

I drove back to the station house pondering life and death and how ill-prepared most of us are for either one and the role unfinished business plays in grieving for someone we've lost, whether we most regret things we said and did or things we didn't say or do.

So far in my thirty-something years, I'd had some significant losses. My parents died when I was too young to feel the guilt and loss and regret so common to people left behind, leaving it to my daddy's mother to raise me. The death of my new young husband in a hunting accident hit me a lot harder. That brought me back to Ogeechee and what I hoped would be a cocoon protecting me from more pain. We hadn't parted on bad terms the day he died, but I hadn't gotten up to say goodbye that morning, either, and we'd never gotten around to taking that wonderful honeymoon trip. Regret. My grandmother took me in again and was too smart to let me stay in a cocoon. After a while, she and Aunt Lulu ganged up on Hen and made him give me a job. It probably surprised all of them, and disappointed Hen, when it turned out to be more than shock therapy for me. I like my job. Grandma's death a few years after that, more predictable at her age, came with different regrets. Every selfish, mean, disrespectful thing I'd ever done to disappoint her made me grieve in a different way than I'd grieved before, knowing I'd never be able to tell her I was sorry. I was not comforted at all by pious assurances from well-meaning friends that she was in Heaven now and knew and forgave everything, even if she hadn't already done it.

CHAPTER 14

After the bustle at Gordon and Annie Stubbs's house, and the melancholy it had triggered in me, it was a relief to get back to the station house.

Hen was hard at work. Glad for something to help me shake off my mood, I joined him, hoping for a colorful account of his search of the Rankins' room. He disappointed me.

"Dennis looked like he had a stomach ache the whole time, hardly said a word, not that he coulda said much, the way Inez just kept sputtering and spitting. I got Willie up there, too, to make sure nothing else had migrated to someplace it hadn't oughta been. Everything seemed to be in order."

"That's too bad. It would have been nice to be able to arrest Inez Rankin for something."

He sighed. "The best I could do was invite the pair of 'em to come down and be fingerprinted and give us a statement."

"I take it you didn't find anything interesting in Bradley's room, either."

"Nothing outside of some underwear he ought to be ashamed of, a few T-shirts, some running shorts, and a couple of pairs of britches. He's either innocent or smart enough not to put anything incriminating somewhere connected to him," Hen said. "That doesn't let him off the hook for the things we found in the bag on the veranda, though. He'd have known Shawna and Frank were already gone and nobody was likely to spot it."

"But why would he have bothered hiding it instead of packing it? And he did go through that room on his way out of the house," I pointed out. "Did you think he was acting peculiar when we caught him downstairs trying to get in the house? He didn't react to your statement that we had found some stolen property, but he was pretty specific about what he'd been doing, like he was setting up an alibi before we had even said anything about suspicious circumstances."

"You have a suspicious mind, Trudy. Good. Don't worry. We'll be able to find him if we need to talk to him again," Hen said. "But even if we find his fingerprints all over this junk, we'd look pretty silly in court trying to prove he stole something that was still right there at the house."

"Okay, then, what about Mr. Stubbs? Do you think Bradley pushed him down the stairs?"

"I don't know what to think, I'm so tired. No chance at all he'd be able to name anybody he talked to, being a stranger in these parts, and all. I'm so tired of this whole bunch, I'm purely looking forward to some quiet, thoughtful investigation."

Given that we weren't sure what we were investigating— possibly nothing more than a practical joke or two gone awry and an accidental fall by an Alzheimer's victim—and given the recent bereavement of practically the entire pool of what could generally be considered the suspects, the Ogeechee Police Department was in serious need of some objective evidence.

We scrutinized the earrings, bag swag, and the framed family tree for fingerprints and any other clues they might offer. Our efforts were rewarded in interesting ways. As Hen had said, there were several clear fingerprints on the silver, the book, and the framed family tree; some smudges on the bugle; nothing useful on the necklace or the watch; only fragments on the earrings. All that remained was to identify the fingerprints and talk with the people who put them there. Piece of cake.

"Looks like we've got us several distinct and different lines of inquiry, Officer Roundtree," Hen informed me.

"Please enlighten me," I begged effusively, but humbly.

As usual, he ignored my phony groveling tone and took me literally. "In chronological order, Inez Rankin's earrings and other migrating objects. We've got the earrings, but don't know who put them where we found them."

"Check. Line of inquiry number one: migrating objects." I wrote it slowly, trying to get a rise out of him. It didn't work.

Turning to the items we'd found in the bag, Hen picked up *My Life in Baseball* and opened it to the flyleaf. He held it so that I could see, above a scrawled signature, the words: 'To my cousin Gordon from Tyrus.' "What do you make of this?" he asked.

"Well," I said, pointing at the family tree, "Cousin Gordon is probably Gordon Stubbs. Would a copy of this book auto-graphed by Ty Cobb be valuable?"

"Wouldn't surprise me," Hen said. "Maybe we'd better find us somebody who knows."

"That's line of inquiry number two," I said.

"Don't be in such an all-fired hurry," Hen said. "That's just item one in inquiry number one, the migrating objects. I think it's safe to group the necklace and the silver with the book, but we have that photograph."

"Right. Migrating, but not with the earrings or the other things. And don't forget the missing vases."

"Right," he agreed. "We have three sets of migrating objects— bag swag, photograph, vases." He raised three fingers as he counted, then added a fourth. "And the earrings, if you want to count them."

"If we count the earrings and group the other items the way you list them, we can claim a twenty-five percent success rate."

"Let's count 'em, then. And there's Julian Stubbs."

No joking matter.

"And finally, this family tree," Hen said. "Lookee here."

He adjusted the lamp so that the light fell fully on the family tree. The black calligraphy stood out in sharp contrast to the cream-colored paper, but there were lighter marks which looked like they'd been made with a pencil and smudges that looked like erasures. "You notice these pencil marks before?"

"No," I admitted. "Haven't had time to really look at it till now."

"Does that mean you can't say if the marks were there when you were looking around the house with Shawna the other day?"

"No." Why did I feel so defensive? "We actually did look at it pretty closely, but the light in that hall isn't the best, so I wouldn't want to swear to it."

"Can you make out any of it?"

I leaned closer. "Not very well. It's pretty cramped. It looks to me like maybe somebody was trying to bring the family tree up to date. Willie said they'd talked about doing that. Maybe whoever it was—Julian?—was trying to add the people who hadn't been born when the thing was made in the first place, the marriages, everything, but not doing a very good job. See here—this word could be 'Gretchen,' but it's in the wrong place."

Hen squinted at the marks. "If this word is Gretchen, it would mean whoever wrote it did it after the announcement last night about Kevin and Gretchen running off. Willie said Julian and Roddy Holland went upstairs with this thing. Maybe they were fixing it up together."

"From what I heard, Julian and Roddy might have gone upstairs just to get away from the ruckus downstairs," I said.

"Maybe."

"It's a shame anybody would deface something like this."

"Maybe it was somebody whose thinker wasn't working very well," Hen said.

"Julian? Yes. Maybe that's what he was doing when he fell. If he took it down off the wall to write on it, that would explain why it fell down the stairs with him."

"But not why he fell," Hen pointed out.

"No. Except that holding it might have thrown him off balance."

"Willie didn't say anything about the marks?"

"No. But we were all paying attention to Julian Stubbs at the bottom of the stairs. Nobody was looking at this."

"Ask her about it," he said. "Maybe these marks have been there a long time and have nothing to do with us."

"Yes, sir." I made a real note to myself.

"The way things keep squirming around on us where the Stubbs family is concerned, we better make us a systematic plan," Hen said. "Let's get everybody in here and check their alibis and see if they can tell us anything useful."

"Who do you mean by everybody?"

"Everybody who was at the party the other night, everybody who's been at the Stubbs house lately, and anybody else we can think of until we figure out what-all's been going on over there."

"Yes, sir," I said smartly. "A lot of the people we need are probably at Gordon Stubbs's house, or will be."

"We'll call over there, then," he said. "I'll get that goin'. You go talk to Roddy Holland and see what he has to say about the family tree."

"You don't want to round him up with the others?"

"Yep. You give him that message while you're there. We want them to come in for fingerprinting, him and Jean both, along with everybody else, and we'll get statements about this junk—" he gestured at the items "—but go on and talk to Roddy about him and Julian and this family tree, sort of casual. We'll go over it again when he comes in."

"Yes, sir. Whatever you say. I'm on it! You want me to talk to

Willie Lanier first?"

"Suit yourself." A rare concession to my own sense of priorities.

I called Willie, who said she needed to go to the grocery store anyway and would come to the police station first, if that would be okay. I said it would.

"Willie's coming right now," I reported. "How about I do some busywork till after she's gone and then talk to the Hollands?"

Busy-work not being my favorite thing, I was glad to see Willie just a few minutes later.

"Thanks for being so cooperative," I said.

"If being cooperative will get this whole mess behind us, I'll cooperate my backside off," she said.

"Come on in and let's talk a minute," Hen invited, when he saw Willie. "I want to show you something."

"The family tree? I've seen it before," she said.

"Have you seen this before?" Hen pointed to the pencil marks.

She took a closer look. "No. No, I have not! Who'd do a thing like that?"

"We were hoping you could tell us," Hen said. "Do you have any idea how long the marks might have been there?"

"No, not really."

"Not to comment on your housekeeping," I said, with a smile so she'd know I wasn't being judgmental about it, "but could it have been there a while? Would you have noticed, in that dim hall?"

"I don't know," she said. "Maybe not. Not to comment on my housekeeping, but something like this thing, hanging there so long it's practically invisible, is lucky to get a fast pass with my duster if I happen to see a cobweb on it. I don't know when's the last time I really looked at it. You'd think somebody would have noticed the other night, though, wouldn't you? When they were passing it around."

"Yes, you would," Hen said. "Well, let's get you fingerprinted, and we'll cut you loose. Thanks for coming by."

Willie's dismissal cut me loose, too. I found Jean Holland, wife of Roddy, adoptive mother of Gretchen, in her kitchen.

Untidy and under a strain, she was still pretty, and it was easy to imagine that she'd looked like Gretchen when she was younger—willowy, blonde, blue-eyed. I reminded myself she was biologically Gretchen's aunt, so the resemblance shouldn't have been a surprise. She was baking a cake to take over to Annie Stubbs's house for the family.

"Have you heard from the newlyweds?" I asked, meaning to be pleasant, forgetting she wasn't happy about it.

"No." She reached for the switch on the mixer.

"I need to talk to Mr. Holland. Is he around?"

She directed me to the backyard. The mixer started whirring before I was out the door.

I found Roddy working on his barbecue grill with a wire brush. He'd wisely prepared for the dirty work by putting on grimy gray overalls. His hands, forearms, and even his cheek, were grease-stained. The grease and the ferociously intent expression on his face as he attacked the grill were the most noticeable features in a man neither especially large nor small, with coloring neither especially light nor dark.

"Might ought to leave this crud on here and let the people who want their food grilled, instead of fried the way God meant for it to be, take their chances with the carcinogens," he said in greeting. "You get a pot for boiling shrimp or a pot full of hot grease, now that's easy to clean up."

I had a feeling Jean might not have agreed with Roddy's opinion of how easy it is to clean up grease, but I didn't want to start an argument with a wrought-up man wielding a wire brush, so I got down to business. "You've heard about Julian Stubbs."

"Yeah. Too bad. I kind of liked him." He gave the grill another swipe. "They send the police around to let people know that kind of thing?"

"Not necessarily, but I happened to be at the Stubbs house when Julian fell. Inez Rankin—"

Roddy Holland gave a snort that I interpreted as an opinion about Inez.

When he didn't add words to his snort, I continued. "Inez reported a theft, and I went over there to see about it. So we have a death and a theft, and we want to find out if they're connected."

"And where do I come in?"

"When Mr. Stubbs fell, the family tree that had been hanging in the upstairs hall fell with him. Willie Lanier said he had been talking about how it needed to be brought up to date, and you went upstairs with him during the party. Did he seem to have anything in particular on his mind?"

"On what was left of his mind, you mean? No. Just what Willie said. You get a bunch like that together, they all get to talking about family connections, but Jean and I aren't part of their family. Well, maybe we are now, if Gretchen and Kevin really did get married, which I reckon they did. You know what I mean. I wasn't interested in all their family stories. I just went up to look at the thing to humor Julian."

"It looks like somebody had been writing on it. Was that Mr. Stubbs?"

"Could have been, I guess, but I didn't see him doing it, if that's what you want to know."

"Did you notice any writing on it?"

"No. Which doesn't mean it wasn't there. I wasn't paying much attention."

"It looks like somebody added Gretchen's name."

"No kidding?" He took another swipe at the grill with the

stiff wire brush.

"Have you heard from Gretchen and Kevin?"

"No."

Prying into that did not fall within the scope of my responsibilities, so I was going to let that line of conversation go, but Roddy added, "You probably heard Jean was upset when she heard about them running off. We've got nothing against Kevin. It's just that, well, we, especially Jean, had different ideas for Gretchen. Big wedding, all that. You know how mothers can be." He waved his wire brush recklessly. I stepped back.

"Jean's killing herself, cleaning out closets, scrubbing floors, baking, going crazy because she doesn't know how to get in touch with Gretchen. I'm cleaning my grill. Never have done it before. Had to go buy a brush."

Pretty sure no words I had would help, I merely smiled. I didn't even comment on his foresight in getting the grill cleaned up so far ahead of cookout season.

I invited both Hollands to come down to be fingerprinted, and when I got back to the station house, it was apparent that the parade of suspects had begun. Inez Rankin was erupting from her car when I got out of mine.

"Who does Henry Huckabee think he is?" she asked.

I took that to be rhetorical, and it was. She didn't wait for a reply.

"Breaking into our mourning like this, treating us like a bunch of criminals!"

"Miz Rankin," I said as mildly as I could manage, "being fingerprinted isn't just for criminals, you know. There's a lot of confusion about what's been going on at the Stubbs house, about your earrings and some other things, and the best way to clear it up is to eliminate from suspicion the people who had business being in the house. We call it 'taking elimination prints.' "

I was surprised she let me string two sentences together without interrupting, and more surprised that she seemed to see my point.

"Oh, all right. Those earrings cost Dennis a bundle. Let's get it over with."

I followed her into the station house. To my surprise, Dennis Rankin was inside talking to Hen. His back was to us, and Inez and I weren't making much noise—having already said all we had to say to each other—so we had no trouble hearing what Dennis was saying.

"I don't want to get Inez in trouble for making a false police report or anything, but nobody stole her earrings."

A look from Hen stopped me in my tracks and my restraining hand stopped Inez.

Dennis continued. "I thought it would teach her a lesson, not to leave her jewelry lying around like that. Never occurred to me she'd call the police. I was going to wait till she'd made a big fuss about it and then show them to her, hanging on the Christmas tree, hoping to embarrass her. I shoulda known better. I don't guess you could give her a warning about making a false report to the police, or something like that, and still teach her a lesson?"

Hen grinned but shook his head. "I purely do sympathize with a man who wants his wife to be careful with her valuables, Dennis, but she didn't knowingly make a false report. Unless you think she knew you did it and wanted to get you in trouble?"

Inez couldn't stand it another minute. "Dennis Rankin!"

His shoulders slumped, and it was a long moment before he turned.

Hen intervened before the situation could get uglier. "I have some good news for you, Miz Rankin," Hen said. "We've found the thief and recovered your earrings."

She didn't seem to think that was funny.

CHAPTER 15

Shawna and Frank Kersey and their son, Tommy, arrived with Shawna's parents, Tom and Nancy Purvis, just in time to keep Inez Rankin from committing spousal abuse in front of witnesses. In spite of what Inez had said about our intruding on the family's mourning, the people who'd been at the Stubbs house for the after-the-mayoral- marathon party agreed to come by to be fingerprinted. In my opinion, they may have been relieved to have a break from dredging up old stories about Julian Stubbs and logging in the casseroles and phone calls of condolence. Those things would wait.

In one of those subtle indications that Hen does believe I make a positive contribution to crime fighting in Ogeechee, he decreed that someone even lower on the pecking order than I am would do the fingerprinting so that I could help take statements. This crowd was giving us far more business than we usually have, and the effect was something between a carnival and a cattle drive, as we shuttled people between the waiting room and the fingerprinting station and on to the conference room where we asked them to take a look at the bag swag and the family tree and tell us what they knew.

Young Tommy Kersey's enthusiasm for being fingerprinted was contagious, very helpful. Even Inez Rankin stopped acting childish and responded positively, if not enthusiastically, rather than set a bad example for the boy. Tommy was the only one, for instance, who wanted to make several sets of prints.

He even made a game of cleaning his fingers with the little moist towelettes. It was a shameful waste of moist towelettes, but it added to the festive atmosphere. I appreciated it when Frank borrowed a stamp pad and some paper, produced a handful of colored pens, and showed Tommy how to create fanciful pictures incorporating his fingerprints. I recognized a snail, a heavy-bodied bird, and a turtle among their more outlandish creations. Shawna exuded boredom. I stifled the impulse to suggest to Frank that he show her how to make pictures. Their family dynamic was no business of mine.

The statements?

Dennis Rankin, grateful to be separated from Inez, tried to make the separation last as long as possible by swiveling back and forth in the upholstered chair as he considered his every comment. He treated us to an unnecessary but impassioned defense of his behavior, but he didn't have anything to add to what he'd already told us about his whereabouts when Julian Stubbs tumbled down the stairs. He denied having anything to do with the bag swag and there was no way in creation we were going to find his fingerprints on any of it. Unless maybe the book. He might have looked at the book some time or other. Would we be able to tell if he'd handled the book years ago? He was sure he hadn't touched the family tree. I was inclined to believe him, pending evidence to the contrary.

If either of the Rankins had wanted to take things from the Stubbs house, I'd have bet on it being Inez, but she also claimed innocence. But we shouldn't be surprised if we found her fingerprints on anything in particular, and it wouldn't prove anything because she liked touching things.

Tom Purvis, following his grandson's lead, showed an interest in having his prints taken, but couldn't, or wouldn't, swear he'd ever noticed "any of that crap," and believed we were "making a mountain out of a molehill." To hear him talk, you'd think he kept his hands in his pockets at all times. He was sure he'd never touched any of the significant items. Furthermore, he'd been at home all morning with Nancy, hoping to hear from Kevin. And Gretchen. You could have knocked him over with a feather when he heard about Julian. I was not struck by Tom's originality of expression.

Nancy Purvis did recognize, with a shrug, the book, necklace, maybe the candlesticks but she wasn't sure, and of course the family tree, but she was far more interested in her son's elopement and seemed slightly surprised and aggrieved that we didn't share her interest. Kevin had, finally, phoned home and been told about his great-uncle's death, so he and Gretchen were cutting their honeymoon short, and Nancy wanted to go home and kill the fatted calf. Or something.

Shawna Purvis Kersey became more animated when we took her statement, because she was getting more attention, I assumed.

Unfortunately, she was only interested in the same general topic as her mother, with one glaring difference. Whereas Nancy seemed bent on welcoming her new daughter-in-law (adopting a strikingly different attitude from the Hollands' reaction to the wedding), Shawna still had her nose out of joint. "Where do the Hollands get off acting like Kev isn't good enough for their precious princess?"

Even if I'd thought I had an answer for that one, I wouldn't have had a chance to offer it.

Shawna raved on. "Mama says Roddy Holland dated Jean's sister before he took up with Jean, and Jean's always been jealous. Did you know that?"

"Actually, I did."

She might not have heard my interruption. "Don't you think it's creepy that she married her dead sister's ex-boyfriend?"

"I'm asking the questions here," I said in heavy police-officer voice, but that didn't even slow her down.

"I think it's strange. Mama says he broke up with Karen and people said she wasn't careful who she slept with after that and that's what got her in trouble and would also explain why she never would say who Gretchen's daddy was. Maybe she didn't even know."

"That's pretty serious gossip, Shawna."

"Gretchen will chew him up and spit him out, make his life a living hell, take him for all he's worth, the self-centered princess of a b—" As she paused, apparently looking for a word she was willing to say in front of the police, I couldn't help thinking she'd inherited her way with words from her father. Family tree.

Frank had nothing much to say about anything. Maybe living with Shawna had made that an unnecessary skill. A few years down the line, if they didn't watch out, Shawna and Frank Purvis would take over from Inez and Dennis Rankin as an example of strange bedfellows.

Tommy Purvis insisted that we take his statement, which focused mainly on how much he liked the back stairs at the Stubbs house. He had no idea what he might have touched. His eyes lit up when he saw the old bag and the collection of objects. Did he recognize these things?

"Sure. They were in the house when we were there for the party." Bright, observant kid.

He hadn't put the stuff in the bag, no, not even as a joke. Tommy's statement wasn't really any less helpful than his father's or his grandfather's. Or his mother's or grandmother's, come to think of it.

Hen and I said goodbye to that group, promising Tommy that if we decided to arrest him, we'd come with sirens screaming.

"I'll bet you we find that young'un's fingerprints on every surface in the house," Hen said.

135

"Okay, then, I'll match that bet and raise it with the theory that Inez gathered that stuff, planning to get it later, because she thought she deserved to have it. You want to arrest her?"

Hen was, I'm sure, weighing a thoughtful, reasoned response to the suggestion when he was saved from answering by the arrival of Annie and Gordon Stubbs, who brought the new widow. The three of them reeked of tobacco, and I couldn't help wondering if Vera's desire to stay with them had as much to do with the fact that Annie and Gordon had a more open-minded attitude toward smoking than Della and Willie as it did with their years-long friendship. These three went to the head of the line.

Everybody was so eager to make the widow comfortable in the waiting area that we talked to Gordon Stubbs first.

Gordon gave a short bark of laughter when he caught sight of the items we'd laid out for viewing. "Good Lord, I haven't thought about that in I don't know when."

"What?" I asked.

"Which?" Hen asked.

"That book."

"Something special about the book?" Hen asked.

"Probably nothing special about it in actual fact, but it goes to show that you can count on your family not to ever let you live down a mistake."

"Sounds promising," Hen said, leaning back in the swivel chair he always occupied in the conference room we share with the city council. It's the one the mayor uses because it looks something like a throne. "Tell us about it."

Gordon leaned forward in his humbler chair and laughed again. "Well, there are Cobbs way back in the Stubbs family tree, and so I naturally assumed The Georgia Peach was one of those Cobbs. Never asked anybody, you understand, since it was so obvious. Well, one time I said something to that effect,

136

and I never lived it down. Everybody else, for some reason, either knew better all the time or knew better after I'd made the mistake."

He gestured toward the book. "Years later when somebody or other ran across this book, they couldn't pass it up. Mighta been Vera or Julian. Sounds like something one of them would do. Anyway, whoever it was wrote that inscription in it and gave it to me for Christmas. Everybody got a good laugh out of it. Even me, since it was such an old joke by then."

"You're saying it isn't even Ty Cobb's autograph?" I asked, to get back to the point.

"If I had to guess, I'd say it's more likely Julian's autograph," Gordon said.

"No chance this book is worth anything?" Hen asked.

"It would sure surprise me if it turned out that way," Gordon said. "Even if Julian or whoever it was hadn't written in it. You never can tell, though. Ask a book dealer, but I doubt if a book where Ty Cobb, a mean old ba—a tough competitor," he amended with a glance at me, "a man like Ty Cobb tries to paint himself as a good guy would be worth much. I wonder if anybody remembers where it came from. Brings back memories, I'll tell you. That's when I learned not to take things for granted—not even about your own family. You may not know as much about your kinfolk as you think you do."

Except for the book, and the family tree, of course, nothing struck a chord with Gordon. He went on his way, marveling at the unexpected appearance of the old family joke, assuring us that if he'd ever touched even those items he couldn't remember when.

We talked to Vera next. She also said she hadn't handled any of the items. She had nothing to add to what we already knew, but was surprisingly insistent that she'd heard voices in the hall just before Julian went head first down the stairs.

"We'll keep that in mind, ma'am," said Hen, whose mama raised him to be polite to his elders.

Next up, Jean Holland, still wearing the slacks, shirt, and harried expression she'd had on when I'd last seen her, back in her kitchen.

There was strain in her voice, an edge that suggested she was holding herself in tight control and trying to behave. "I've been so distracted about Gretchen, I don't know where my head is. Yes, it's too bad about Julian, but I imagine if he'd had anything to say about it, he wouldn't have minded going like that—right after everybody'd been making a big fuss over him. He always did like seeing himself as a big, important man," she said through tight lips.

Apparently oblivious to how harsh that sounded, she added without emotion, "It was a big shock to me to see how far gone his mind was. He's known me all my life, and he kept wanting to call me Karen. I corrected him a time or two, and then let it go."

"Were you and your sister that much alike?" I asked, wondering if his getting her name wrong could explain her coldness about Julian Stubbs's death.

"I never did think so, but there's probably a resemblance. Karen worked for him one summer, so it's natural he'd remember her better. But it got on my nerves that he kept asking about Gretchen. I was so shocked about them running off— still am, if you want to know—that I wasn't in any mood to try to be patient with him. I'm sorry about it now, but how could I have known?" She said she had never been in the Stubbs house before and wouldn't have recognized any of the items we were displaying.

Pending incriminatory fingerprints, we were content with that, although I did note that, in spite of her words, she didn't sound particularly sorry about having been impatient with the soon-to-be-dead man.

Roddy Holland gave us a preemptive confession of sorts. "I got to thinking after we talked, Trudy. You might find my fingerprints on that picture frame there with the family tree in it."

"Why would that be, Roddy?" Hen asked.

"Probably got everybody's prints on it, if it comes to that. I think they were passing it around at the party. I put it back up."

"Anything particular Julian wanted to show you about it when y'all went upstairs during the party?"

"Hard to say. Even if he'd had something in mind, he might have forgot it by the time he got his mouth open. He was in bad shape."

"You told Trudy you didn't see him write on it?" Hen asked.

"That's right."

"Did you write on it?"

Roddy shook his head. "Why would I? I couldn't even draw my own family tree past a generation or two. I sure wouldn't know anything about the Stubbs relatives."

That made it unanimous. Nobody would admit to writing on the family tree or noticing that anybody else had.

That left Della Stubbs, who hadn't got back from Savannah, and Kevin and Gretchen Holland Purvis.

"Pure as Ivory soap, every last one of 'em," Hen said when they'd gone.

CHAPTER 16

It was much quieter at the station house the next day, which was helpful to my thought processes. I set about catching up on some paperwork and was grateful when Hen summoned me to his office.

We'd received the autopsy report on Julian Stubbs.

"The poor old fella had an ulcer, an enlarged prostate, and diabetes, but it looks like what killed him was the shock of the fall. Landed on this picture frame with such a whomp his poor old heart couldn't take it."

Hen was sitting at his desk and freely paraphrasing the report he'd salvaged from the sea of other papers.

I stood in the doorway.

"Too bad it wasn't the frame that gave out instead of Mr. Stubbs," I responded.

"There is also that head wound you observed, an injury not inconsistent—" Hen raised his eyebrows to show his opinion of the helpfulness of that phrase, and repeated "—not inconsistent with the notion that somebody hit him with something. The blow to his head might have done him in eventually, if the whomp to his heart hadn't got to him first."

He peered at me over the drugstore glasses he's reluctantly taken to using to help him read.

"Is the head wound consistent with having come into contact with the frame of the family tree?" I asked. "Could he have hit his head on it as he fell?"

"Hmm. Looks to me like the wound is inconsistent with that possibility. Something with a sharp edge hit him—too sharp for that curlicue frame. Mighta been the side of a door, or something like that. In addition, there are some other minor scrapes and contusions that make it look like he was a victim of abuse."

"Mrs. Stubbs said he used to bleed easily, from his blood-thinner medicine or something. Probably bruised easily, too, from bumps that wouldn't leave a mark on most of us."

"Look at this." Hen indicated where the photo showed a patch of small, evenly spaced prickle marks on the upper chest. "What the report calls multiple fine punctures. Looks like somebody used him for a pin cushion."

"Maybe his wife was beating him with her hair brush," I suggested.

"You're kidding, aren't you?"

"Probably, but it's hard to say what frustration and unhappiness might drive a woman to."

Hen nodded and made a note. "It's an ugly fact of life, sure enough. We'll look into that."

"Can you tell if the marks were made on his bare body?"

"Fuzzy edges. Looks like they came through the fabric."

"Miz Stubbs hitting him playfully?" I asked.

"Rough play, if that's what it was," Hen said. "Now that wound on his head. He might have got it when he fell down the stairs."

"Right. But I went over the stairs with a magnifying glass and didn't find any sign of that. It might have been a blow to the head that sent him down the stairs in the first place."

He nodded. "Okay, then, what are our options?"

It may sound elementary—probably is elementary—but the way Hen likes to work is to ask questions to see what I'll say. By the time we've argued as many sides of every question as we

141

can think of, trying to outsmart each other at every turn, we've usually covered the possibilities. It's a good way to keep from jumping to conclusions.

"Accident?" I asked, just for the sake of being able to eliminate it. I sat in the hard wooden chair across from Hen's desk as I answered myself. "I don't think so. A blow to the head pretty much rules out an accident."

"What about that blow to the head being an accident?"

"Let's see." I tried to picture it. "He's holding the family tree, bumps into something hard enough to knock him down the stairs, and falls, holding on to the family tree. It could happen I guess, but I don't know what he could have bumped into."

"A door frame?"

"He bumped into a door frame, and instead of dropping the family tree and clutching his head, he staggers around until he falls down the stairs? I didn't find any evidence of that, either."

"You don't like it?"

"There's no door frame right there, remember? The entrance to the Brewton Suite is the nearest to the stairs, but it's several feet away. Falling down the stairs because you bumped your head on that door would call for some serious staggering."

"Okay, then," Hen said. "What about somebody hitting him accidentally?"

"Like they're looking at the family tree, and the other person has a muscular spasm and winds up conking Mr. Stubbs?" I'm sure the expression on my face conveyed my opinion of the idea. Still, I tried to give the possibility serious consideration.

"Let's try that," I suggested. I took one of Hen's many framed certificates of achievement from the wall. He eyed me warily.

"Just thought we should try to see how that might work," I said.

"File room," he said, leading the way out of his tiny office.

We closed the door to the file room behind us and spent the

next few minutes working on the problem, taking turns holding the framed object, making assorted unexpected moves in erratic directions. I'm glad there were no witnesses who might later be called on to testify that our family tree seemed to be suffering from some sort of blight. In spite of our enthusiasm and creativity, nothing we could concoct would explain how Julian Stubbs would have that head wound. Except: "Somebody clobbered him," Hen concluded, wiping the sweat from his brow with the back of his hand.

"Yep," I said, kindly fetching him a glass of water to underscore the fact that I hadn't worked up a sweat. "On purpose, too. If it really was some kind of bizarre accident, whoever it was would have rushed down the stairs right behind him, trying to help, wouldn't they?"

"Uh huh. You'd think anybody without bad intentions would act like that." He put the empty water cup on top of the file cabinet. "Let's say it was somebody who was up to no good, somebody who shouldn'ta been there. Then it could be a kinda-sorta accident."

"Okay, I'll play," I said. "Maybe Julian Stubbs caught somebody defacing that family tree, and they struggled, and Julian took it away from him. Or her. Or—wait—say it was the other way around. Julian was defacing it, and somebody caught him at it and tried to snatch it."

"Okay, that works. They're struggling over the family tree, and Julian snatches it away and falls down the stairs."

"The other person lost his or her grip?" I suggested.

"Could be. Probably. So what we have could be called involuntary manslaughter," Hen said.

"That accounts for everything but the head wound."

"Yes, indeed," he said. "Whatever happened, I'm inclined to rule out an act of God or a pure, unadulterated accident. Too bad. I don't like it at all. I like it better when somebody with a short fuse gets pushed beyond endurance and pulls a gun or a knife on the spur of the moment in front of a cheering section, proud of himself—or herself—for the moment, at least. This looks more and more like a genteel, sneaky murder where somebody is not proud of it and is trying to get away with it."

"Looks like it to me," I said. "We're going to need to find some actual evidence of something, aren't we? Have we identified any fingerprints on the family tree?"

"Oh, yeah." He smiled and led the way back to his office, where he rummaged around in the sea of papers again before leaning back in his chair at a dangerous angle so he could put his feet up on the desk. I know Aunt Lulu didn't teach him that. "In addition to several prints we haven't been able to identify on the different items—it is a more or less public place of business after all, so it's no surprise there'd be stray prints around—in addition to them, specifically on the family tree, besides a lot of smudges, we have plenty of Julian Stubbs's fingerprints, and contributions from both Jean and Roddy Holland, Willie Lanier, Bradley Booth, Vera Stubbs, Shawna Kelsey, Dennis and Inez Rankin, and, last but not least, you," he told me.

"I think they had it downstairs, passing it around. I'm surprised your prints aren't on it."

"I musta been in another room getting something else to eat."

"Well, for the record, Hen, I didn't use the family tree to kill Mr. Stubbs. I hardly knew the man and had no reason at all to wrestle with him over that family tree. I must have touched it when Shawna was showing me around the other day. I did not touch it, except by the hanging wire, after Mr. Stubbs fell."

"Instinctively a good investigator. Noted."

"What about on the other things?"

"I've got a list of whose prints we found on what," he said.

"Some of it's just what you'd expect. What would you expect? Want to start with the stuff in the bag?"

"Sure. I would expect nothing useful from the necklace. Most people would hold it by the chain."

"Right. What else?"

"Probably prints on the candlesticks, the bugle, and the book. And the watch. I nearly forgot that. Unless whoever it was handled only the chain."

"That's pretty good, Officer Roundtree. Not that what we found will do us much good. Let's see here, now. On the candlesticks, Willie Lanier, Bradley Booth, and some unidentifiable smudges and partials. On the bugle, Willie, Bradley, Tommy Purvis, Gordon Stubbs. On the book, just smudges. Nothing on the watch or chain. What would you expect on the picture frame you found in Julian's suitcase?"

"Julian's prints, of course. Willie's."

"Not perfect, but not bad."

"Where'd I go wrong?"

"You were right about Willie and Julian. But . . ."

"But what?"

Hen grinned. "Want to guess who else's prints we found on it?"

"Tommy Purvis?"

"That woulda been my first guess, but, no. Come on now, Trudy."

"Give me a minute. Bradley? He seems to have had his hands on just about everything else."

He shook his head. "Give up?"

"Give up."

"Inez Rankin."

"What? Why?"

"You got two good questions, there, Trudy. One of us is going to have to ask Inez why. I'll take my little list of whose

145

prints are on what and give everybody a chance to explain, if they haven't already. Almost anybody in the house could have a perfectly innocent reason for touching anything."

"But Inez wouldn't have had any business in Willie's room touching that picture."

"Right. I'll want to hear what she says about that."

"You'll talk to her, then? What do you want me to do?" If he said I could hang around the station house and respond to calls about dogs running loose, he'd have a screaming mutiny on his hands. I'd even rather talk to Inez Rankin.

"We haven't talked to Della Stubbs or the newlyweds since everybody on the Stubbs family tree started going loony. You get to talk to them."

"Yes, sir," I said. "I'll see if any of them can shed any light on all the wandering knickknacks. Who knows? Maybe one of 'em will know why somebody would want to pitch Julian Stubbs down the stairs."

"We got us a tangled mess here, Officer Roundtree," Hen said, gloomily surveying the junk.

"Uh huh. Glad it's not my family."

"Just my in-laws, Trudy, and not all of them. Bradley Booth ain't even a distant cousin, far as I know, but just to be safe maybe we ought to get him back and see if we can pin everything on him."

"Good idea. I like it so well I hate to bring the subject back to the Stubbses, but do you think Inez Rankin might have committed more or less accidental murder over a pair of earrings that weren't missing, after all?"

"Kinda far-fetched, ain't it? You think she accused Julian and he denied it and they got in a tussle over it?"

"Sounds pretty lame, I know."

"I've seen stranger things right here in Ogeechee," he said.

Thus encouraged, I offered another theory. "Or maybe Vera

Stubbs, in a brief regrettable fit of frustration over her husband's increasing limitations, gave him a shove? You mentioned a lot of bruises and scrapes on the body. You don't suppose she was habitually abusing him, do you, and things got out of hand?"

"Breaks your heart to think about it," Hen said, "but it could have happened. No," he amended, "I don't think that."

"Vera Stubbs and Inez Rankin are our best suspects, though. They're the only people who were upstairs with Julian when he fell—or was pushed."

"Didn't you say you heard a ghost?" The expression on Hen's face was thoughtful.

Was he trying to see if I believed in ghosts? The thought sparked an idea.

"I'd rather find a live person to blame it on, but maybe it was a ghost of some kind, Hen, something way back in Julian Stubbs's past. You know how it is when you get to stirring up old memories. There's no telling what'll float to the top. And they say when people start losing their minds, they lose it from the most recent and go back. Maybe Julian was clear back in his childhood thinking about something that happened then and stumbled into a wall or something."

"Far-fetched. I like it better than your ghost theory, but not much better."

"It's all I have right now," I admitted.

Hen sighed and took his feet off the desk, which I took as a hint for me to go talk to Della Stubbs and the new Mr. and Mrs. Purvis and see if I could come up with a better theory to explain the murder.

CHAPTER 17

I'd need some luck if I were to get to Kevin and Gretchen before they'd been tainted by everybody else's version of the recent events at the Stubbs house, so I made them my first priority.

I found them at Kevin's parents' house, which was in an advanced state of confusion. They had elected to come to the Purvises instead of the Hollands for reasons that did not need to be explained, but, of course, the decision wasn't without its complications. Before their return, Shawna, Frank, and little Tommy Kersey had already vacated their space at the Stubbs House Bed and Breakfast and taken occupancy of Kevin's room at the Purvis house. Judging from the uproar when I arrived, I must have come in near the end of a rousing family discussion about sleeping arrangements. Nobody seemed particularly glad to see me, not even my bosom buddy, Shawna.

"What do you want?" she asked.

"I want to congratulate Kevin and Gretchen," I answered. "And I need to talk to them."

"Y'all go on, Kev," Nancy Purvis said, waving a hand in my direction and, apparently, immediately forgetting me. "We'll sort things out here. Maybe Shawna and Frank can go back over to Willie's."

"Maybe they should get the honeymoon suite," Shawna said with, I thought, unnecessary force.

"Is there a honeymoon suite?" Gretchen asked.

"We can go stay with my folks, Shawna," Frank said. "Or go on back home, like we planned in the first place, before all this came up. That would simplify everything."

For this sensible suggestion, he earned a glare from his loving wife, who, even if she was green with jealousy over the attention her brother was getting, wouldn't want to miss anything that was going on in Ogeechee.

"You go on if you want to," Shawna told Frank. "You probably need to get back to work, anyway. I'll stay here and help out."

Aware that I was an outsider, I was choking back the question of what Shawna would be helping out with. I doubted she'd be called on to make funeral arrangements for her great-uncle, and I couldn't see her helping anybody with cooking or cleaning or solving the many puzzles facing the OPD.

Gretchen Holland Purvis spoke up. I got the idea she'd prefer a police interview to more wrangling with her new family. "What do you need to talk to us about? Do you want us to go to the police station?" she asked, hopefully, I thought.

"You could talk in the living room," Nancy Purvis said.

Gretchen looked disappointed. Maybe the living room wasn't far enough away from her in-laws.

"We need to get their fingerprints," I said. "So if it's convenient for Kevin and Gretchen, we could go on down to the station house and do that now."

"Fingerprints?" Tommy Kersey was avid.

I smiled at him. "No, we don't need yours again. You did a good job the first time. But we need to have good prints from everybody else who's been at the Stubbs house lately, so we'll know if there are prints from somebody who shouldn't have been there."

"A burglar?" Tommy's eyes grew big.

"Maybe. Maybe a bank robber. A space alien."

"Really?" He was practically jumping with excitement.

"No telling till we've checked." I grinned at him.

"Don't encourage him, Trudy," Shawna said.

"We could go with you now," Gretchen said.

"Good. I'll get statements from you while you're there, then, instead of doing it here. I won't keep 'em long," I assured the others. "And we'll skip the bright lights in their eyes and the rubber hoses, since they're newlyweds." That sounded like something Hen might have said. Coming from me, it fell flat, but it did get the three of us out of there. We barely escaped without Tommy, who, in spite of—or, okay, maybe because of—our recent moment of rapport, seemed to believe I was arresting his uncle Kev, and, besides, he really really really wanted to ride in a police cruiser.

The station house isn't especially comfortable. It isn't supposed to be. But at least it was quiet—quieter than the Purvis house and much quieter than it had been the day before. Kevin, Gretchen, and I took care of the fingerprinting, and retired to the conference room. With the mayor and Hen both out of the way, I settled myself in the mayor's throne and was able to look down upon the newlyweds. To my surprise, the position did seem to confer a sense of power and wisdom.

"This is a weekend that will go down in your family lore," I said. "I realize you've probably heard some version of what happened after you left, but just in case you've missed anything, being on your honeymoon and all, I'll remind you that besides the Bicentennial celebration, Mr. Stubbs's death, and your wedding, there have been several things going on that the police are looking into."

"Mama told us about Aunt Inez's earrings, if that's what you're talking about," Kevin said.

"That's part of what I'm talking about," I admitted, "but to tell the truth, there's a whole list of things connected with the

Stubbs house and this family reunion that need to be explained."

"We weren't here for much of it, you know," Gretchen said. "So I don't know what good it'll do to get a statement from us."

"Let's start with y'all telling me about your friend Bradley Booth." I swivelled magisterially.

"Bradley? What's he got to do with anything?" Kevin asked. He reached for Gretchen's hand.

"Maybe nothing," I said, unmoved by this display of young love. "But he was around for most of the weekend, and he's one of the few outsiders in the middle of things."

"Is that some sort of crime?" Gretchen asked. "Being an outsider?"

"Not from my point of view," I answered. "Maybe from his. Maybe he's feeling like a victim. He took a lot of heat for the two of you when he made your big announcement."

Gretchen inched a bit closer to Kevin.

"Yeah. We heard," Kevin said.

"My detective instincts tell me you expected the announcement to be unpopular and that's why you found a fall guy."

Gretchen squeezed Kevin's hand. Apparently that made him the spokesman. "See, Mama and Daddy were dead set on having me at this big family thing this weekend, and it seemed like—well, we thought it would be a good time to tell them. That's why we got Aunt Willie to invite Gretchen's folks, so Bradley could tell everybody and get it over with."

Get it over with? I glanced at Gretchen and noted that she'd withdrawn her hand. Kevin also noticed, and noticed me noticing, and rushed to explain.

"I mean, we wanted to get married, and we didn't want to wait." He looked earnestly from me to Gretchen and back.

I waited.

"And we really didn't want to have to be there when they

151

found out, to tell the truth. You're right. We knew her folks and mine would both have wanted a big blow out of a wedding, social event of the season, like that, especially her mother. Right, Gretch? So they wouldn't like us running off."

"Why not give them what they wanted? You don't strike me as a couple who'd object to a splashy wedding and all the hoopla."

"We just didn't want to wait," Gretchen said.

"Okay. I believe in letting people make their own decisions about their lives, as long as they aren't breaking any laws, but why not leave a note? Why involve an innocent bystander? Bradley must be a good friend. He had to know he wouldn't be very popular for breaking the news."

"That wouldn't matter to Brad," Kevin said. "You'd have to know him. When we—Gretch and I—were talking about it, the Bicentennial and the family reunion and all, he got kind of interested. It was like he was hinting for an invitation, wasn't it, Gretch, practically invited himself?"

"His folks are in Bermuda or somewhere, and he wasn't in a big hurry to get home," Gretchen said.

"Yeah," Kevin said. "Yeah, and you invited him, didn't you, Gretch? Feeling sorry for poor, pitiful Brad?"

"I don't remember whose idea it was, Kevin." Now that we were away from her new in-laws, I seemed to have risen to the top of Gretchen's list of people she wasn't interested in being near. Shy new bride, interested only in her husband? Maybe.

Kevin looked disappointed, but persevered. "Well, whoever's idea it was, Brad's usually up for whatever'll break the routine, willing to help a buddy, and he doesn't care what people think, especially if it's people he doesn't know and especially if whatever he's doing will stir things up. So, we got to thinking this would be a good way to sort of make our big announcement."

"It was his idea?" I asked.

"I don't know. You know how it is when you're hanging out and kidding around. It just came up, and it seemed like a good idea, and Gretch pulled out all the stops, batted her big ol' baby blues at him and he couldn't resist. Nobody can resist her baby blues."

I could, but I understood the new husband's point.

"I didn't feel sorry for him," Gretchen said. "It just sounded like fun. Brad's family runs an antique store. He's really into old stuff. Maybe he thought he could find some—what do you call it, stock?—stock for their store or something. Yeah, now that I think about it, I think you're right, Kev, it was kind of his idea to come. We'd been talking about the old house, and he asked if he could stay there and talk to all these old people. His family is just his parents, so he doesn't have all this family, and that clinched it, made it sound like a big adventure or something. I think he said he was going to do a research paper about it or something like that."

"Yeah, I'd forgotten that part," Kevin said. "So, it wasn't like we invited him to come down and be the guest star at a family lynching or anything. He was doing us a favor and helping himself at the same time."

"Okay." I resisted an impulse to see if a hard kick would make the throne chair swivel all the way around. "That seems to cover your friend Brad." Not that I'd learned much.

The rest of their statement was simple, straightforward, and quick. They both said they hadn't even been to the Stubbs house. Gretchen said if their fingerprints turned up on anything, it would have to be a frame up. I got prompt shrugs and a casual, offhand, "yeah, sure," when I asked if they trusted Bradley.

That was more than I did, but I let them go and moved on to my next interview.

I found Della Stubbs at home, holding the fort while Willie made a grocery run. She led me to the family room/sitting room where she had her desk and computer workstation.

I happily accepted her offer of coffee and a pecan muffin and took an armchair within easy reach of a side table. Della put her coffee and muffin on the desk, but turned to face me. Was this her way of being sure I knew she was a busy woman with more to do than chat? Looking past her, I couldn't help seeing the computer screen, alive with a screen-saving school of small fish being chased by a much larger one.

"I'm sure Miz Lanier filled you in on everything," I said after I'd assured myself that the quality of the refreshments was what I'd come to expect. I'd been doing pretty well at the Stubbs house lately.

"Lord, I hope it was everything! We've had a death in the house—a death in the family, at that—maybe a burglary, and definitely some things that weren't where they were supposed to be. We don't need anything else right when we're trying to get a business off the ground."

"Too bad you missed the excitement."

She took a sip of her own coffee. "Not that my being here would have made any difference. We thought almost everybody would be leaving, and, to tell the truth, even if they didn't leave, I'd had about enough of some of them. Not Uncle Julian, though. He was still a nice man. But I had some bank business to do in Savannah and didn't see any reason to put it off. Willie can cope." Another sip.

I matched her sip. "It doesn't sound very convenient to do your banking in Savannah."

"Maybe not, but when I was working there, I got used to dealing with Savannah people and didn't want to change." She smiled. "Anyway, I don't like the idea of banking here in town, where everybody knows your business."

"You don't trust the bank to be discreet?" I said it with a smile so she wouldn't take it wrong.

"I just don't like the idea of too many people knowing too much about my business."

"The curse of the small town," I said. And the blessing, too, sometimes. "Sounds like you and your sister have the work divided up the way I'd want to do it, having somebody else doing the cooking and cleaning."

"It suits us," she said so sharply I guessed maybe it suited her better than it did Willie.

Okay. I'd get down to my own business. "You'll need to come to the station house and give us your fingerprints, but I can get a statement here, where it's more comfortable." I lifted my coffee cup.

"I don't know what good it'll do to get a statement from me." She glanced at the computer. Another reminder to me that she had work to do?

I broke off another bite of muffin and washed it down with a sip of coffee. "This shouldn't take long. You never know what might turn out to be useful. You weren't here when Mr. Stubbs fell, but you were here most of the time you had a house full of people. Did you notice anybody acting strange?"

"In this family who'd notice somebody acting strange?"

"A lot of items turned up in odd places—or didn't turn up at all. You didn't see anybody acting like they were up to something, anything to make you think anybody was stealing things?"

"No, but that night when everybody was over here, anybody could have been up to anything. Things got really crazy when the grownups got upset over Kevin and Gretchen, but even before that, with the kids all over the place, and everybody wanting to see what we've done with the house, somebody could

155

have walked through leading an elephant, and I might not have noticed."

"I see your point. I guess it shouldn't surprise anybody that some things got moved around—although some of them wound up in strange places—but one of the weekend's mysteries is that Willie says some expensive vases are missing. That's more serious."

Suddenly, friendly Della Stubbs, who'd given me coffee and a muffin and made jokes about her family, couldn't meet my eye.

"You know what happened to the vases." I tried not to make it sound like I thought it was a serious crime.

She looked uncomfortable. "It's nothing to cause a ruckus about. I just hadn't gotten around to telling Willie."

"Telling her what?"

More confidently now, meeting my eye: "I took them to Savannah to have them appraised for insurance."

Apparently, she didn't even want her sister knowing too much about what I had thought was their business, not her business.

"If they're all that valuable, wouldn't it have been a good idea to tell her so she wouldn't worry?"

"It was just a last-minute impulse, since I was on my way to Savannah anyway. I swear, with all the hubbub lately, we haven't had a minute to talk."

Sure. We were finished. She promised to come by the station house to be fingerprinted, and I left. Whatever was going on, Della couldn't have stolen the vases from herself; I'd leave her to make peace with her sister. By the time I closed the kitchen door behind me, she'd already turned to the computer.

Feeling mildly pleased with myself for having solved another one of our mysteries, I returned to the station house ready to learn how Hen had done. He hadn't been having any more fun than I had, but he'd worked off his frustration on the mess of papers on his desk. It was now possible to see parts of the surface. It did cheer him up to learn that I'd solved the mystery of the missing vases.

"Is every blessed person in this family afflicted with the irresistible impulse to move things?" he asked.

"Della's the only one who's confessed, Hen. Dennis Rankin isn't technically in the family, not in the way you mean," I reminded him. "And speaking of Dennis, how'd you do with Inez?"

"Inez Rankin tried to make like her fingerprints were entitled to be on anything in the house, maybe had been there since her childhood when she visited her grandparents, since she doesn't have a high opinion of the way her cousin Willie keeps house, and I can make whatever I want to out of it."

"I know you didn't let her get away with that."

"Oh, I let the crack about Willie go, but I told her she'd have to do better about the fingerprints since they really do not last forever when exposed."

"Did you tell her where-all we found her prints?"

"Now, Trudy," he said sadly. "Give me more credit than that. I know not to lead the witness. When I told her we'd found her prints in some unexpected places, she reminded me she'd already said she'd probably straightened up the family tree, if that's what I meant. Then I asked her if she could think of any other unexpected places, and I waited her out."

"She brought up the photograph?"

"She did, but not directly. She said she'd probably handled all the old family keepsakes, especially pictures."

"And you said?"

"I said I could understand that because she was obviously a sentimental kind of woman and those things would mean a lot to her."

"And you didn't choke?"

157

"No," he said, looking pleased with himself. "It wouldn't hold up in a court of law, but I'm convinced she knew we had her prints on that photo. She didn't give me anything else, though. Didn't volunteer that she'd put it in his suitcase."

"Maybe she didn't do that."

"I think she did."

"Why?"

"Maybe she felt sorry for Julian and wanted him to have it."

"More likely, she was trying to frame him—or convince the unconvinced that he was off his nut. Maybe make him think he'd done it. Or maybe she was planning to take some things for herself and thought she could call attention to this and he'd take the blame."

"You've got a devious mind, Officer Roundtree."

"Occupational hazard," I said. "Comes from associating with scum and worse."

"I warned you this was no job for a lady."

"And I warned you I was no lady, remember?"

"Oh, yes, I do remember."

I smiled sweetly at him. "As for Inez Rankin, then—"

"Much as I dislike her, without a confession or something that could pass for a reasonable explanation, I guess we'd better keep an open mind about who put the photo in the suitcase."

"This is all so messy, Hen! Most of what's occupying us isn't criminal activity. We can't charge anybody for moving things from one place in the house to another, can we? No matter how much we dislike them?"

He seemed to consider before delivering his verdict, with a sad shake of his head. "It's better if we can find some kind of criminal intent."

"Oh, heck. That's what I thought. Della gave me a muffin, but I've burned through it. I think I'll go get some lunch. Maybe that'll clear my head."

CHAPTER 18

I'm sure you can imagine my surprise and delight when I stopped by the *Beacon* office to see if Phil was free to have lunch with me and found Shawna there, one haunch possessively dominating a large corner of his desk. I grimaced in sympathy for whatever poems, articles, ads, opinion pieces, and photographs were trapped between the two unyielding surfaces.

"Hello, there!" I said, interrupting a high-pitched, trilling, purely artificial laugh from Shawna and the baritone underscoring that Phil was contributing.

Shawna turned just in time to catch the grimace that must have accompanied my greeting. She cut off her laugh in mid-trill. "Oh, hi, Trudy," she said, giving me the same look my more aggressive cat uses to convince the timid one that it's more than her life is worth to try for the catfish scraps.

"Hi, there, Shawna," I said. "Hi, Phil."

Phil peered around the obstacle that was Shawna's chest. "Hey there, Trudy. Uh, I asked Shawna to come by so we could discuss the story *The Beacon* will be doing about Julian Stubbs."

So he'd asked her to come by, had he? I couldn't quite picture Shawna as a good family resource.

"Is that what you were laughing about? Mr. Stubbs must have been more of a cut-up than I realized," I said.

"Oh, we got to talking about school, you know. Haven't seen Phil to really talk to in years and years." To insure that I would get the full force of her smile, Shawna shifted so that her rear end took up even more of Phil's desk top. I'm sure it was purely accidental that her skirt hiked up in an unattractive bunch, revealing an acre of thigh.

One thing you could bet your mother's Social Security check on: even if Phil and Shawna were doing legitimate business, I wasn't going to leave *The Beacon* till Shawna did. I'd wait, if I had to, till they'd exhausted the apparently hilarious topic of their old school days.

"Y'all go ahead and finish. I'll wait. There are a couple of things I wanted to talk to you about, Shawna. Police business," I added, like an idiot.

She grinned at me, then at Phil. "We're just about through for now, aren't we, Phil? Do you want to talk about it some more over lunch?"

"I'm a little behind here," Phil said. "Why don't y'all go on to lunch without me. I'll see you later."

"Sure!" Shawna said. "Trudy and I have tons of catching up to do. Let me call Mama and tell her I won't be back for lunch. I think Frank's already gone back home, and Tommy went somewhere with Teri and Delcie Huckabee. Teri's been really nice. I was worried that Tommy didn't really have any friends here, so it was a relief when he and Delcie hit it off. You can't ever tell about kids, can you?"

"I sure can't," I said.

Shawna slid down off the desk, hiking that skirt up even more, and stretched her arms high overhead, again making me think of the behavior of cats. This posture clearly says, "Rub my stomach. I know you're my friend." Verbally, she said, "You're sure you don't want to come to lunch with us, Phil?"

"I'm sure," he said. He's a coward, but not an absolute fool.

Shawna turned to me, arms still overhead, enhancing her bustline for whoever might be interested. I halfway expected her to bend over and touch her toes in order to call attention to her seductive rear end, but she merely brought her arms down and embraced herself before she asked, "Where do you want to go, Trudy?"

Downtown Ogeechee consists of three or four blocks of businesses clustered around the intersection of Court Street and Main Street. Roughly speaking, the businesses—including a general store/hardware store/garden supply store, Kathi's Cafe, a gift and card shop, and a dry goods/clothing store—straggle south from the courthouse to just north of the Stubbs House Bed and Breakfast. The courthouse and grounds occupy the northwest corner. The *Beacon* offices are on a side street just south of the courthouse. A small shopping center with a grocery store, a furniture store, a movie rental place, and a sandwich shop, occupies the northeast corner.

"How about The Lunch Pail?" I suggested. "It'll be quick. I really don't have all that much time."

Phil and I would have gone to Kathi's for home-cooked comfort food and pie; Shawna didn't deserve that. The Lunch Pail is a cute—cutesy—place, heavy on decor and craftsy touches—with country crafts for sale in the back, as a matter of fact—and light on cooking skills, which fit my mood perfectly. It was just a bonus that it has uncomfortable hard plastic booths and is in the shopping center across from the courthouse, about as far as we could reasonably get from the *Beacon* offices without making a point of it.

Shawna must have sensed my irritation and realized she'd be even more irritating if she ignored it and pretended we were sixteen again, girlishly absorbed in going out to lunch together. "Ooh," she gushed. "This place is darling! Has it been open long?"

"Not long. They used to be just crafts and added the lunch part to see how it would go."

"So, how's the policin' comin'?" Shawna asked when our

161

waitress, a high schooler whose enthusiasm for her job suggested she might be a felon on work release, left with our order—a pastrami sandwich for Shawna, a hot roast beef sandwich for me. It's one of my favorite foods. There wasn't much chance The Lunch Pail would do it as well as Kathi, but it was the most appealing thing I saw on the menu. We both asked for Cokes.

"An arrest is imminent," I said, not caring whether Shawna would recognize the stock evasive police answer or not. She didn't seem to, any more than she seemed to be aware that she was one of the fish swimming around in our pool of suspects.

"Really? Who? For what?" Or maybe she was throwing my attitude right back at me with this wide-eyed innocence.

I relented. After all, we had been friends for a long time. "No, not really, Shawna. No arrest is imminent. We're still investigating, collecting statements and evidence. You want to save us some time by confessing?"

"Why would I want to hurt him? If you ask me, y'all are making way too much out of an old man falling down some stairs."

"Oh, that's not all we're investigating. There's a whole passel of other mysterious goings-on. Most of it probably doesn't have anything to do with his death, but we can't just ignore anything suspicious. After all, we're so far in the backwoods we have to make the most of every opportunity we get to investigate something," I said.

"You're being sarcastic, aren't you? You'd better watch it. A lot of people don't like sarcasm. It makes them feel uneasy. Especially men, when it's coming from a woman."

"I appreciate your expert advice," I said sarcastically. "I do try to keep it down whenever I'm seducing anybody."

"You are so funny!" she said. "I've always liked that about you."

Our work-release waitress brought the Cokes and slopped only mine when she set them down.

"Anyway," Shawna said, smiling as she watched me mop up the sticky liquid, "I think he was a dirty old man and deserved a push."

"No, you don't think that," I said, irritably, I'm sure.

She backed off just a smidge. "Mama says Uncle Julian never could be trusted around a pretty girl, and everybody always said Gretchen's real mother never would say who the daddy was because it was him, and she knew it wouldn't do her any good to try to get him to do anything about it."

"You are referring to your esteemed uncle, Julian Stubbs, ex-mayor, pillar of the community, and subject of the forthcoming laudatory memorial article in *The Ogeechee Beacon,* about which you were just conferring with the editor?"

"There's that sarcasm again, Trudy! Of course, that's who I mean. That's who we're talking about, isn't it? Uncle Julian might have been all that other stuff like you say, but this would explain the way Jean Holland acted when she heard her precious Gretchen had married Kevin. It would be incest, wouldn't it?"

"Slow down, Shawna. Even if what you're saying is true—and it's just gossip, juicy, but just gossip—Kevin and Gretchen would be . . . what? You're the one who's supposed to be up on all this genealogy. What would Kevin and Gretchen be to each other? Besides husband and wife, I mean. Third cousins?"

"No. Not that far apart." Taking my question seriously, Shawna sketched on The Lunch Pail's cute country-print place-mat with her fork as she worked it out, then grinned at me. "If Uncle Julian was Gretchen's father, that makes Mama and Gretchen first cousins, so Kev and Gretchen would be first cousins once removed."

"Give it up, Shawna. I don't know how close the relationship would have to be for it to be incest. I'd have to check the statutes, but I don't think that's close enough for anybody to kill over it."

"Who cares what some old statutes say? Everybody knows you're not supposed to marry your kin. I can see Jean Holland killing Uncle Julian because of that."

"Not if she's thinking straight. If she wanted to kill him for carrying on with her sister, she's had twenty years to do it. And if she was worried about incest, she'd have had to kill Kevin, not Julian."

"Well, I think it makes sense."

"Sense? What part of it do you think makes sense? I think what you really think is that Gretchen isn't good enough for Kevin because her mother got into trouble she couldn't deal with. And another thing," I continued, "if she is the killer, then you'd better not go around talking about it. You might be the next target."

Shawna shivered in overdone mock fear, making fun of me and the whole idea.

"As a matter of fact, Shawna, the investigation is still wide open. For all I know—officially, as a police officer—you could be the one who pushed your uncle Julian down the stairs. That would explain why you're trying to talk me out of investigating."

Shawna interrupted her sputter when our waitress arrived with our sandwiches. I wasn't thrilled with the look of the pale brown gravy on my sandwich. At least there was a lot of it, enough to drip over the edge of the plate.

"Anything else I can get y'all?" our waitress asked as she licked my gravy off her fingers.

"Not for me," I said.

Shawna shook her head at the waitress and turned back to me to resume sputtering in outrage over the suggestion that she was a killer, but I beat her to the punch.

"So tell me, Shawna," I continued, when the waitress had shuffled off. "Where were you on Monday morning right after breakfast?"

"You can't bluff me, Trudy. You know perfectly well, Frank and I were moving our stuff over to Mama's."

"I'll check your alibi," I said.

Her look of disgust was surely meant for me and not for the pool of gravy beside my plate. I decided to give up my poor imitation of Bad Cop.

"You've had a busy morning, haven't you?" I said. "Did you get all the room arrangements straightened out before you came to talk to Phil?"

"Huh? Oh, you mean with Kev and Gretchen coming. Yeah. They didn't really want to stay with Mama and Daddy or with the Hollands, as if Jean Holland would let them, even. I mean, it's their honeymoon! Well, it turns out they went back to Willie's." She shivered. "I don't know that I'd want to have my honeymoon in a house where somebody just died, but everything else is so weird they probably haven't gotten around to thinking about that. I think they're getting the room Frank and I had." She gave up trying to pretend to be horrified and giggled. "They wouldn't want the room—I mean the suite—with twin beds, or the one where Julian was staying, and I think Inez and Dennis are still there, so they couldn't have that room. And the la-di-dah Brewton Suite has a private entrance. They'll probably like that."

"Going over there sounds like a good idea," I said. "They can be here in Ogeechee for the funeral, but they can have their privacy, too. You're staying with your folks, then?"

"Uh huh. Me and Tommy. I'm no detective, but I'll bet I can clear up a mystery for you," she said.

"Which one is that?"

"The one about why Kev and Gretchen ran off."

"I don't know how to break it to you, Shawna, but that is not a police matter. I put it down to starry-eyed, passionate young love."

"Maybe that, too, as well as the fact that Gretchen's pregnant and the sooner they make it legal the less people will have to talk about."

"Don't be mean, Shawna."

"Me? I don't know what you're talking about. Mama and Daddy—and the Hollands, of course—are hacked off now, but when Gretchen starts showing, they'll be glad they didn't wait for a big wedding, with everybody in town counting the months and then having to pretend the kid's premature."

"I'll hand it to you, Shawna. You solved a mystery I didn't even know I had. Not really a matter for the police, though."

"Probably not." She giggled. "Although I think it would be fun if you arrested Kev for scandalous premarital sex."

"I think Gretchen would have to be the one to press charges," I said.

"More likely she's the one who led Kevin down the garden path, anyway," Shawna said.

"Make up your mind whether you're on his side or not. Are you saying he's such a catch she'd have to trap him?"

"Well, I like him a lot better than I like her. She's got a sneaky side."

"Probably genetic," I said, trying everything I could think of to irritate her. "If her mother was a loose woman, maybe Gretchen is, too."

I was ashamed of myself almost instantly, when I saw Shawna falling in love with the idea.

"You think?"

"No. I was just—"

"It's not very likely Kevin's the first guy she's been with,

166

Trudy. She's a girl with a high opinion of herself. I bet once she got out of Ogeechee and the limited choices she had here, she ran wild."

"And Kevin's too starry-eyed or too unconscious to suspect he's just another casual notch on her garter belt? Come on, Shawna. A joke's a joke. I was just kidding. Leave her alone. You don't want to be enemies with her, do you?"

"You're right. She's my sister-in-law now, a member of the family. But I still wouldn't put it past her," she insisted with a grin.

My gravy was too salty, obviously an attempt by the kitchen staff to add flavor of some kind, and the meat was tough, but I ate it with some enjoyment because I had the added sauce of watching Shawna try to wrestle with the gristle in her pastrami. Altogether I was in reasonably good humor, and I thought I was being subtle when I said, "I'd better get back to work now, but maybe we can get together again before you leave. How long do you think you'll be staying?"

"I don't know exactly, but I'll keep you posted. I don't have to be in a hurry. Frank's already gone. After all, this is my family mess, not his."

I didn't ask what she meant by "family mess." I wanted to think she had in mind her uncle's death, or possibly the migrating objects from the Stubbs house, but I was afraid she was still thinking of her brother's marriage.

"And to tell you the truth, Trudy, I may just take advantage of this excuse to stay for a while."

"Oh? Through the school holiday, you mean?"

"Maybe longer than that. I'll have to see. Frank and I haven't been getting along all that well, and I could use some time to think about things." She took a bite from her sandwich, and most of the meat pulled out from between the bread.

"Think about what things?"

"Oh, you know. Whether I'll be better off with him or without him, like Dear Abby says, or Ann Landers, or whoever it is that says it."

She attacked the pastrami with a knife and fork, trying to separate the fat and gristle from the edible part. I nibbled on the parsley garnish that came with my sandwich, hoping to cut the salt.

"What's wrong with Frank?" I asked. I realized I didn't know him well.

She made that irritating empty slurping sound with her straw, which roused our waitress from her coma so that Shawna could signal for more Coke, before she answered. "He's just Frank."

"He seems like a perfectly nice man to me," I said, thinking of how good he seemed to be with Tommy.

"You wouldn't understand, Trudy."

"Probably not."

"Here you are, footloose, not tied down with a kid, with an exciting job . . ."

"Don't glamorize it," I said, not that I thought for a minute she was sincere. I hadn't been enjoying my role as confidante even before the conversation took this turn.

"And a great man in your life," she persisted.

"Well, yes," I began cautiously, but stammered to a stop when it became obvious that Shawna wasn't listening. She pushed the pastrami aside, sat up tall, and smiled at something over my shoulder.

Darned if Phil Pittman wasn't coming through the door.

"Thought I'd invite myself to your girl-fest," he said.

Gag me. Without waiting for actual encouragement, he grabbed the chair from behind the cashier's station and joined us.

"So, what are y'all taking about?" Phil asked, looking expectantly from Shawna to me.

"You, of course," Shawna said. It was the literal truth, or close enough, but coming from her it sounded like blatant flirtation.

Phil sat up tall and flexed his muscles in a lame strongman pose. He had the good sense not to ask what we'd been saying.

But then, he'd probably taken Shawna's comment as a joke, and he was just playing up.

At this delicate moment, my belt radio started crackling at me. I was not happy to hear the voice of the police dispatcher.

"What? Where? Okay. I'm on my way."

From Bradley Booth's enthusiastic departure from our town on Monday, I hadn't expected to see him ever again, but for some reason, a mere two days later, he had returned to the Stubbs house and become the subject of an assault. If it turned out he'd been trying to break in again, I'd assault him myself.

"I'll talk to y'all later," I said as I dropped some money into the sticky Coke residue by my plate and headed for the door. Only later did I realize it might have sounded like a threat.

But, then, surely both Phil and Shawna would have recognized that my first duty was to my glamorous job.

CHAPTER 19

I hit the siren and got down to Stubbs Street, just a few blocks
south of The Lunch Pail, in time to see Bradley Booth run out
the front door of the Stubbs house and become the victim of a
flying tackle by his old buddy Kevin Purvis.

From what it looked like, Bradley would have been better off
if it had been I who assaulted him. Something about the way
Kevin jumped on top of Bradley and started beating his head
against the ground made me think he was out to do serious
harm, whereas I would merely have been venting frustration at
a slow learner. Luckily for Bradley, he'd landed in a flower bed,
and the soft pine-straw mulch cushioned the impact.

I leapt out of the car yelling. Kevin stopped beating his friend
long enough to look up and register the presence of the police.
With a look of disgust, he gave Brad's head one final thump
against the pine straw and climbed off him, giving him a
sideways kick I was probably not supposed to notice as he
turned to face me.

First things first. "You all right, Brad?" I asked.

"I think I broke something," he said.

"Don't move," I said, including both of them in the order. I
called for an ambulance. Except for raising one arm to shield
his eyes against the sun, and groaning in a convincing manner
when he did it, Bradley didn't move. He closed his eyes, and it
seemed to me his breath was labored, but it was regular.

"I thought you left town," I said, to pass the time.

"I came back," he said, and groaned again.

Hands up and out in a surrender pose, Kevin sidled toward the front steps and sat. Once seated, he clasped his hands together between his knees and glared at his victim. He was panting.

Behind Kevin, Gretchen, Willie, and Della were clumped together near the door, wide-eyed. Eager as I was to find out what had been going on, I first called in to the station house to report and waited till the ambulance had arrived and Bradley was being attended to before I began asking questions.

"Y'all go on back inside," I said to the women as the ambulance pulled away. "I'll talk to Kevin and be there to talk to you in a few minutes."

Willie and Della turned to go.

"But—" Gretchen began, starting toward me instead of toward the house as instructed.

"Go on."

"I don't see why—"

"Go on, anyway."

The look she gave me might have withered kudzu, but she gave in. "I'm sorry, Kev," Gretchen said, as she turned to go.

I started my conversation with Kevin at that point. "What's she sorry about, Kevin? What's going on here?"

I know better than to ask two questions at once, and the lapse met with the usual success. He answered the one he wanted to answer.

"I was beating up on Bradley," he confessed.

"I may not be Sherlock Holmes or Jane Marple, but I'd figured that out. Were you trying to kill him?"

"I don't think so. Maybe."

"Why?"

By now the fight and adrenaline rush had gone out of Kevin. He probably wasn't much of a fighter in the first place; this

171

fight had left him pale and shaky. He sagged, leaning forward, supporting his head in his hands, his hands covering his face.

The words were muffled. "Do I need a lawyer?"

"I'm just trying to find out what happened."

"I was beating up on Brad."

"Uh huh. And?"

Hen's car slid to a stop in front of us, to my relief, if not Kevin's. I met Hen at the sidewalk and told him the little I knew.

"I'll talk to Kevin," he said. "See what you can find out from the women."

The three women were in the kitchen, but in the few minutes since I'd seen them, they might have traveled to different planets, each dealing with the aftermath of the recent violent outburst in her own way. Willie was moving aimlessly from the stove to the sink to the refrigerator; Della was at the desk by the window, tapping at the computer keyboard; Gretchen was sitting at the kitchen table making pellets out of what looked like muffin crumbs from the plate in front of her.

They all looked up at me.

It was Willie who asked, "Is he all right?"; Della who said, "I wonder what brought that on"; Gretchen who asked, "Are you going to arrest Kev?"

"We'll see," I answered them all.

Even in something that seems as routine as this, it's best to talk to witnesses separately so that they cannot influence each other's recollections and impressions of what happened, with or without malicious intent.

"Gretchen, let's go talk in the library," I said.

Willie nodded and turned back to the sink; Della shifted her gaze through the window and out into the backyard; I led Gretchen into the library. We sat in the faded-rose easy chairs near the Christmas tree, where Hen and I had been sitting when we spotted Inez Rankin's missing earrings.

Gretchen was wearing jeans and a silky-looking pink sweater that made her look angelic. She slipped off her shoes and pulled her feet up under her, her knees leaning against the arms of the chair in an awkward V. I'm limber enough to sit like that if I want to, but I didn't think it would go well with the dignity and power I needed to invoke at the moment, not to mention the restraint of my uniform.

"Brad won't press charges, if that's what you call it," Gretchen told me.

"Tell me what you meant when you told Kevin you're sorry," I began with a smile.

She suddenly seemed mesmerized by the Christmas tree.

"Come on, Gretchen. Tell me. Did you sic Kevin on Bradley?"

"No." She didn't stop looking at the Christmas tree.

"I'm going to talk to Willie and Della and Kevin and Bradley—and the mayor and the president of the board of education—if I have to, to get some answers. You might as well give me a little help here. Do I haul Kevin in for assault? Do I charge him with running amok? Temporary insanity? Was it self-defense? Was he provoked? Pick one of those questions and answer it."

"I don't know."

"You don't know anything? Okay. Start with this. Where were you when the uproar started?"

Finally, she looked at me. "I was here."

"Here where?"

"Right here by the Christmas tree." She pulled her knees together and hugged them. Ah! Animation!

"Good. Why were you here?"

"By the Christmas tree?"

"Let's start with why you were here at the house."

"We're going to stay here, in what they call the Brewton

Suite. We brought our stuff."

"Okay. So you and Kevin were here in the library?"

"No. Not right then. Kev had gone back to his folks' house to get my makeup case that I forgot and left over there, and we were just talking—"

"Who's 'we'? Not you and Kevin?"

She let her knees flop back into a V. "Me and Brad."

"Okay. That's a start."

"We were just talking, I swear we were, right here, not in anybody's bedroom or anything, and I got something in my eye and Brad was trying to get it out, that's all we were doing, and Kev came in like, I don't know, like Ghostbusters or something, and he was all over Brad before we knew what was happening. It was like, I don't know, he went ballistic. I mean, he just lost it! It's like he went crazy or something. He pushed me out of the way and went after Brad like he wanted to kill him."

Hearing herself say that, Gretchen's sixty-mile-a-minute recitation screeched to a stop. She took a deep breath. "I mean, I don't mean he really wanted to kill him. I mean, they're friends."

"Uh huh."

"Well, I know that doesn't sound like it."

"No."

"He's always been jealous, but there's no reason."

Hen likes to quote from the Old Testament, the Book of Proverbs: "The wicked flee when no man pursueth." The application to modern police work is that when people look guilty even though you haven't suspected them of anything, they're probably guilty of something. It's the same thing when people start denying something you haven't accused them of.

"Why would Kevin be jealous of Brad?"

The complacent look on Gretchen's face told me she's the kind of woman who interprets the actions of a jealous man as a compliment, as a measure of her worth. Some women even provoke fits of jealousy in order to prove to themselves how important they are to the other. Her words strengthened my suspicion that she might be this kind of woman. "I went out with Brad before I started going with Kevin, and Kevin thinks maybe I'm not over him."

"Why would he think that?"

A complacent shrug.

"Why would he think that now?" I persisted. "They've been getting along. What set him off today?"

A complacent smile. "I really don't know."

I wasn't ready to let go. Could I shake her complacency? "Brad left Ogeechee a couple of days ago. Maybe Kevin was surprised to see him. Maybe he thought you and Brad were sneaking a meeting."

"We weren't." She went back to looking at the Christmas tree.

At this point, Hen and Kevin joined us. Kevin and Gretchen, appropriately enough, had eyes only for each other, although from where I sat the eyes seemed to be sending different messages.

Showing more life than I'd seen from her before, Gretchen was out of her chair and wrapping herself around a haggard Kevin before they were well inside the door.

"Kevin's calmed down," Hen told us. "I'll have to talk to Bradley before we decide about charges. For now, we're through with you."

"Both of us?" Gretchen looked at me.

I nodded.

"Did you find out what this is all about?" I asked Hen when the newlyweds had disappeared, clinging to each other, but quiet, up the stairs.

"Nah. Insisted it was just between him and Bradley. How'd you do?"

"Not any better. All I got was that Kevin went to his parents' house and came back looking for Bradley's blood. I'll see if Shawna can shed any light."

"Shawna Kersey, shedder of light," Hen said. "Not the way I picture Shawna."

"In this case, maybe," I said.

"You may have a point," Hen said. "You finish up here with Della and Willie. I'll go talk to our victim."

Back in the kitchen, I found only Della. A slight disarray in the usual careful arrangement of her curls was the only clue to the recent turmoil, unless you count what looked like a game of Texas Hold 'em on the computer screen, instead of business.

Willie, she said, had gone upstairs to get some work done.

Della had had plenty of time to get her thoughts organized, and her statement was clear.

"Yes, Bradley was here with me having a glass of tea when Kevin dropped Gretchen off. She seemed surprised to see him, but they left and I got back to work. When Kevin came in a little while later I told him Gretchen and Bradley were up front somewhere. The next thing I knew there was all this screaming and yelling, and it sounded like things were getting knocked around, so I called the police. We've got a lot of valuable things in there and I don't need a bunch of rowdy college kids wrecking the place."

"No."

"I tried to break them up with a broom, but I couldn't do it."

"Wish I'd seen you try."

"Me, too. It might have looked funny to somebody just watching, but it didn't feel funny, I'll tell you." She smiled. "Sweeping's usually Willie's job, but I'd just swept them out of the house when you got here."

"Quick thinking," I said. "Just one more thing and I'll let you get back to work."

She looked politely patient.

"I thought Bradley left Ogeechee on Monday. Do you know what brought him back?"

My question seemed to surprise her. "You'd have to ask Willie about it, but I think he called on Monday, yes, after he'd left town, to see if he could keep the room after all. I think that's right. But we didn't see him again till late yesterday."

That didn't answer my question. I tried again. "Do you know what brought him back?"

She smiled a nice-little-old-lady smile that made me think she was hiding something. "He's a nice boy. He likes old things. I think he liked Willie and me . . ."

She waited for me to get the self-deprecation. When I smiled she continued, ". . . and he likes our house. I think he said his folks were away somewhere and wouldn't be back till just before Christmas. Maybe he just liked the way we took care of him."

Unfortunately, since she'd had so much time to think about her statement, I wasn't going to get any more out of her.

Willie wasn't doing housework upstairs when I found her, as I'd expected. She was in her sitting room working on the jigsaw puzzle. I noted the rise and fall of Kevin's and Gretchen's voices from behind the closed door of the Brewton Suite.

"Jigsaw puzzles are calming," Willie said.

"Mind if I join you?" I asked.

She gestured toward the chair across from her, and I sat. "I thought Bradley left town," I said as I studied the puzzle and tried to find a point of entry.

"If you want my first-hand experience and not hearsay, I can't say I know about that." She smiled up at me when she said it. "All I know for sure is he checked out of here and left with you and Hen on Monday. He called later, though, and said he'd lost a camera and wondered if I'd found it. Well, I hadn't. So he asked if he could come back here to stay while he looked around for it. Didn't make a lot of sense, if you ask me, but I never did pretend to understand kids that age. Maybe he's just at loose ends with his folks off on a trip somewhere. I don't know. Anyway, he came back and was just hanging around. Almost made me sorry for him. Everybody else has their own business to tend to, and nobody was able to spend any time with him. He went back and talked to Della, which got on her nerves, I imagine, but she didn't run him off. I got on with my work upstairs, to make sure things were nice for the newlyweds in the Brewton Suite. I'm finding out there's always something needs to be done in the hotel business."

"The price you pay for having customers," I said.

"That's exactly right, so I'm not really complaining. Anyway, I was running the vacuum off and on, and I heard some coming and going but didn't pay much attention since I knew Della was downstairs, and then the first thing I knew there was this banging and slamming from downstairs, and then I heard your siren. I don't know what led up to it, if that's what you want to know."

She'd been trying to fit pieces of a pair of tinselly angels together as she talked. Now she joined two sections and looked up, pleased.

"We're getting this bed and breakfast business off to a rousing start, with police and ambulances here every other day. And this is the second time today for you." She left the angels for the moment and started on a star, almost the same color as the angels, but not tinsel.

"I'm getting a little tired of it, myself. But look on the bright side, at least everybody in town will know you're here," I said in consolation. I reluctantly gave up on my search for a teapot-shaped puzzle piece that would fit into one section of the cookie jar, and went back to the station house.

Hen's report on his talk with Bradley was entertaining and enlightening only because it reassured me that Hen hadn't done much better at clearing things up than I had. He set the scene for me—Bradley in his hospital bed, cleaned up, fresh from X-ray—then he read from his notes, the lack of expression in his interpretation telling me all I needed to know about his irritation:

Me: You want to tell me what that was all about?

Bradley: Nothing to tell.

Me: Your buddy attacks you, and there's nothing to tell?

Bradley: It's no big deal. He just lost his temper.

Me: You got any idea what set him off?

Bradley: He didn't tell me.

Me: So he just lit into you and tried to kill you with no reason. Has he ever exhibited homicidal tendencies before that you know of?

Bradley: It was . . . it must have been a misunderstanding.

Me: You want me to arrest him?

Bradley (smiling): Not unless I die. Then I want you to pickle his hide.

"And that's that," Hen said, slapping his notebook shut. "The doc said the worst of it seemed to be a broken rib and possibly a mild concussion. Some scratches and bruises that don't amount to much. They wanted to keep him overnight to make sure there was nothing else wrong."

"Oh, there's something else wrong, Hen. It might not be the kind of thing they can test for at the hospital, but there's something wrong. The way I got it from Gretchen, it might have looked to Kevin like Bradley was moving in on her."

"Simple as that?" He looked hopeful.

"Simple as that," I said. "But, it doesn't look good for their marriage if Kevin doesn't trust her any more than that."

"You got a romantic streak you've been hiding from me?" Hen asked.

"I don't think that's romantic, just good sense. If they don't trust each other, why did they get married?"

"Romantic and idealistic!" Hen said. "I never would have guessed. Does Phil know about this side of you?"

"What's Phil got to do with anything?" I asked, imprudently letting Hen know he was annoying me.

"You want me to have a talk with that boy, persuade him to make an honest woman out of you?"

"You want me to tell Teri you've been sneaking donuts?"

"Just asking," he said. "Wouldn't want to fall down on my duties as the man in the family."

"Excuse me while I go see if Kevin still has any fight in him. Maybe I could get him to beat you up for me, me being a helpless female and all."

His guffaw was so contagious I had to join in. Peace officers at peace with one another once again.

CHAPTER 20

After a day that had felt more like a week—starting with going over the autopsy report with Hen; going through the interviews with Kevin, Gretchen, and Della in the morning; running into Shawna at *The Beacon*; eating lunch at The Lunch Pail; and ending with the assault at the Stubbs house—I was ready for some serious decompression.

I had just stepped inside my back door and picked up a cat when my phone rang.

"I didn't think you liked The Lunch Pail," Phil said.

"I thought Shawna would like it," I said.

"Really?"

I didn't feel like going into that, so I said, "I was thinking of a quiet evening with my cats and my jigsaw puzzle."

"How quiet? What about something to eat?"

"Pizza? Here?"

"Works for me. What time?"

"Whenever you get here will be fine. I'll just sit and vegetate till then. It's not like I'm going to clean house for you or anything."

"See you later, then."

Phil brought pizza with everything on it but the kitchen sink, actually the one Wanda's Pizza Kitchen calls "The Kitchen Sink," but he had them hold the anchovies, the way I like it.

We ate at the old round oak table that occupies the space between the stove and the pantry, since the dining room table still had Grandma's embroidered tablecloth on it from Sunday and I wanted to spare myself the chore of trying to get pizza sauce and grease out of it and since the table on the porch had the puzzle on it.

We dived into that pizza like neither of us had eaten in a week. It was a good antidote to The Lunch Pail's hot roast beef sandwich. I was looking at the last stringy fragment from the pizza box, trying to decide whether it was cheese or extremely greasy cardboard, when Phil asked, "Are you feeling better now that your feeding frenzy is over?"

"Somewhat," I said. "How about you?"

"I wasn't as bad off as you were," he said. "I didn't have lunch at The Lunch Pail." Sometimes he's almost too smart for his own good.

I offered what I had finally decided was cardboard to a cat, who also refused it.

"How's the investigation coming?" Phil asked.

"The investigation? Make that plural. We're investigating a dozen things. The hardest part is trying to figure out how many different investigations there are and which parts are connected to which, very much like that old crime-fighting analogy, the jigsaw puzzle. But we are making some headway, on some fronts."

"Such as?"

"Phil, exactly what I do not need this evening is to keep going over and over this messy case."

"What do you need? A massage? Some reflexology?"

"Keep your hands off me, you cad!" But I smiled when I said it.

Responding in kind, Phil held his hands over his head in a mockery of terrified surrender. "Yes, ma'am. Whatever you say, ma'am. But what do you want to do that doesn't involve hands?"

"What I'd like to do does actually involve hands. You want to work on the puzzle? Willie Lanier says jigsaw puzzles are calming."

"Sure. Calm is good."

"Let me just do the dishes first," I said, piling the greasy napkins into the pizza box and cramming it into the bulging trash bag. "There. Done!"

The cats followed us to the porch. Dumplin wanted to sit in my lap. Biscuit was content for the moment to watch from a nearby chair. Phil got his own chair.

"So," I said, surveying the puzzle to get my eye and brain back in tune. "How was your day?"

"Not bad. More varied than usual, with the Julian Stubbs death to cover. It's been interesting talking to people who remember him and can give me anecdotes for our story."

"I could see that." I started collecting pieces for the whitish-grayish background behind Santa's head.

"What do you mean?" Phil hadn't found a focus yet. He looked at me.

"Shawna," I said. "I don't know what she was telling you, but she told me that the younger Julian Stubbs was . . . let's say he was a ladies' man."

"Really? Shawna said that? It doesn't sound much like her."

"Those might not have been her exact words."

"If you're not actually quoting her, I think you can do better than that. Are you saying he was a cad, a bounder, a tomcat?"

"Let's say she strongly hinted that back in his younger, more virile days, he was not above using his position to help him have his way with women."

"That's an interesting angle. She didn't mention anything like that to me."

"Trying to protect the family honor from the sensation-mongering media, probably. Why don't you work on Santa's pack?" I pointed to the picture on the box and then to the blank area on the table where that section would go, but he ignored me.

He asked, "You believed what Shawna said about Julian? Just took her word for it?"

"It was her mother's word, actually."

"Which makes it hearsay, doesn't it? Or maybe she was paraphrasing. Which means you can take it with a grain of salt. Which means I'd be out of my mind to suggest anything like that in *The Beacon*."

"You think you're pretty smart, don't you?"

"Comes from hanging out with the cops. But there might be something to what she says."

"Even if it is hearsay?" I challenged.

"Right. We aren't talking about the rules of evidence or the rules of slander or libel. We're talking about who'd commit a crime, aren't we?"

So there we were, back at the Stubbs murder.

Phil persisted. "That's how an investigation works, isn't it? Doesn't any kind of investigation—and especially a murder investigation—always hinge on what led up to it? If somebody murdered that old man, it's bound to be because of something in his past. I've heard Hen say it takes a lot of emotion, strong emotion, to make a person want to commit murder, and I don't think Julian could have done anything on this trip that would have sent anybody into a rage."

As he talked, Phil had finally started collecting brownish pieces to make up Santa's pack.

"You're right," I said, no longer resisting talking shop. "Even if his fall was semi-accidental, and—or—somebody just got carried away in the heat of the moment, there had to be a reason for what happened. If it was murder, deliberate murder, maybe somebody got worried about what Julian might remember, or that he would forget there was something he wasn't supposed to talk about, some old scandal, since his thought processes weren't what they used to be."

"The possibilities are endless for a man like him," Phil said. "He had his finger in all the town politics—county politics, for that matter. Lots of potential there."

I was happy to see that Phil could fit pieces together and carry on a conversation at the same time.

"Annie Stubbs hinted at old enemies," I said. "Do you know of any?"

"No." He turned a puzzle piece every possible way before putting it down and returning to his thought. "I'll see if Daddy remembers anything like that." Phil's father and his father before him had run *The Beacon*. If there were any skeletons in Ogeechee's political closets, Mr. Pittman would probably know.

"If there'd been any serious enemies, most of them would be gone by now," he continued, "and the others wouldn't exactly be in the kind of shape where they'd be able to sneak into the Stubbs house and push him down the stairs."

I smiled, thinking of how lively Annie and Vera Stubbs were. "Some of his contemporaries might surprise you, Phil. Mainly, the way I see it, we're limited to somebody who had access to the house."

"You mean somebody in the family?" Phil asked.

"Maybe not, now that I think of it. Anybody in town—anybody who cared—could have known where Julian was staying."

"Could anybody in town have gotten in to do it?"

"I think so. Somebody—maybe Julian—could have let the killer in, and in spite of what Willie and Della claim about one of them always being there for security, that wouldn't keep anybody out—not somebody who really wanted in. There are three entrances to the house and somebody in one part of the house wouldn't necessarily hear somebody coming in somewhere else. The door into the Brewton Suite from the upstairs porch wasn't locked when I went up there to investigate, and just before Julian fell, I thought I heard somebody overhead. Somebody—anybody—could have come up the back stairs and left the same way."

"What if it was Vera or Inez? Either one of them could have had it in mind and been watching for an opportunity."

"But why?"

I gave up working on that boring background and started looking for pieces of Santa's hand.

"Oh, good grief!" Phil startled me.

"What?"

"You don't suppose his mind was so far gone he started groping Inez?"

I shuddered. "No, surely not. But if he did, it's no surprise he wound up at the bottom of the stairs."

Phil grinned at me. "Well, then, you have a good suspect. I think you ought to ask her about it. And if you don't like Inez, there's Vera, in a fit of jealousy."

"Much as I like it, Phil, and I really do like it, my imagination will not stretch far enough to cover either of those motives."

"Okay, I'm not proud. Ignore my theories. But if you do, all you have left is a sneak, and if it was an outsider, robbery is the obvious motive. Anybody might have known there were extra people staying at the Stubbs house, and they might have brought valuables with them. Inez was flaunting those earrings in front of the whole town on Saturday, just inviting somebody to try to snatch them. And any low-level punk worth his street cred knows that where there are diamond earrings, there might be other small valuable things."

"Maybe, but I don't know, Phil. Most thieves—even low-level punks—would rather do their thieving without having to confront somebody."

"For obvious reasons! Just look what happened when this character came upon Julian!"

"Exactly. Got any other theories?" I asked, turning a piece that looked exactly right but wouldn't quite fit.

"Okay," Phil said. "Maybe it was a thief, and whoever it was couldn't wait till nobody was around for some reason."

"Maybe."

"There's a lot of stuff that needs explaining. You've found the earrings, but what about the missing vases you told me about? Or that other stuff you and Hen found?"

"The vases weren't stolen, either. It was a lack of communication. Della took them and hadn't got around to telling Willie. And for the other things—why would anybody collect them and put them out on the porch instead of leaving with them— especially if they'd just committed murder?"

"Got rattled? Didn't want to get caught with stolen property that would tie them to the murder? You're the police officer, Trudy, not me."

"Ah. Copping out, I see. Well, as long as you're so intent on assisting the police, explain why Julian was holding on to the family tree when he fell."

"You're suggesting somebody killed him over the family tree? With the family tree?"

"I'm doing no such thing. I'm simply asking questions. What do you think?"

While he thought, Phil lifted Biscuit, who had decided to eat a piece of the puzzle—apparently more inviting than the grease-soaked cardboard—and put her on the floor. I took the rescued piece and fit it into the puzzle. Had Biscuit been trying to help?

"It seems pretty extreme to think that somebody whacked him for defacing that old piece of calligraphy," Phil said.

"If he was the one who defaced it."

"Right." Phil was now holding Biscuit in his lap, his hand between the cat and the table.

We worked in silence for a bit.

"Why do the same things keep coming up?" I asked.

"In your investigation?" he asked, pausing with a puzzle piece in his hand, the shape I think of as a silly hat—knobs on three sides and a hole on the fourth.

"No, I mean in puzzles. It's like there's a rule, or some stock everybody has to pull from."

"You aren't making a lot of sense," Phil told me, studying the silly hat.

"Well, just look. Holly. Evergreens. Ribbons. Candles. Bells. Angels. Santa Claus."

"You mean the picture on the puzzle? It's a Christmas puzzle, Trudy. What else would you put on a Christmas puzzle? Motorcycles? Dragons?"

"Maybe toy ones. Why not?"

He just looked at me. He is so patient.

"Okay. You're right. But out of all the possible playthings in the world, why books?"

"I just see one book," he said.

"Why did I say books?"

"You're asking me? Hey look!" He slid the silly hat into place and gave me a triumphant grin.

I was feeling triumphant, myself, but not because we were doing so well with the puzzle. Why had I said "books" when this puzzle only had one book? Because the reason some of the same things seemed to keep coming up was suddenly obvious to me. Many of the things that were pictured on my puzzle were pictured on Willie Lanier's puzzle. The important thing, though, was that actual touchable versions of some of these same items had also turned up in a battered old leather bag that had the Ogeechee Police Department trying to work out a different kind of puzzle. Eureka! I had a flash of insight into what had been puzzling the police.

Furthermore, before Phil and I called it a night, we had everything put together except a patch of featureless background. It's always the parts without colorful details that are hardest and take the longest. We didn't mind stopping with only a small portion left. We'd finish it, but there was no hurry. We'd have other times to work on it. Maybe we'd stall around, save it till Christmas Eve.

Sometimes life is good.

CHAPTER 21

I gave some thought to the most gentle, tactful way to lead Hen to the same puzzle-oriented epiphany I had experienced.

Here's what I settled on.

"You're guilty of blatant favoritism, dereliction of duty, a serious lapse in judgment, and failure to follow good police procedure," I told him as soon as I got to the station house and had poured myself a cup of coffee. The coffee would give me something to hurl at him in case my planned goading went past the limits of his endurance and he went on the attack.

But he's used to me, merely glanced up from what he was doing and asked, "Is that four separate charges or just one?"

"Four parts of the same lapse." It annoyed me that in spite of being distracted, and with part of his brain on something else, he'd managed to count my four charges.

"Ah. You're not bringing up discrimination against women again? I told you I'm about to hire Dinah Witherspoon, didn't I?"

"Yes, you told me. No, this is not about gender equity in the workplace. It's more urgent than that."

He put down the papers he was holding and arched his back, apparently trying to make his elbows meet behind his back. I wondered how long he'd been hunched over his desk.

"Even more urgent than that?" he asked. "Must be serious, then. What is it?"

"I've realized you didn't bring in everybody for statements

about what went on at the Stubbs house on Saturday night."

"And that leads to these wild charges?"

I sipped and waited.

"Who'd I miss?" He focused his gaze on the far wall, obviously running through the cast of characters in his mind. When he focused on me again, he looked puzzled and a touch impatient. "Who?"

"Teri and Delcie were there, weren't they?"

"Uh huh." He was focused on me now, all right.

"Let me put this to you another way, Chief."

"Good idea."

"Better yet, let me show you. Get the bag with the swag, the bag swag, the swag bag. I want you to see something at the Stubbs house."

"I don't want to go back to the Stubbs house," the Chief of Police whined. "Just stop acting so cutesy-cute and tell me what this has to do with my wife and daughter."

"I'm getting tired of the Stubbs house, myself," I said, "but I think it would be better if I show you something and see if you come to the same conclusion I did."

Maybe it was the mystery that got to him. Ten minutes later, with me carrying the old bag with its assorted swag, we were at the Stubbs house again, upstairs, with Willie Lanier, looking at the jigsaw puzzle on the table in her sitting room.

The puzzle wasn't much further along than it had been the last time I saw it, so it was the picture on the box that I called to Hen's attention.

I gave him a chance to make the connection I had made, and he rose to it, but then he'd had me to point him in the right direction, mentioning Delcie and asking him to bring the bag.

"I'll be a pot-bellied pig!" he said, which passes for strong language if you're a Methodist.

"What?" Willie asked.

191

Like a practiced magician's assistant, I held the battered bag open so that Hen could reach in. He made the most of it, too, for Willie's benefit. First he gestured toward the bag itself, and then to the traveling bag at the doll's feet in the puzzle picture. There was a definite similarity, which made the rest of the revelations almost unnecessary, but he followed through: the bugle, the pocket watch, the candlesticks, were directly comparable; the amber necklace was more subtle, but it had a clear resemblance to the garland that wove around the candlesticks and through the evergreen needles, draping gracefully into the doll's section of the shadowbox.

"I see what you're telling me. These things look like the things in the picture. But what does it mean?" Willie asked.

"Child's play," I answered, probably smugly. "It means your crystal candy jar might have been the next thing to disappear." Hen pointed to the candy jar in the picture.

"Ah, I see," Willie said, frowning in a way that said she didn't see.

"We'll return these things to you when we've satisfied ourselves they don't have anything else to do with our investigation," Hen told her. "Shouldn't take too long. I believe we know who's responsible for this, and I'm confident we'll have a confession within hours."

"Take your time," Willie said. "No telling how long it would have taken me to miss some of that stuff. I can get along without it. It's that much less to dust."

Hen was uncharacteristically quiet as we drove back to the station house.

"Do I get a commendation or something for solving—for helping you solve—the mystery of the Bag Swag?" I asked, to break the silence.

Hen made a sound somewhere between a grunt and a snort.

"Aren't you glad to know it doesn't have anything to do with

Julian Stubbs's death?"

"As far as we know, it doesn't," he said, "but the way things have been going lately, the Lord knows it might."

"You're not mad at them, are you?"

Grunt. Snort.

"Even if they did it, Hen, it's not really a police matter, is it?"

He didn't answer.

"It was just a couple of bored kids entertaining themselves at a family party," I explained.

He still didn't answer.

"They didn't damage anything or steal anything. It's not a reflection on you as a father or your position as Chief of Police."

That was all I had, so I was relieved when I finally got a response from him.

"You get Shawna and Tommy down here," he instructed me. "I'll get hold of Teri and that daughter of hers."

"Her daughter?"

"Obviously these criminal tendencies don't come from our family, Trudy." I took that comment as a sign that he was returning to normal. Surely he was joking.

"I'll defend the Roundtrees, Hen, but I can't say I know all that much about the Huckabees."

"I'll vouch for the Huckabees," he said.

"Okay. We leave out the Huckabees. That leaves . . . yeah. Maybe you're onto something. We do have Stubbs blood in both suspects."

He grunted at me, and I pretended that meant he didn't know what I was talking about.

"That's right, isn't it? Shawna's mother was a Stubbs before she married Tom Purvis."

He grunted again.

"So Tommy's got bad blood. But maybe Delcie isn't what they call a direct descendant."

193

"How can somebody be an indirect descendant, Trudy? Either you're a descendant or you're not."

"People use that phrase all the time. I was hoping it meant something, so you'd have an out, but there it is. She has Stubbs blood, all right." I heaved a huge theatrical blockbuster of a sigh. "So how are we going to handle the interrogation?"

"We've already fingerprinted the daylights out of Tommy and gotten his statement. We'll do that with Delcie. We'll see where it goes from there. I want those little boogers to learn the difference between the truth and a lie, and especially not to lie to their parents or the police."

"Good idea, Chief, as long as you keep in mind that they have not committed a crime."

"It's a crime to lie to the police," he said.

"Be fair. Maybe Tommy did, but you didn't ask Delcie about it, did you? Directly? And you're annoyed with yourself, aren't you? And you know it's not a big deal, but you're trying to save face, aren't you?"

"Officer Roundtree, fetch your friend and her son."

"Yes, your majesty."

Rather than call, I opted to appeal directly to Tommy and head off what I foresaw as Shawna's knee-jerk resistance to coming back to the station house. I drove to the Purvis house and offered to bring Shawna and Tommy back to the station house with siren wailing so they could help us clear up a couple of points in our investigation. My plan worked. Shawna might have been able to resist me, but she couldn't resist her son who headed for my cruiser as soon as the invitation was out of my mouth.

I don't know what Hen said to Teri, but whatever it was obviously put her in motion and in high gear. By the time I got to the station house with Shawna and Tommy, Delcie and Teri were wiping the ink off their fingertips.

Henry Huckabee isn't the man to take an accusation of favoritism lightly, not when it comes to his professional reputation.

CHAPTER 22

Delcie wiggled her fingers at Tommy in greeting. He's a couple of years older than she—making him about nine—so it came as no surprise that she'd be delighted with the attention she was getting from him.

"Hey, awesome," Tommy said. "Now we both have police records."

"No, you do not have a police record," Shawna said.

"That's right, Tommy," I said. He looked so disappointed I tried to soften the blow. "To be completely accurate, Tommy, you and Delcie, your mother and her mother, are assisting the police in their inquiries. Inquiries are the questions we ask to help us find out the truth. You do not have a police record unless you've been legally pronounced a criminal. It's a record of your contact with the police. Trust me, you do not have a police record, and you do not want one."

Tommy didn't look convinced.

"Helping the police again?" Shawna said. "We already did this."

"The investigation has taken another turn," I said.

"Where's Hen?" Shawna asked.

I'd been wondering that myself.

"He had to take a call," Teri explained. "Said he'd be right with us."

"The police do that all the time," Tommy said to Delcie. "It's supposed to make us nervous so we'll confess to anything they want us to."

"Stop it, Tommy!" his mother said.

"He's just kidding," Delcie explained. "Aren't you, Tommy?" Tommy shrugged.

"How long is this going to take?" Shawna asked.

"Depends on how long it takes us to break them down," I answered.

"See there!" Tommy said.

We were at the back of the City Council chambers/police conference room, talking in more or less muted tones while we waited for Hen.

Teri's only a few years older than Shawna and I, but compared to Shawna, she looked matronly, positively boring.

Teri wears autumn colors that go nicely with the reddish tones in her hair and her pale complexion. Her wardrobe runs to comfortable, practical clothes that accommodate the range of activities called for from an elementary school teacher. She'd come to the station house wearing neat brown slacks and an orangey T-shirt.

Shawna was in a very short black skirt, patterned black hose, and a tight red sweater. I don't know what profession she was trying to suggest.

Naturally, I did not compare myself to either of them, since I was in uniform and, therefore, sexless, not in the game at all, although I happen to know that the dark blue uniform goes pretty well with my iceberg blue eyes and brown hair.

To complete the catalog, Tommy and Delcie were both wearing: jeans, blue; T-shirts, multicolored; sneakers, formerly white. Tommy and Delcie were making themselves at home in the august chamber. From where I stood, it looked as if they were having a swimming race. Each was on one of the recycled church pews that serves as seating for the members of the public who attend City Council meetings, on their stomachs, inching and scootching along, giggling the whole time.

Hen joined us, and Shawna attacked. "I do not appreciate it that you bring us down here again and then make us wait!"

"Believe it or not," Hen said, "there's more going on in town than your one-family crime spree."

He turned to me. "That call was about a gaggle of teenaged girls who decided to extend their Christmas-shopping dollars by making themselves the beneficiaries of unattended Christmas packages in cars outside the Food Lion. 'Tis the season."

"You want me to go see about it?" I asked.

"Nah. Got it under control."

We'd obviously been ignoring Shawna for too long.

"You so desperate you have to hassle little kids?" she asked Hen. "We already gave you our statements and told you everything we know, which isn't anything. Isn't it police harassment to make us come down here again?"

"I think of it as the police asking good citizens for information in the interests of justice and instilling a healthy respect for the truth," Hen responded, a smile on his face.

Sometimes I think the more unreasonable other people are, the easier it is for him to be unflappable, secure in his own superiority.

"You've already tried and convicted them," Shawna said. "I'm going to call a lawyer."

Even Shawna had to know that was nonsense, that whatever trouble Tommy was in, Delcie was in it with him, but in view of the escalating hostilities, I offered the calm voice of reason as a way for her to save face.

"Oh, for crying out loud, Shawna, back off. Don't be ridiculous. Do you want to raise a punky hoodlum with an honest-to-god police record or somebody who has respect for law and order?"

"No need to get worked up," Hen said, turning on *me* for

Pete's sake! Back to Shawna: "Now, I'm at fault, as Officer Roundtree has kindly called to my attention, and I admit it, because I overlooked a couple of people who were at the party at the Stubbs house on Saturday night when I was taking fingerprints and statements. I take responsibility for that, and I'm about to make up for it."

"By hauling me and my son in for questioning again?"

"Come on, Shawna, you know Tommy loved every minute of that," I said.

"There are some inconsistencies I think Tommy can clear up for us," Hen said.

As usual, Teri had been quiet, but now she spoke up, without apparent rancor. "He's hauled me and my daughter in, too, Shawna. Why don't we go ahead and get this over with, and when Hen's through with us, I'll take the kids over to Vidalia for some lunch and a movie?"

Shawna acknowledged and accepted this friendly offer with a nod, then went to the front of the room and sat in a pew. The children stopped swimming. Hen assumed the throne-like chair and addressed the assembly.

"Now Tommy Kersey and Delcie Huckabee, I want you two little heathens to understand why we're here. I want to make sure the two of you know what it's like to be in trouble with the police."

"Why're we in trouble?" Tommy asked.

"Because you lied to the police—yes, you did!—and made us waste time we should have been spending on something else. Now, we're going to separate you and interrogate you—"

"What's that mean? Interro—" Delcie is unquenchable.

"It means we're going to question you one at a time, so we can compare your stories and find out the truth."

Delcie nodded, solemn. Tommy smiled.

"Any questions?"

"No, sir, Daddy," Delcie said.

"I'm acting as the Chief of Police of the town of Ogeechee, right now, not your daddy," Hen said.

Delcie made a face.

"Are you going to handcuff us?" Tommy asked. The rascal was enjoying himself, confirming once again the wisdom of separating the suspects so that they can't influence each other by word or attitude.

"We're going to interrogate you separately," Hen continued. "And you'd better be sure you tell the same story."

"Cool," Tommy said.

"We'll have to see about that. We'll talk to you first," Hen told him. "Teri, you and Delcie go wait in my office. Delcie, don't mess with anything."

While he waited for Teri and Delcie to leave, Hen tapped some papers against the tabletop, scowling and frowning in a menacing manner.

When he turned to speak to Tommy, Hen waved what I now recognized as a fingerprint card. "Since you are a minor—that means a child—your mother must be present when the police talk to you, to look out for your interests."

"What's that mean?" Tommy asked.

"It means she'll make sure we don't mistreat you or try to trick you or make you say something that isn't true, or anything like that. Right now the only trouble you're in is for lying when you came down here before and gave your statement."

"I didn't—" Tommy began.

"Wait just a—" Shawna started, but Hen flapped the fingerprint card and frowned at her, and she subsided.

"Yes, son, you did. This fingerprint card tells me you did handle some of the things in that bag that we asked you about."

"I forgot," Tommy said, not even bothering to try to make it sound convincing.

"No, you did not forget. You lied on purpose because you didn't think you'd get caught. That's a real bad habit to get into."

Hen looked toward Shawna, who tightened her lips in an unbecoming scowl. "So what's the big deal? It's not like they stole the stuff."

"The big deal, Shawna," I said, trying to keep Hen from climbing over the table and throttling her, "is lying. To anybody. Heck, a boy who would lie to the police might lie to his mother."

"Maybe he didn't understand what you were asking him," she said. "He's only a little kid."

"See, now," Hen said. "That's why we like to have a parent present. If you'll check with Frank, I'm sure he will confirm that this is what Tommy told us." Hen consulted the statement Tommy had given us earlier. He read, without inflection, "Officer Roundtree: Do you know anything about the things in this bag? Tommy Purvis: Yeah, I saw that stuff around. Officer Roundtree: You didn't put it in the bag? Tommy: No. Officer Roundtree: Not even as a joke? Tommy: Uh uh."

"Okay," Shawna said. "So?"

"So, we've got his fingerprints on some of those things," Hen said. He let that sink in for a moment.

"All right," Hen said, settling back in his chair in a pose that invited friendly conversation. "Now that we understand each other, I want you to tell me what you know about this bag and the things in it."

"It was Delcie's idea," Tommy said.

"What was Delcie's idea, son?" Hen asked.

With a glance at his mother, Tommy continued, "We saw that puzzle, and I wanted to hide some of the pieces, a joke, you know, so people wouldn't be able to find them, but Delcie said it would be more fun to try to find things like on the picture. So we did. We took turns finding things."

201

"So there," Shawna said. "Big deal. Is that all you want to know?"

Hen ignored her. He spoke to Tommy. "Is that all you have to tell me?"

Tommy shrugged. "That's all we did. We were just playing. We didn't hurt anything."

"You going to bring out the thumbscrews now?" Shawna asked.

"What's a thumbscrew?" Tommy asked. "Can I have thumb-screws?"

"We don't do thumbscrews," Hen told him. "They hurt. Now, son, having your mother here while I talk to you is a good idea, because then nobody can say I mistreated you. But it's a bad idea in one way, too."

"Why?" Tommy asked.

"Because I might ask you something you don't want your mama to know. You see what I mean?"

Tommy darted a look at Shawna, then nodded. "Uh huh."

"You know we're trying to find out why Mr. Stubbs fell down the stairs," Hen said. "Is there anything else you think you ought to tell me?"

"Did somebody push him?" Tommy asked.

"Why would you ask that?"

Tommy squirmed, and I could almost see discretion warring with pride. Pride won.

"We had to sneak, so people wouldn't catch us taking the things."

"I remember doing that when I was a boy," Hen said with a warning glance at Shawna. "Makes you feel like you're invis-ible."

"Yeah! We were on a secret mission, so nobody could see us, so when Uncle Julian came up with that other man, we hid.

And they started arguing. Maybe that man pushed him down the stairs."

"Uncle Julian didn't fall down the stairs that night, Tommy," Shawna said, earning a sharp glance from Hen.

"Could you hear what the men were arguing about?" Hen asked.

"No, not really."

"Do you know who the other man was?"

"I'm not sure."

"But you knew most of the people who were at the party, didn't you?"

"Most of 'em."

"I think that's enough," Shawna said. "You're not getting anywhere with this."

"You may be right," Hen said. "One more thing. I asked you about this before, but I'm giving you a chance to change your answer if you need to."

"Okay," Tommy said.

Shawna looked disgusted.

Hen showed Tommy the pencil marks on the family tree. "Y'all do this while you were sneaking around? Either one of you?"

Tommy smiled. "No sir. I didn't. Maybe Delcie did."

For some reason, I thought he was telling the truth.

"Okay. Now, just in case I didn't ask that question the right way, I'm asking again: Did you see anybody else writing on it?"

"No."

"Thank you, son. You've been very helpful." Hen wound things up by reminding Tommy how important it is to respect the police and not to lie, and by putting handcuffs on him. I was pleased to see that Tommy didn't like it much.

Hen removed the handcuffs, and he and Tommy parted friends. I noticed Hen didn't thank Shawna for being helpful.

Teri and Delcie were next.

"You just sit there and pretend I'm not your daddy," Hen told Delcie. "No special favors. Just tell me the truth and answer my questions."

"Yes, sir," Delcie said.

"Was it was your idea or Tommy's to collect these things and put them in the bag?"

I could tell she wasn't happy about it, but she said, "Mine, I guess."

"You guess?"

If this kid's not careful, she's going to grow up to be a manipulative flirt, a heartbreaker. Her eyes grew moist, the corners of her mouth drooped. I don't know how Hen stood it, but he waited for her answer.

"I didn't think it would hurt anything. We were just playing."

Hen's stern mouth relaxed a bit at this confession. He was probably proud, as I was, that Delcie hadn't tried to shift whatever blame there was on to Tommy.

"You must have been a couple of really good sneaks to gather up all these things without anybody seeing you," Hen said.

Delcie knew this might not be a compliment. She nodded slowly.

"Tommy says y'all were hiding upstairs and heard Mr. Stubbs arguing with somebody," Hen said. "Do you remember that?"

"It wasn't a big argument," Delcie said. "They weren't yelling."

"But they sounded angry?"

"Well, the other man sounded more angry."

"Did you know the other man?"

"I think it was Mr. Holland."

"Do you know what they were arguing about?"

"It might have been about that thing on the wall where they were standing."

"Where were you hiding?"

"In Tommy's room."

"Where were the men?"

"Right outside the door."

"Could you see them?"

"No. We were afraid to peek."

"Whose idea was it to hide the bag with the things in it?"

"Both of us, I think. We put it out on the porch when we heard somebody coming, and we were going to get it, but then it was time to go home, and we didn't get it."

"Okay. Good. You and Tommy have helped us clear up one of the strange things that's been going on," Hen said. "Now, is there anything else you noticed while you were sneakin' around that the police ought to know about?"

"Do you really want to encourage her to repeat everything she heard at that party, Hen?" Teri asked. "I've been trying to teach her not to be a tattletale."

"I'm sure you and Mama are doing a good job raisin' her," Hen said, "but this is a police investigation, and I'm the ruling authority here, not Miss Manners. Delcie, you can tell the difference between helping a police investigation and just tattling on people, can't you?"

Caught between her parents, Delcie sided with the one with the piercing iceberg blue gaze, who also happened to be the one that wanted her to tattle. "Miz Della was talking to that other guy, that friend of Uncle Kevin's, and they seemed to be sneaky about it."

"Were they arguing?"

"No. They were real quiet, like they didn't want anybody to hear."

"But you're a good sneak. Could you hear them even if they didn't want anybody to hear?"

"Uh huh, but they were just talking about football."

205

"Football?"

"Uh huh, football teams, and stuff. Stuff, like the stuff Tommy and I were getting to put in the bag."

"Any particular stuff?"

"I don't know."

"Where were they when they were talking so quiet?"

"In the dining room."

"Where were you that you could hear them so well?"

"I was under the table."

"You really got around, didn't you?"

"Yes, sir."

"And you didn't hear anything else they said?"

"I didn't hear any more words, but I did hear a kind of a squeaky noise, like a door."

"The front door?"

"No. It was closer than that."

"The china cabinet?"

"Maybe."

Hen directed her attention to the family tree. "Tommy says he didn't do this writing. Did you?"

"No, sir." No bravado, no tell-tale body language. I believed her.

"You know anything about it at all?"

"No, sir."

Having wrung out every scrap of tittle-tattle and grilled both suspects enough to make an impression on them, Hen turned them loose. Teri left with the kids. I waylaid Shawna as she reached her car and tackled her on the question Bradley wouldn't answer about the assault.

"From what I've been able to find out, Kevin was perfectly sane and normal when he went over to your folks' house to pick up something for Gretchen yesterday, but a raving homicidal maniac when he got back to the Stubbs's house and attacked

Bradley Booth."

Shawna nodded thoughtfully.

"I've been asking myself what could have happened," I said.

She went on nodding while she sucked in her stomach and smoothed her sweater.

"But it would have been smarter to ask you, wouldn't it?" I asked.

"Why do you think I'd know?"

"Just a wild guess. Did you see him at your folks' house?"

"Yes."

"Did you talk to him?"

"Yes."

"What did you talk about?"

"Isn't this an invasion of privacy or something?" She reached to open the car door. I moved closer.

"Not if it has something to do with a police investigation. You heard Hen. Tell the truth so we can stop wasting our time if it doesn't have anything to do with Mr. Stubbs's death."

"I don't like your attitude, Trudy." She made as if to push me away.

I didn't budge. "Come on, Shawna. It isn't like you to be so close mouthed. You must really be ashamed of yourself. Do you know what set Kevin off?"

"I can't imagine."

"You want me to guess?"

"Sure. Guess."

"I guess it had something to do with Bradley . . ."

"Wow! I'm impressed! You must be a real credit to the force."

"Bradley and Gretchen," I said.

Suddenly Shawna didn't look quite so pleased with herself. She jerked the car door open.

"Did you give Kevin that load of bull you gave me, about Gretchen being promiscuous?" I asked. "With Bradley?"

"Well, I'm pretty sure I didn't say promiscuous, but I might have suggested that Gretchen was taking advantage of him. He's my brother, my little brother, why wouldn't I try to look out for him?"

"And you think telling him his brand-new wife has been carrying on with somebody else is looking out for him?"

"I thought he ought to know."

"And you know this? Actually know it? It's not just one of your evil troublemaking fantasies?"

"Honestly, Trudy, the way you dramatize things! Anybody can see Brad is more Gretchen's friend than Kev's."

"What's wrong with that?"

"Maybe nothing, but maybe something, if he got her pregnant and wouldn't marry her and she had to go looking for somebody stupid enough to come to the rescue."

"So you're saying your brother is stupid?"

"Where Gretchen is concerned, yes."

"This is your idea of trying to welcome her into the family and get along?"

"It's a question of loyalty, Trudy."

"That's another load of bull."

"It is not a load of bull."

"Were you trying to incite Kevin to murder?"

"Don't you blame me for this."

"Just asking."

"Here's something you didn't ask. He's going to ask for a paternity test on that baby."

"What?"

"You know, Trudy, so they can know for sure who the father is."

"Yes, I know what a paternity test is. Was that your idea? Your troublemaking has reached new heights. Or depths."

"I might have suggested he could do that if he's worried

208

about it. He has a right to know if it's not his, doesn't he?"

I couldn't argue with that.

"Have you heard how Bradley's doing?" Shawna asked.

"You're belatedly worrying about inciting your brother to murder?"

"No. I mean, I just thought I'd ask."

"I called the hospital. They're not happy with his tests overnight. They're keeping him another day. It isn't like there's any place for him to go to if he leaves the hospital."

"Well," Shawna said, the sudden change in mood revealing the depth of her concern for Bradley, "I could stay here and talk to you all day, Trudy, but I've got to go now. I've got a date with Phil Pittman." She slid into the car.

"A date? With Phil? You sent Frank back home so he wouldn't get in the way of your hitting on Phil?"

She looked up at me and batted her over-mascaraed eyelashes. "It was Phil's idea, Trudy."

I stared down at her.

"Well, he wanted me to come back and go over his story about Uncle Julian with him," she said.

That explained her get-up.

"Tell him hello for me," I said, stepping back.

"I'll do that little thing." She slammed the car door shut and gave me a parting smile that I didn't like a bit.

We'd been pretty sure of the culprits in the bag swag before we hauled this crowd in, so maybe all we'd accomplished— besides giving Shawna another opportunity to grate on me— was identifying some of the previously unidentified fingerprints. It was too much to hope that the incident would scare Tommy away from a life of crime.

CHAPTER 23

"What are you muttering about?" Hen asked as I stomped past his office door.

"Nothing," I answered through clenched teeth.

"Shawna getting to you?"

"What makes you ask?"

"It was the smoke coming out of your ears that made me wonder."

Oh. Change the subject. "Hen, do you believe what Delcie and Tommy said about Roddy and Julian getting in an argument on Saturday night?"

"They both mentioned it, so I believe they heard something that sounded to them like an argument, but I wouldn't want to try to send anybody to jail on the strength of it. Anyway, as Shawna pointed out, that was Saturday night. That's a long way from saying Roddy pushed Julian down the stairs on Monday morning."

"What if Roddy and Julian were having an argument about something, something so serious it brought Roddy back on Monday to finish it?"

"Remember, Trudy, Julian Stubbs hasn't lived here in years. I don't know what they had to talk about, much less get in a fight about."

"Uh huh. It would have to be something pretty important. Delcie said she thought they were arguing about the . . . what did she call it . . . that thing on the wall outside Tommy's room, where they were hiding. 'That thing' has to be the family tree. And we know somebody had been marking on it."

Hen laughed. "You suggesting Roddy criticized the calligraphy, and Julian took it wrong?"

"Well, no, but something. Roddy's daughter just married into the Stubbs family. Maybe Roddy was adding her to the family tree, marking it up, and Julian was trying to keep him from ruining it."

"It's not much of an incitement to murder," Hen said.

"I'm just brainstorming, Hen. Don't make me do all the work. You're the big cheese."

"Okay, little cheese. Let's take another look at it and see if we missed something. Lordy, this whole mess is getting on my nerves."

"That's just because you think your daughter has bad blood, and it's getting you down. I'm sure environment will turn out to be more important than heredity, and Teri and Aunt Lulu are doing a good job with her." Then I had another thought. "Or maybe you could re-direct those criminal tendencies. Put those kids on the payroll. Nobody'd ever suspect."

"I'll give it serious consideration. For now, you go over what we've got," the big cheese said to me. "I'm going to go have another talk with Bradley Booth."

He, the boss, went off into the clear December sunshine and fresh air while I, the underling, buckled down to the tedious task of going over all of what passed for evidence in the Stubbs case—the statements, the fingerprints, and our own observations of the people involved.

The best I could hope for would be that, like with a jigsaw puzzle, if I just kept moving things around and trying to put pieces together, even if I didn't see ahead of time where a particular piece would fit, it would all come together at the end.

I stalled—I mean I started—by making a couple of charts.

On the first chart, I listed the items we'd determined were significant to the investigation down the side and the names of all the suspects—all the people associated with the Stubbs family party—across the top, with one column left over for unidentified. Then I filled it in. Boring.

I made a similar chart for alibis for the time of Julian Stubbs's death. This was marginally less boring because I included everybody I could think of so I could give myself the pleasure of crossing off a lot of names, which would feel like progress. I started with the easy ones. I crossed off Teri Huckabee, Delcie Huckabee, and Henry Huckabee because I'm prejudiced. Willie Lanier was with me when he fell. Cross her off. Everybody else, however unlikely, would stay on the list until I could find a way to check. Here's what they claimed:

Della Stubbs was supposed to have been in Savannah.

Bradley said he'd been out running.

Frank and Shawna Kersey had been moving from the Stubbs house to the Purvis house. Much as I'd like to find Shawna guilty of something illegal—as distinct from just awful, like a wagging tongue, trashy taste in clothes, and unprincipled flirtation—I really hoped I'd be able to cross off Frank, Shawna, Tommy, and Shawna's parents, Nancy and Tom Purvis, all at once, with one phone call.

Dennis Rankin was supposed to have been fishing with Tom Purvis.

Kevin and Gretchen Purvis had been off on their honeymoon.

Jean and Roddy Holland were both at home when I went to talk to them later that morning. Had they been there all morning?

Inez Rankin and Vera Stubbs were undeniably upstairs when Julian tumbled. No way I could cross them off.

Annie Stubbs, Gordon Stubbs. Not likely, but not crossed off.

I picked up the telephone and started chipping away at the alibis.

Della Stubbs wasn't pleasant about it, but she gave me the name of the banker she'd met with in Savannah, and he confirmed the meeting. Heavy line through her name.

When I called, Annie Stubbs said she and Gordon had been together all morning. I doubted I'd shake either of them from that story, true or not, if that's what they'd decided on. I wasn't desperate enough for a theory of the crime to believe Annie Stubbs would have pushed Julian down the stairs to help out her old friend, Vera. But, as long as I was talking to her, keeping in mind that Vera and Inez were unquestionably upstairs with Julian when he fell, and remembering that conversation between Annie and Vera on the porch of the Stubbs house—

"Is Miz Vera there right now?" I asked.

"No. She and Gordon went over to pick out a casket. I figured I'd stay out of that, let Julian's widow and his brother decide how much money to spend. Tell the truth, much as I love Vera, having anybody in your house every minute gets old fast. It's bad enough having Gordon underfoot all the time, and I'm used to him. It's good to have a minute all by myself. You want me to take a message?"

"No, but if you would, you could answer a question for me."

"Sure. Always happy to stay in good with the police."

"I wish everybody had that attitude, Miz Stubbs. You remember that night I talked with you and Miz Vera out on the porch after the party?"

She gave a little laugh. "That was just about the last peaceful minute we've had for a while. I sure do remember it."

"Y'all were talking about her husband and how bad he was getting with his memory."

"I remember. Yes."

"You were around him, around them both, quite a bit, and I

want to know if you think his disease was making him ornery."

"Ornery? Julian? Not that I ever saw." She gave a short laugh. "Not that he couldn't be a tease, ornery in that way. But that's not what you mean, is it?"

"No, ma'am, I meant ornery as in mean and hard to get along with, hard to control."

"I don't know about hard to control. Don't know that anybody ever tried to control him."

"Not even Miz Vera?"

"What are you getting at, Trudy?"

There was a distinct chill in her voice, now that she'd sensed what I was after. I rephrased my question, as gently as I knew how. "He had a lot of bruises on him, marks that are hard to explain. Now, if his wife had to get a grip on him to help him, or to help restrain him, it would explain some of those marks."

"He bruised easy. Talked about it himself. Laughed about it." Cautiously now, much more guarded than she'd been, even if she did want to stay in good with the police.

I kept on. "So if anybody suggested that his wife was mistreating him, you'd have a hard time believing it?"

"Who suggested that? Just tell me! Who'd say such a thing?"

"And if somebody suggested she might have gotten so frustrated with him that she pushed him down the stairs?"

"Vera! Not ever in this world. She's a saint."

I should have known better than to start that conversation over the telephone, where I couldn't see tell-tale signs of evasion revealed through body language. Still, they say if you're deprived of one sense, the others grow more acute. I had the distinct impression that Annie Stubbs wasn't as sure about that as she wanted me to believe. Or she might have been pure out lying to me, regardless of any suspicions she might have had. She is Shawna's grandmother, after all. Bad blood.

That was the only even mildly interesting conversation I had.

Nancy Purvis told me Frank, Shawna, and Tommy got to her house about ten o'clock and stayed there. She claimed they'd all been in sight of each other the rest of the morning and there was no way any of them could have gone off—to run an errand, for example—without being missed. More dark heavy lines.

I was about to call Jean Holland when Hen returned.

"How's Bradley this morning?" I asked.

"His same old ingratiating self," Hen said. "Had a heck of a time finding him, though. He'd left the hospital and gone back to the Stubbs house."

"Have Willie and Della adopted him?"

"Maybe. Ol' Bradley's tucked back into what I'm coming to think of as his room over there, said his folks aren't back from their trip yet, so he'll stay there another day or two."

"Did he tell you why Kevin went after him?"

"No change in his story. Still says it was a misunderstanding."

"Did you try out Shawna's theory on him—the theory that Kevin thinks he's the father of Gretchen's unborn child?"

"Yes, ma'am, I did. He stuck with misunderstanding. Said he can't help what Kevin thinks."

"Poor misunderstood boy. Good thing Willie and Della are so taken with him."

"Della, maybe. I didn't get the idea Willie's crazy about him."

"Hen, judging from what Delcie said about them whispering together, does it sound to you like Della and Bradley are up to something?"

"You're not going to claim Della's his long-lost mother, are you? I've had about all I can stomach of mixed- up family trees."

"No, not that, but there's something going on between them."

"You aren't suggesting that Della and Bradley connived at the murder of Julian Stubbs for some reason?"

"All we're missing is motive and opportunity," I said.

215

"We only have Bradley's word for it that he was out of the house when Julian fell. Maybe Julian caught him and Della stealing antiques." Hen's shaking head revealed his distaste for this theory.

"Could Della steal from the house? It mean, it's her house."

"Depends on what it is. She could be stealing from Willie."

"Bradley might have pushed Julian, but Della couldn't have. She was in Savannah," I reminded him.

"Have you corroborated that?"

"Yes. I started checking on alibis after you left."

Before he could quiz me any further, the dispatcher interrupted.

"Chief, there's something going down at Wilson's. Jerome's on his way."

Wilson's is formally known as Wilson's Bait and Beer; informally known as a trouble spot out near the south end of the city limits. Jerome is Officer Jerome Sharpe, a hunk of babe magnet with a voice like a freight train and a size and shape that qualify him as a one-man riot squad.

Hen sighed. "Looks like I'll be heading home by way of Wilson's."

"Want me to come?" I asked.

"Nah. You go on home. I'll go take a look and call you if we need more muscle."

I wasn't about to argue. It's an undisputed fact, which has nothing to do with equal rights or discrimination, that Jerome Sharpe has a much more dampening effect on hi-jinks at juke joints than I do. And, not that I let the memory of it slow me down on the job, but it's also a fact that I once got a broken wrist from slipping on a beer bottle after a juke-joint fracas.

I was much happier going straight home from the station house than taking Hen's detour.

CHAPTER 24

When I got home, I was greeted, as usual, by cats. Dumplin and Biscuit have different ways of showing their high regard for me. Dumplin's way is to watch with apparent boredom as I go about my business, unless my business brings me near her bowl, and then to approach with appropriately measured steps and emit one measured meow. Biscuit's way is to get underfoot as soon as possible whenever I come inside.

I'm as predictable as they are. I automatically stoop to pick up Biscuit. On this evening, tired as I was—and tired especially of the Stubbs case—I especially liked holding something soft and warm, something purring. Something predictable. As my fingers stroked and scratched the cat, they came upon a knot in the fur. Had that rascal gotten into the pizza cheese, after all? No, just one of the inevitable tangles a cat like Biscuit, long-haired and lazy, will have.

I found the stiff grooming brush in the basket next to the TV and set to work on the knot, brushing gently at first, then more and more firmly, digging deeper and deeper into the knot until it was untangled. Surprisingly, Biscuit enjoys this attention. Unless I'm careless enough to dig too deeply into the knot before it's ready to untangle, that cat will lie there like a sports car with its motor idling while I work. Alas, the accumulating tensions of the week must have gotten the better of me. I wasn't careful enough. With a yowl, Biscuit leapt away, leaving only a brush full of hair and a look of reproach.

As I sat there, half asleep, pulling cat hair from the wiry brush, trying to decide whether I was hungrier than sleepy, or the other way around, I pricked my finger on the brush. Watching the drop of blood form, I realized that if I'd been even more careless, I'd have made a pattern much like the odd punctures on Julian Stubbs's chest.

I treated the puncture with an antibiotic, the ointment Hen calls Cat Tail Medicine because if you use it, he says, "A skint tail will heal up and hair over in two days." I was less interested in infection than I was jazzed because I'd put together another piece of our murder puzzle.

I decided to talk to my boss about letting me do my work at home. Obviously, that's where I'm having all my good insights.

I slept well.

CHAPTER 25

I was disappointed to find that Hen wasn't at the station house when I arrived next morning, since I was rested, fed, and ready to share.

"He'll be in later," Dawn told me. "That mess at Wilson's kept them out pretty late."

"What happened?"

"Somebody got cut, but not too bad." She grinned. "Everybody calmed down pretty much when Jerome got there. The way he tells it, there wasn't but two men with knives and not more than a dozen or so cheerleaders, so he had it all under control, and there wasn't anything left for the Chief to do by the time he got there except interview some of the witnesses."

"I'll bet that's at least half true," I said. Like most women, like me, Dawn is half in love and fully in awe where Jerome Sharpe is concerned, in a purely unemotional way, you understand. He's wisely close mouthed about his private life, but we're pretty sure he has a girlfriend in Glennville. From various hints Jerome has let slip—probably intentionally—Dawn and I think she's really a composite of several women. Either that, or she must be some woman.

My delight over the insight I'd had the night before had moderated somewhat this morning. I was happy about it, but insight is merely insight; evidence is something else entirely. In search of evidence, while I waited for Hen I spread out all the objects we'd accumulated in the Stubbs case and started the tedious job of comparing statements with prints on objects. I could devise no chart to help me with it, and tedious is an understatement. Too bad this slice of real life wasn't more like a TV crime show, where camera shots would fade in and out on different bits of my tedium, showing time passing without anybody actually having to endure it.

We'd taken everybody's fingerprints so we'd know who'd handled things, and we'd more or less accounted for the prints.

What we hadn't done in all the uproar was analyze the position of the prints. To keep myself from falling into a hypnotic trance, I began trying to position my hands on the objects in such a way as to match the fingerprints. Most of that was just as paralyzingly tedious as going over the statements. But when I got to the family tree, I discovered something that struck me as useful.

To keep from handling the family tree excessively, I took the time to make a dummy of it, and drew in the fingerprints we'd lifted, selecting a different color for each person's prints. It made an entertaining change from the charts. Then, remembering that I'd not quite finished checking on the alibis before I'd stopped the day before, I turned back to that chore. I had the phone in hand to call Jean Holland when Hen barreled in.

"Remind me not to wish for a nice, clear-cut crime in a public place again," he said, creating such a stir with his entrance that both Dawn and I knew he was prepared to regale us with tales of derring-do. He does love mixing it up with the bad guys. It's much more fun than the administrative work that is such a big part of his job.

"Made you lose some of your beauty sleep?" I inquired, putting the telephone down.

"Jerome made it sound pretty wild," Dawn said. She's a better audience than I am, unequivocally delighted to listen, uncritical. I enjoy Hen's performances, too; I just don't like for him to know how much.

"Lord, yes," Hen said. "We got the stab-ees and the stab-ors separated into different piles and hauled off and started trying to find out what had happened, only to discover that, due to some mysterious virus, the entire population of the place had gone deaf, dumb, and blind. The combination of moonshine and pharmaceuticals Josh Wilson dishes up mighta had something to do with that, but some of it was an entirely unreasonable instinct among that particular population not to cooperate with the police, just on general principles. The best statement I got—the *best* statement—was something like 'Uh huh, Chief, T-Bone and Zook got into it.' Well, heck, I already knew that."

"Is his name really Zook?" Dawn asked.

"Short for Zucchini," Hen said. "He's got squashy brains."

Dawn laughed.

I suppressed a groan. "Did all that lack of cooperation hurt your feelings?" I asked, with a glance at Dawn.

He gave us a self-satisfied grin. "I don't take it personally. And it don't hurt my feelings at all that before we were finished with that pack of low-functioning riffraff, we'd hauled in not only the two main characters but confiscated about a bushel of stuff Wilson did not have written down up there on the menu board, caught up with a couple of gentlemen who'd been eluding us for reasons unrelated to the main event, and scared the religion plumb out of a couple of poachers we accidentally ran across on the way back."

He yawned.

"Y'all did a good night's work," Dawn said.

"Yes, ma'am, that's the kind of night makes a man glad he decided to go into law enforcement. Except for the paperwork."

"Let me get you some coffee," I offered.

"You up to something?" he asked, stifling another yawn.

"You have a nasty, suspicious mind."

"Can't deny it. Occupational hazard, but it helps me in my work. So, what are you up to?"

"I want to show you a couple of things, and I want you to be awake enough to appreciate them, so I don't have to spell everything out for you. I missed all the fun at Wilson's, but I wasn't wasting my time, either."

"Glad to know the department can run without my constant supervision," he said, turning toward his office. "Bring my coffee in here."

"Jerome called. Said he'd be in later," Dawn said.

Hen nodded, but kept ambling toward his office. "The paperwork'll wait for him."

I hurried to get to his office with the coffee and my revelations before he fell asleep.

"Here. Hold this." I put his coffee in front of him and held up my colorful dummy family tree.

He reached for it. "What is it?"

I ignored the question, knowing when he got his eyes open he'd be able to see that I had clearly written STUBBS FAMILY TREE across the front.

"It's a facsimile," I volunteered. "Notice how you're holding it."

His thumbs were near the bottom corners, his fingers splayed on the back. His fingerprints, if we had taken them, would have been roughly where various other sets of prints were found. Willie's. Julian's.

Hen looked up at me with a slight frown.

"That's how you'd hold it if you were looking at it. Right?" I asked.

He gave me a withering look. "Yep. I'm holding it this way, and I'm looking at it."

"Now, say somebody was passing it around, showing it to

222

everybody. Where would you expect prints?"

He handed it back to me. I took it, holding it upside down, my thumbs near the top, my fingers on the back. I handed it back to him; he took it casually, sideways and put it down so he could pick up his coffee.

"And?" he asked.

"Most of the prints are just where you'd expect—thumbs on front, fingers on back. Between y'all passing it around at the party and different people going past it in the hall and stopping to straighten it out, we can account for most of the prints. Even most of the smudges can be explained that way—that or Willie's cleaning."

"You have my attention, and I'll keep listening if you'll go get me some more coffee."

When I got back, he was matching his hands to one of the patterns that could not easily be explained. There were prints from a left-hand palm and fingers near the center of the family tree, a smudgy right-hand palm print a few inches below the scratchy word "Gretchen."

Hen looked up. "These prints would belong to whoever wrote in Gretchen's name."

"Yes, sir. That's what I think. Want to guess who?"

"Julian."

"Too easy."

"Yep." He turned my facsimile over. "What we have left here, what's got you so revved up this morning, would be these thumbprints on the back."

"Yes. Whoever was holding it that way wasn't looking at it."

"What was that person doing?" He put down the facsimile and leaned back in his chair.

"That person was either making off with it or using it as a club. Maybe both."

"Interesting theory, but does it fit our facts?"

"It is not inconsistent with our facts," I said. "I've reviewed the autopsy notes. It won't surprise you to learn it's inconclusive. Julian Stubbs unquestionably fell on the frame; he hit his head on something sharp that was not the frame; and he has multiple fine punctures. Oh! That's the other thing!"

How could I have forgotten? I presented my cat brush.

"Uh huh," he said.

"I'm not saying somebody hit him with a cat brush."

"I'm glad to hear that."

"Those multiple fine punctures can't have been made by a hairbrush, not Vera Stubb's hairbrush, anyway. Her brush—the one Willie and I found when we were packing up for Vera after Julian fell—has nice soft bristles. But when I went to talk to the Hollands on the day Mr. Stubbs died, Roddy was cleaning his barbecue grill with—"

"Let me take a wild guess. A wire brush."

"Yes!"

"You're suggesting Roddy Holland sneaked into the Stubbs House with a wire brush looking for somebody to assault?"

"No. Not exactly. Doesn't sound very likely, does it?"

"Maybe it would go down better with another cup of coffee." He held out his cup.

When I returned this time, he was back to the facsimile family tree, holding it in that awkward, upside down position. "These prints are Roddy Holland's?"

"They are."

He sipped thoughtfully at his coffee and grimaced. He was now awake enough to notice how bad it was. "But remember, there are other suspects here."

"I do remember. Our pint-sized informants said Roddy and Julian were quarrelling, but it sounds like Della and Bradley were up to something, too. Maybe it wasn't Roddy at all. Maybe it was Bradley. He's just got to be guilty of something! Maybe

Julian was just standing there holding the family tree and Bradley came up and pushed him. His alibi is about as substantial as . . . as one of Aunt Lulu's biscuits."

Hen looked amused. "Crumbly?"

"Uh huh. Crumbly. Won't support much weight. You know what I mean."

"I'm afraid I do." He sighed. "Thanks to you, it looks like we've got more on Roddy than anybody else, but not enough. The position of the fingerprints could be explained away, and you yourself have thought of several implements that might have inflicted those prickle wounds."

"I guess I'll get back to slogging through the alibis, then," I said with a sigh. "I was working on everybody's whereabouts, just about to call Jean Holland."

"Don't do that. Don't call. Give me a few minutes to make a phone call, and then we'll go over there and talk to the pair of Hollands."

Impatient to see how Roddy Holland responded to my evidence, I grumpily went off to tend to other business and was pleased to see Jerome arrive. Listening to him supply details about the bust at Wilson's would help pass the time.

Snazzy in his sharply pressed uniform, earring stud gleaming, curly hair neatly trimmed, Jerome exuded confidence, as well he might. Jerome had barely gotten started on the tale when Hen joined us, ready to put in his two cents' worth. The bust at Wilson's was already assuming mythic proportions, sure to become one of Hen's stock policin' stories.

"I went by to talk to Miz Virgie," Jerome said.

"Who's that?" Hen asked. "I don't remember that name from last night."

"Miss Virgie Hall. She wasn't there. Wasn't anywhere near the place, wouldn't be caught dead in a devil's hangout like that. She's T-Bone Jackson's sister's aunt's cousin's grandmother, if I have it right. Everybody in the family's scared to death of her, and she's not scared of anybody but the Holy Ghost, so she didn't have any reason not to tell me what she knows. Which isn't much," he added, raising a cautionary hand the size of a tennis racquet. "But it helps some. She said she thought T-Bone and Zook—who'd rather be called Zook than the name his mama gave him, which was Sharon, which sounded all right to her because Jesus was the Rose of Sharon, and, anyway, she was on drugs when they asked her what name to put down—T-Bone and Zook, according to Miz Virgie, had been at each other over how to divide up some money one of 'em got paid for a job where he did all the work using the other one's equipment. She wouldn't tell me which one was which, but she hoped they'd both learned their lesson."

"Blood's thicker than water," I said.

"And some people's brains are thicker than blood," Hen answered, so wound up in the story he didn't seem to realize that didn't make any sense.

"Good work, Officer Sharpe," Hen said. "Officer Roundtree and I are just about to go interview the prime suspects in the Stubbs killing."

"Want me to go along?" Jerome offered.

"I think we can handle this one. Your fun's over for a while. You'd better write this all up while it's fresh."

"I'll go get you some coffee," Dawn said. If she was trying to console Jerome for missing our action, she should have offered him something else.

CHAPTER 26

Hen and I made a quick stop on the way and were soon ringing the front doorbell at the Holland house.

"What now?" Roddy Holland asked when he saw us standing on his porch. "I'm guessing y'all didn't come by to sing Christmas carols."

"Just a few things we think y'all can help us clear up," Hen said. "Is Jean here?"

"She's in the kitchen. I'll bet I could talk her into giving you some hot chocolate if you'll sing 'The Little Drummer Boy.' "

"Maybe later," Hen said. "Can we come in?"

"Be my guest. I'll go get Jean."

The Hollands' Christmas decor was very stylized, neither the old-fashioned Victorian version that reigned at the Stubbs house nor the haphazard accumulation of nostalgia-laden things I use. The silver aluminum tree with revolving color wheel was solidly retro. Were the Hollands stuck in the 1950s?

"Do you know when Mr. Stubbs's funeral's going to be?" Jean asked, after she'd invited us to take seats and laughed off Roddy's suggestion that we'd sing if she'd give us a treat. "I've been waiting to hear."

"There was a delay because of the autopsy," Hen told her. "Then I think they wanted to wait till the paper came out so people could see the announcement. Probably this week sometime." He gave her his iceberg stare. "I got the feeling you didn't care much for him."

She darted a glance at her husband. "That's right, I didn't, personally, but I'd go and pay my respects, for the family."

"You mind telling us what you had against him?"

"It's personal, and a long time ago."

"About your sister?" Hen probed.

"That's right."

"Go ahead, Jean. It's not like it's a big deal," Roddy said.

Hen settled himself back in the easy chair to listen.

Jean looked embarrassed, but seemed to be encouraged by Roddy's calm. "I didn't like his friendship with my sister, but that's old news."

"That's all? I got the idea there was more to it than that."

"I really didn't like it." She tried a smile.

Still friendly, still relaxed, Hen asked, "You dislike it enough to push him down the stairs at the Stubbs house?"

Jean looked stunned, but it was Roddy who asked, "Have you lost your ever-lovin', cotton-pickin' mind? What in the world would make you ask a wild-eyed question like that?"

"Here's what we've got, Roddy," Hen said. "Jean got very upset at the news that Gretchen had married into the Stubbs family, enough to cause a scene at the family reunion. I know. I was there. That indicates strong feelings, and it would take strong feelings to make somebody push an old man down a flight of stairs."

"That's crazy," Jean said. "I wouldn't."

"If that's what you call evidence, I'm not impressed," Roddy said.

"Oh, we have evidence," Hen said. "Y'all remember coming down for fingerprints and statements? We have her fingerprints on the frame of that family tree he was holding when he tumbled."

"Hers and everybody else's, I'll bet. Everybody in the house handled that thing!"

Hen turned to Jean. "You want to tell us about it?"

She looked at her husband, panic in her eyes. "Tell you about what? I don't know what you're talking about."

"Where were you on Monday morning?"

"Right here making Christmas cookies. Trudy, you know that. I was here when you came by."

I wasn't enjoying this interview much more than the Hollands were, but Hen and I had agreed that this approach was the one to take. "That was later, Miz Holland, after he fell," I reminded her.

"Were you here all morning?" Hen asked.

"Yes. I told you. I was doing my Christmas baking."

"Read it in her statement," Roddy said.

Hen ignored the interruption. "Can you prove it?"

"How would I prove it? We ate the cookies. I took the cake to Gordon and Annie's for the family. But, anyway, Trudy, I was making that when you came. I'm not making any sense." She still looked stunned. "No, I can't prove I was here all morning."

"Can you prove she wasn't?" Roddy asked. "Isn't that how it's supposed to work? Innocent until proven guilty?"

"Can Roddy vouch for you?" Hen asked Jean.

"Hold it!" Roddy said. "Don't you need to give her a Miranda warning or something—something to remind her that what she says can be used against her and she ought to have a lawyer?"

"You've just done a good job of that, Roddy. I'm not happy about this, but we've got to follow up on what we have. We're still getting our facts together. You want a lawyer present, Jean?"

"I don't mind helping them, Roddy," Jean said. "I didn't think much of Julian Stubbs, but I don't think somebody ought to be able to get away with killing him."

"It's a matter of principle," Roddy said. "They can't come in here and try to intimidate us—you—without anything to go on. They need to get their facts together before they go off half-cocked and start accusing people of murder."

"What if I told you we had witnesses that heard you arguing with Mr. Stubbs before he died?" Hen asked Jean.

She shook her head in wonderment. "I'd say I must be in the middle of a nightmare. Maybe I do need a lawyer. Roddy?"

"We're not to that yet," Hen said, waving a calming hand as Roddy drew breath to respond. "Maybe we can clear this up. You were here all morning, Jean?"

"Yes. I was upset that Gretchen ran off with Kevin like that, no point in denying it, and I was working it out in the kitchen. I told you."

"Roddy, can you vouch for that?"

"Of course, I can. You satisfied?"

"Roddy, tell the truth. We don't want to get in trouble. You can't vouch for me. You weren't here the whole morning."

"Sure, I was."

"No. Don't you remember? You went down to the hardware store to get that brush for the barbecue grill?"

Bingo.

"Oh, right. Yeah. I think that was later, though."

"Oh."

"You had it when I came by to tell you about Mr. Stubbs," I reminded him. "You were cleaning your grill. Remember?" I turned to Jean. "So you don't have an alibi for the whole morning. You could have gone back over there."

"Where?" Jean asked.

"Julian Stubbs was pushed down the stairs at the Stubbs house," I said. "On Monday morning. While Roddy was off buying a wire brush at the hardware store. You had an argument with Mr. Stubbs on Saturday night."

"No, I didn't," Jean protested.

"So, is that it?" Roddy asked, standing in an obvious effort to tell us we'd overstayed our welcome. "Or do we move on to the next stage—like getting the lawyers in to protect us against what is beginning to look like police harassment. Y'all under pressure to settle this case and can't find anybody else to blame?"

"No," Hen said. "We generally like to take our time till we're sure of getting the right person."

"If you're accusing Jean based on fingerprints and somebody who claims Jean argued with Julian, you must be desperate," Roddy said.

Hen went on without missing a beat. "She has motive, means, and opportunity. Jean, I think we need to take you in."

"You can't do this!" Roddy said.

Jean still looked like she was in shock.

Hen stood, shifting his weight inside his uniform, seeming to expand in size and authority. "I think we understand each other."

"Leave her alone," Roddy said.

"Just doing our job," Hen said. He jerked his head in my direction, plainly conveying that I should clap Jean in irons and haul her off with us.

There was a long dramatic pause, a tableau, before Roddy spoke.

"Wait," Roddy said.

Now Jean looked confused. Hen winked at me as he turned to Roddy. "Yes, sir?"

"It was an accident."

"Roddy? What do you mean?" If possible, Jean looked more bewildered than she had at the notion of her own arrest.

"An accident?" Hen inquired. "No kidding? How'd it happen?"

"Take me away." Roddy held out his hands.

"Even if we were going to take you away, we wouldn't use cuffs, Roddy. I'm not a feeble old man and neither is Trudy."

"Roddy?" Jean seemed on the verge of tears.

"Don't worry about it, hon," Roddy said. "I'll tell them all

231

about it down at the jail."

"No," Jean said, going to his side, taking his hand. "You don't have to face this by yourself."

"Yes, hon, I do," Roddy said. "I pushed him."

"But it was an accident." She turned to Hen and me. "It was an accident."

"We'd like to hear all about it, Roddy," Hen said. "Mirandize him, Trudy."

"You have the right to remain silent," I began.

"Save your breath," Roddy said. "I'll tell you what happened. I'll get my own lawyer, when it comes to that."

"Maybe you ought not talk to them, Roddy," Jean said.

"I want you to know what happened, honey," Roddy said. He turned back to Hen. "When we went upstairs to look at that thing, that family tree, at the party on Saturday night, Julian started writing on it, putting Gretchen's name on it. At first, I thought he was putting her in because she married Kevin, but when I looked, I saw he was putting her name like a descendant, not somebody who married in. I know he was just an addled old man, but that's what he was doing, and I couldn't talk him out of it. Addled old man or not, I wasn't going to stand there and let him bring up all that about him and Karen. Yeah, I heard all that."

"Roddy, honey, none of that was important," Jean said.

When Hen and I first arrived, Roddy had been genial and friendly. When we started pointing a finger at Jean, he'd been defensive, aggressive. When he started confessing, he'd been resigned. Now, for the first time, he seemed apologetic, and his words were so painfully private and moving I thought he'd have done well to keep them for his trial.

"Jean, you know Karen and I broke up before all this Julian stuff, before Gretchen was born. You know that was over. You know I married you because I loved you, not because you reminded me of Karen."

Jean was crying, silently.

"But Julian Stubbs wasn't a good man." Roddy seemed to remember Hen and me. "I didn't mean to kill him. I stand by that. But he wasn't a good man. Deep down, I've always thought it was his fault Karen did what she did. If he'd helped her, stood by her, she wouldn't have had to take that way out. And then to have him forget what he'd done and start putting Gretchen into the family tree . . . well, I couldn't stand it."

"What was the big deal?" Hen asked. "Probably nobody much would have noticed it."

"Yeah, but the more I thought about it, the more it seemed like he really knew what he was doing—or thought he did. If he was trying to claim he was Gretchen's father, it would humiliate Gretchen and insult Karen's memory, and bring up old junk for Jean, all right now when Gretchen was getting married and ready to start a new life. I let it go that night, and fuzzy as his brain had gotten, I figured he'd probably forget all about it, but I didn't want to leave that thing like that, so I decided I'd go back and get it."

"Just to be clear," Hen said. "You decided to break in and steal this family tree?"

"Well, yeah. Or maybe take an eraser to it. And I almost got away with it, too, mistimed it a little bit and got there after breakfast instead of while they were all downstairs eating like I meant to. Julian caught me with it, and he wouldn't let me have it. We got in a sort of tug-of-war with it, and then he jerked it away from me and took a header down the stairs, and I got out of there."

"But, Roddy—"

Roddy took Jean's hand. "I know, honey. I know. It was stupid. Stupid to go over there. Stupid to run away when he fell. But I wasn't thinking straight. All I was thinking was how much I love you and Gretchen, and I didn't want this old man bringing up all that old stuff about Karen—about me and Karen—about him and Karen—and causing you more pain. I couldn't stand by and let that old goat claim my daughter. All I meant to do was take the family tree—maybe clean it up and put it back. I figured he'd go back home and it would all die down."

All the air seemed to go out of him at once. He looked at Hen defiantly. "That's the story. It was an accident."

"I've got to arrest you, Roddy," Hen said.

"No!" Jean said.

"Yes," Hen said.

"I'll get me a lawyer and take my chances in court."

"Good idea," Hen said. "Whatever spin you put on your story, you killed a man while in the act of trespassing and attempting to commit a theft. Your lawyer will explain all that to you."

Roddy turned back to Jean, who was pale, still shocked. "Gretchen's my daughter, even if he did give the sperm."

"Oh, Roddy!"

"We're gonna need to take your barbecue brush, Roddy," Hen said, pulling out the search warrant we'd picked up on our way over. "You want to hand it over or make us look for it?"

He handed it over.

CHAPTER 27

You'd think once you have a confession in a murder case, that would be the end of it and the people involved could get on with putting what's left of their lives back together. 'Tain't necessarily so. Or maybe that is what happens, even though it doesn't look that way.

We'd buried Julian Stubbs, settled the question of how he died, and celebrated a relatively subdued Christmas, but the year, instead of limping to a close, still gave us some surprises.

One of the surprises was when Vera and Annie Stubbs showed up at the station house one morning. Vera had prolonged her visit in Ogeechee till Christmas, which was easy for me to understand, since that's where most of the people who meant anything to her were.

"What can I do for you?" I asked.

"I want a DNA test," Vera said.

"On Julian, she means," Annie explained. "I tried to talk her out of it."

"Why?" I managed to ask.

"Because all it'll do is stir things up," Annie said.

I smiled at her and rephrased my question, looking at Vera. "Why do you want to do that?"

"To prove he isn't Gretchen Holland's father," Vera said. "I know what people think, and I want to set them straight."

"Let's go sit down and talk about this," I invited. I led them into an interview room that contained a small table and four

"I want a DNA test," Vera said. "I want you to tell me how to go about it."

"I can put you in touch with a lab that can do it," I said, evading the "why" by dealing with the "how." "It might take a week or two and cost a few hundred dollars."

"I don't care what it costs. I can afford it. And I want to do it." Vera sat tall and stuck her chin out and looked straight at me instead of at her friend. "It's the last thing I can do for him."

Annie tried for humor. "He might not thank you, Vera. He'd probably like it if people thought he was the reincarnation of Don Juan himself."

Vera missed the humor. She looked like she was about to cry. "We had sixty-four years of married life, and I knew my husband. I'm here to tell you he did not father a child out of wedlock."

Annie softened it. "I thought as much of Julian as anybody did, Vera, but I didn't think he was a saint."

"I know what you can't quite bring yourself to say, Annie. I do. Julian was a good-looking, friendly man, and I know people thought he cheated on me. You think it was easy knowing people thought he was that kind of man? That he didn't love me enough to be faithful to me?"

"Oh, Vera!" Annie put her arm around her friend's shoulder. "It wasn't about you at all. It was about Julian. It's just the kind of man he was."

"You're not listening to me, Annie. He was not that kind of man. Now, I'll admit he was the kind of man who didn't mind people thinking he was a glad-hander, and worse, and I'll admit we had some bad moments about it, but he promised me he'd never been unfaithful, and I believed him."

"Good for you." Annie said it in a resigned voice and looked to me for support, but Vera wasn't through.

"Don't give me that poor-Vera look, now, Annie. You're thinking I'm delusional or worse. I'm not."

"I give up, Vera. You do what you want to do. You don't have to convince me. As long as you're convinced, that's good enough for me."

I was definitely on Annie's side in what was clearly a well-worn discussion. What if Vera was wrong? What would it do to her if she learned her beloved husband had fathered Gretchen upon an unhappy young woman in bad circumstances who had turned to him for friendship, driving that young woman to suicide?

"Miz Stubbs," I suggested, "this may sound brutal, but the fact is you can't prove a negative thing—you can't prove he never messed around. All you can hope to do is put to rest the talk about him and Karen."

"I'll do that much, then, Trudy, and I want you to tell me how."

I've seen enough stubborn to be able to recognize it. This woman was not going to give up, so I did.

Maybe I could shock her into changing her mind. "You'll have to give the lab something with his blood, semen, saliva, hair, tissue, bone, sweat."

"He's already buried, Vera," Annie said. "It's too late."

Vera ignored her, bent on cataloguing the possibilities. "Blood? Every one of his shirt's got bloodstains, he bled so easy. Don't know about semen, though."

She cut her eyes at Annie, maybe daring her to laugh.

"Saliva? We buried his dentures with him, so you can't have them. His toothbrush? What else did you say? Bone? We'd have to dig him up for that. But sweat now. One of his awful golf caps? Or I can probably find a dirty handkerchief when I get back home and go through his clothes. He'd stuff them down in his pocket."

For the first time, she seemed about to crack, but she regained control, even tried to lighten the mood. "Snot. Would snot help? What else did you say?"

"Tissue," I supplied. "Hair."

"I don't know about tissue. But hair would be easy. His hairbrush."

"Or dental floss, a cigarette butt, toothpick," I suggested. "And you don't need all of that, just one good sample."

"It won't mean anything if you don't have Gretchen's DNA to compare it to, will it?" Annie asked, obviously still hoping to sabotage the plan.

"I'll talk to her," Vera said. "All she'd have to do is spit on a swab. I expect she'll do it if she thinks it might tell her who her daddy was."

"Kind of mean to get her hopes up, if you're so sure," Annie said.

Vera ignored her.

"I'll put you in touch with a lab," I said.

That was that. They left. I was still sitting there—trying to assimilate the possibilities, thinking of the risk—what if it turned out that Julian was Gretchen's father? What would that do to Vera?—when Annie returned.

"I told her I'd left my glasses," she whispered. "Can't you stop her from doing this? I know Julian wasn't faithful to her."

I shook my head. "I thought of that, too, but it isn't my place to stop her. Hope for the best," I suggested. "Maybe Gretchen won't want to do it."

As it turned out, Gretchen was happy to cooperate. What adoptee hasn't wondered about her parentage? Regardless of how she felt about Roddy Holland, who'd been such a loving father to her that he committed murder (or maybe involuntary manslaughter? It was still to be decided in court.), she'd no doubt wondered who her biological father was. As Aunt Lulu explained it to me later (having gotten the scoop from Willie Lanier), once assured that the consanguinity, if it existed, wasn't close enough to make her marriage incestuous, Gretchen wasn't averse to the idea of a charming old gentleman like Julian Stubbs being her father.

Did it put the issue to rest when the results came back proving that Julian Stubbs's DNA was so dissimilar to Gretchen's that he could not have been her father? Of course not.

The results were mixed for those emotionally involved. Vera Stubbs was vindicated, but Gretchen had to give up whatever brief fantasies she may have built on the idea that Julian Stubbs was her father. Gretchen's parentage, never the main issue, was still a mystery—mercifully, not one for the police.

The Stubbs case was all over as far as the police were concerned, even as far as the community grapevine was concerned, and Vera Stubbs had gone back home, so I was surprised to get a call from Annie Stubbs asking me to come by her house. She had something she wanted to tell me. Mentally reviewing the mess that had been the Stubbs family crime wave, I could think of no loose ends, but curiosity had me at her door within the hour.

"Vera wouldn't want me telling you this," Annie told me, letting cigarette smoke drift out through the slightly open window near the kitchen table where we were sitting.

"I can be discreet," I said, instead of asking why she was about to tell me something her friend wouldn't like.

"Whether you can or not, I want to explain something about when we came down to the police station, with her so stubborn and me worried about her if the DNA didn't prove what she said it would."

"You didn't want her to get hurt," I said. "I understood that."

"Especially since I knew Julian couldn't be trusted around a skirt," Annie said, puffing angrily.

"You don't sound quite as admiring today as you did that day," I said, wondering where this conversation was going.

"Vera knew all along she wasn't risking anything. She just didn't trust me enough to tell me, let me make a fool of myself begging with her."

"What do you mean?"

"You know they never had children. They tried and tried to have children. Went to doctors, clinics, everywhere they could think of. Spent I don't know how much money on it, and it just didn't happen. A lifelong sorrow for Vera. Maybe for Julian, too, for all I know, but he had other things that gave him satisfaction, so I don't think it bothered him like it did her."

"Maybe she was the one who couldn't," I suggested.

"That's what I always thought, but when the DNA test came back and I was so relieved for her, she confessed she knew all along it was his fault. That's what makes me so mad, her letting me worry about her. She found out from the doctors and made sure he didn't know. Said she didn't know what it would do to Julian's idea of himself if he found out he wasn't as virile as he thought he was." She stubbed out her cigarette in the nearly full ashtray and reached for another one.

I laughed. "So her grand gesture really didn't put anything at risk!"

"It's not funny. She didn't trust me." Smoke drifted slowly toward the window.

"Her loyalty was divided between you and her husband," I said, not willing to reassure the woman who was now breaking a confidence that her friend should have trusted her. "It must have been a hard secret for her to keep."

"Well, it hurt me, that's all."

And it explained why she was telling me now. Annie was getting even with Vera.

The year was fading fast, but the best was yet to come.

One of Grandma's traditions which sometimes reached the force of a superstition was that it was important to begin a new year the way you intend to go on with it—start with a clean house and your bills paid. Get the Christmas things put away. Eat a lot of black-eyed peas.

Not a bad approach. Even without those guidelines, I've made a point to try to put the failures and disappointments of the old year behind me and look ahead with good cheer.

On New Year's Day the family gathered at Aunt Lulu's for the black-eyed pea part. Phil spent part of the day with his family—his sister Molly, her husband and children, and their father—and met me at my house later in the day to help with dismantling Christmas.

We cheerfully tore apart the jigsaw puzzle and packed away the tree ornaments. He dragged the tree and other greenery out behind the house to add to a pile of other trash that I'd eventually get around to burning.

It was getting to be late in the day when we finished. "All that's left of the old year is some eggnog and fruitcake," I said.

"Not exactly a balanced meal," he said.

"You were supposed to take care of your food pyramid at Molly's," I reminded him. "I'm dessert."

He leered but issued a challenge: "I can wash down fruitcake with eggnog if you can. Bring it on."

He wasn't complaining about fruitcake. We're fifteen miles from The Fruitcake Capital of the World, and loyalty would forbid us from participating in those fruitcake jokes even if our taste buds didn't. Anybody who's tried a Claxton fruitcake, pecans and candied fruit barely held together with sweet cake, will know what I mean. I am willing to admit that some right-thinking, well-meaning people might not like fruitcake, but it's in Phil's favor that he does.

We spent the last part of the first day of the new year together, cleaning up the traces of the old year, and, like a couple of sugar-starved kids, pigging out on foods that don't appear on anybody's list of what's supposed to be good for you. Grandma would have approved.

I nudged Phil aside to make room for me on the couch, enough room for me to tuck my legs up in what was not an imitation of Gretchen's pose at the Stubbs house. Neither was the fluffy pink sweater I had bought myself for the occasion.

"With all that's been going on lately, I've been doing a lot of thinking," I said.

Phil, who had just taken a huge bite of pecan-loaded fruitcake, nodded encouragingly.

"I'm making some New Year's resolutions," I said, watching him.

He nodded again. "Self-improvement is good," he mumbled around his mouthful of cake.

"I'm gonna finally get this house worked on."

"Home improvement is good," he said. "But I'll believe it when I see it."

"Believe. Furthermore, I'm thinking it's time for you and me to take things to the next level."

He managed to swallow the fruitcake without choking. Then he croaked, "What brought this on?"

While I was trying to formulate an answer, he hastily added, "Don't get me wrong. It sounds good to me."

"Good."

He took another bite of cake and chewed at least twenty times before he asked, "You want to tell me what that means— the next level?"

"How much detail do you want?"

"Only as much as you're willing to let me in on," he said,

grinning. "Just let me know what I need to know when I need to know it."

"Okey dokey."

I'm sure Grandma would have approved.

CHAPTER 28

By mid-January, new traumas had pushed the Stubbs case off the front page (if you're thinking of *The Beacon*) and off the top of the list of concerns for the Ogeechee Police Department.

Acting on a tip from Phil Pittman, who'd become alarmed when the Geezerettes wanted to take out an ad, Hen had to crash (raid?) a meeting of the Geezerettes (I have it on what I consider good authority that, according to Geezerette bylaws, men are not welcome) and explain to them his inability and unwillingness to ignore the illegality of the fund-raiser Super Bowl party they'd been planning.

"Where'd that buncha women come up with all that, anyway?" Hen fumed, to me, not his mother, as a way of decompressing after the stress. "I'da given you odds they wouldn'ta known how to bet on a football game."

"Are you being sexist or ageist?" I asked. "Are mature women not supposed to be sports fans, or are they supposed to be incapable of doing the math, or what?"

I didn't really care, but I didn't see any point in trying to help him out, either.

"It would have been one thing if they'd kept it among themselves, but they were all set to sell chances to outsiders," he complained.

"For a good cause?"

"Oh, yeah. After-school programs at the Enrichment Center."

"You can't get much more public-spirited than that, Hen."

"Oh, yeah, pound for pound they're probably the most public spirited citizens we've got. But that don't make it legal."

"What were they going to do?"

"Had 'em three different angles. One was a big board divided into a hundred numbered squares they were gonna sell and pay off depending on the final score."

"Sort of like the Cow Patty Bingo?" I asked. Not being a gambler, my best reference is the annual event where the football field is marked into squares, chances sold, and a cow let loose on the field. "Is it legal for the fire department to do that?"

"I'll look into it," he said, clearly annoyed at my irrelevant question. "The board the Geezerettes are using is more sophisticated, but basically the same thing," he continued. "Mama was helpful enough to explain to me how the Geezerettes—the house—would keep most of the take—she called it the vig, or sometimes the juice," finally he was laughing, "and just pay out a little, so the Enrichment Center would get more."

"Sounds pretty good," I said.

"And they also had a bunch of ways to bet on the game stats—total yards rushing, longest field goal, total points in each quarter, that kind of thing."

"I'm impressed."

"You like that, you'll love the other one. It's based on the actual outcome of the game, point spread, like the Las Vegas sports book."

"Does one of them know Jimmy the Greek?" I asked.

"I think they've been relying on Della the Stubbs," he answered.

I remembered catching Della with Texas Hold 'em on her computer screen. Who'd have known it meant more than just a way to waste a few minutes?

"What's The Enrichment Center going to do for funds if you

do them out of this?" I asked.

"I suggested a bake sale," Hen said.

"Not nearly up to the potential of that bunch," I said.

"They made that v-e-r-y clear," he said. "I'll be lucky if Mama doesn't quit talking to me—or quit cookin' for me."

"You'd get back on her good side if you'd arrest Della for something."

"Wish I could, Trudy. Oh, how I wish I could."

Except for Jerome Sharpe stumbling across—not literally, thank goodness—all the components of a meth lab not far from the edge of an overgrown dirt road near a peach orchard when he went to see about a domestic disturbance, that's the highlights from January.

CHAPTER 29

In late August, Gretchen Holland Purvis gave birth to a healthy girl she called Alyssa Karen. According to Aunt Lulu, the baby's last name is To Be Determined. Oh, there's no question that Kevin Purvis, Gretchen's husband, is the father. He'd insisted on having a paternity test to make sure of that, but in order to avoid risks to the unborn child, he'd waited till she appeared. That would seem to be good news, but the smart money is betting the young marriage will not survive Kevin's suspicions of his young bride.

And Shawna? After having helped me clarify my thinking where Phil is concerned, she had decided, after all, that life with Frank wasn't so bad. It may have been no more than some kind of hormonal coming back to earth after running on an adrenaline buzz for a while, but it might have had something to do with seeing all the bad-news marriages around her. Even impervious Shawna might have noticed how important love and trust are in a relationship. It's barely possible that she toned herself down out of guilt for her part in stirring up all the trouble between Kevin and Gretchen. Possibly, the idea of raising Tommy without help tipped the scales in Frank's favor.

We'll see how long it lasts.

With all the other testing in the air, something prompted Roddy Holland to have tests run to see if he could have been Gretchen's father. Maybe he belatedly started counting the months between his breakup with Karen and the birth of her child. Maybe it was Jean's idea. It doesn't matter. The irony is that Roddy Holland really was his daughter's father.

What would that knowledge have done to his family dynamics through all those years? Would it—how would it—have changed the moment when he was so overcome with righteous indignation that he shoved an old man down a flight of stairs? And if Julian Stubbs hadn't thought he was Gretchen's father, he wouldn't have tried to update the family tree, and Roddy Holland wouldn't have pushed him down the stairs. If Vera hadn't shielded Julian from the fact of his sterility, would it have spared him that sudden death?

Deceit is a tangled web, for sure, with unforeseeable consequences. When we untangle that web looking for the truth, sometimes we don't recognize it when we find it. And sometimes when we do recognize it, we don't know what to do with it.

Speaking of deceit, according to Aunt Lulu, the ugly brown vases that Della took "for appraisal" were never seen again.

Aunt Lulu had it from Annie Stubbs that Della sold them to Bradley Booth. The conversation between Della and Bradley about football teams and "stuff" that Delcie Huckabee had overheard from beneath the dining-room table probably had to do with turning old family assets into ready cash and not with Julian Stubbs's death. I'd bet—if I could find takers—that there were more Stubbs family treasures missing. I wouldn't have been surprised if Inez Rankin's suitcases contained a pilfered trifle or two when she left.

So far, it looks like Willie and Della are still on good terms and will continue to live together in the Stubbs house, although word has gotten around that they were giving up trying to make a go of the Stubbs House Bed and Breakfast.

Whether or not it had anything to do with Della's gambling losses, as Aunt Lulu claims, the women kept falling further and further behind on getting their bills paid. Naysayers aren't surprised that it didn't work out. Mean-spirited naysayers wonder aloud how they could have expected to make a go of it if they didn't have pockets deep enough to ride out a season or two and give it time to catch on. Business-savvy naysayers speculated that they might have been after the tax write-off all along.

My main thought was that they got a gorgeous house out of it, which brings me to a personal note. Against all odds, against history, I had quit talking vaguely about having some work done on the house and actually got something done. With Teri's help with decorating and finding workmen and with endless consultations with Aunt Lulu about how not to ruin the character of the house with trendy choices, I had modernized the bathrooms and had the floors refinished. I know both Teri and Aunt Lulu enjoyed the process more than I did. After all, neither of them had to live with the mess while renovations were underway. Furthermore, it was not their money. I'm pretty sure they were joking when they tried to convinced me to go for a really cute— even I could see that—faucet that cost nearly a thousand dollars. Let them have their fun. Detached as I tried to be, I still had to make choices, and I regret that I will probably never again be able to look at a faucet as simply a way to deliver water into a sink, but will notice the material, finish, and what kind of knob or handle it has.

Naturally, since I'd talked about fixing up the house for so long without actually doing anything, I had to take a certain amount of loving abuse on the subject when we had a celebratory cookout on Labor Day.

"What happened to make you quit stalling around and take steps to keep the place from falling down around you?" Hen asked.

"I was inspired by the renovations at the Stubbs house," I said.

"You've still got a long way to go, then," Hen said.

"If you'll give me a raise, I'll do the kitchen next," I said. "Teri and Aunt Lulu had a good time, and it didn't hurt for them to have something to think about besides spoiling you."

"You'll want to show it off," Aunt Lulu said. "I could put you on the Garden Club tour next spring."

"With a little more work, you could open up for special events, like the Stubbs house did," Teri suggested. "People love being in these old houses, and if they're not in business anymore, you could take up the slack. You could have weddings and things."

"I'll give that some thought," I answered, using all my self-control not to look at Phil, even when he kicked me under the table.

ABOUT THE AUTHOR

Although she doesn't live in Georgia, **Linda Berry** grounds her Trudy Roundtree mysteries in a fictional town much like the real Georgia town near most of her extended family. Trudy Roundtree and Henry Huckabee (inspired and fueled by Linda's cousin, Johnny Shuman) have appeared in five full-length novels and one novella. Linda also writes plays and short stories and is a community volunteer and arts activist. She lives in Aurora, Colorado, with her husband. Check Linda's Web site at www.ogeechee.avigne.org.

ORLAND PARK
PUBLIC LIBRARY
A Natural Connection

14921 Ravinia Avenue
Orland Park, IL 60462

708-428-5100
orlandparklibrary.org